Light Among the Shadows

BY
JENNIFER LEIGH PEZZANO

Copyright © 2021 by Jennifer Leigh Pezzano

All rights reserved. No part of this publication may be reproduced, distributed, or transmitted in any form or by any means, including photocopying, recording, or other electronic or mechanical methods, without the prior written permission of the publisher, except in the case of brief quotations embodied in critical reviews and certain other noncommercial uses permitted by copyright law.

Any references to historical events, real people, or real places are used fictitiously. Names, characters, and places are products of the author's imagination.

Publishing company: Silver Dawn Publishing

Front cover image by Virtually Possible Designs.

Book formatting by Jillian Michaels.

First printing edition 2021.

www.jenniferleighpezzano.com

SILVER DAWN PUBLISHING

Est 2019

Acknowledgments

To all those who have helped me on this journey.

To my ever-patient partner who has tirelessly supported me.

To my daughter who is my biggest cheerleader.

To my close friends and family who have celebrated and held space.

And to all my wonderful writing partners who have helped this story grow and flourish.

Thank you for being the vibrant color in the landscape of my life.

Chapter One

Night falls on my skin.
My dreams always come when I least expect them to.
I claw at the sheets, my skin damp, limbs shaking.
He lies beside me, eyes closed in sleep.
The space between us an endless chasm.
I can't breathe.
I can't live like this anymore.

My hands gripped the steering wheel as I drove in a trance. Where I was going, I had no idea. All I knew was that I had to get away.

The distortions of darkness rushed past me, the haze of taillights in the distance glowing like embers in the night. My whole body was stiff, and a persistent ache radiated throughout my lower back. The hours had blended into a blur of gas stations, motel rooms and prepackaged food hastily bought in convenience stores. It all tasted the same, bland and dry, nothing more than an anchor to hold down the emptiness clawing around inside.

On the passenger seat, my phone flashed its eager blue light once more. Dozens of missed calls, text messages, and voicemail alerts littered the screen. All from John. Reaching over, I turned it off. The thought of listening to them filled me with dread.

What I had done was extreme, but like a wild animal stuck in a trap, I knew the only way to survive was to relinquish a limb. Leaving was the last frantic vestige of my attempt to keep on living, despite there being nothing left to live for. I was hollowed out. Only tender bruised bone remained as I followed the endless white line of the highway.

Sometime during the night, I crossed through Washington, the tip of Idaho, and into Montana. The incessant pace of the road had quieted. Only the occasional passing car slipped by my rearview mirror. I wondered what stories these people carried with them as they drifted past me, encapsulated in their own silent confinement, their bodies bathed in the soft glow of console lights. Were they returning from a long journey? Driving desperately to a lover? Or running from their own misfortune? There was a sense of comfort in knowing I was not the only one traveling through the dark.

The sky was a clear blaze of stars with a sliver of moon hanging shyly in the sky as I pulled off route ninety and into a sleepy truck-stop town. I spotted a motel ahead, the neon vacancy sign like a faded beacon to weary travelers.

I stepped out of the car and into the balmy warmth of the late July night. Entering the muted light of the lobby with its threadbare carpet and racks of dusty tourist brochures, the smell of stale coffee and cleaning solution hit me as I pushed a button on the worn wood of the counter, watching a silent glow appear beneath my finger.

"Looking for a room?"

A brisk voice startled me, and a woman emerged from the back, her grey hair tied up in a bun. I nodded as the weight of the road settled over my body, a heaviness that spoke of all the miles that stretched between me and the life I had left behind.

Through the cracks of the metal blinds, slanted beams of morning sunlight filtered into the room, stirring me from another restless sleep. The distant sound of the freeway was a comforting hum as I rolled over in bed and stared up at the fractures that crisscrossed the ceiling like a faded road map. Caught between loneliness and a sense of relief, I attempted to take stock of what was left in my life. I knew I needed to call John, to at least tell him I was okay, but I couldn't yet summon the strength to do so.

I quickly dressed and gathered my clothes and toiletries, stuffing them into my duffle bag. The urge to keep moving was a persistent force, compelling me forward without thought.

Throwing my bag into the front seat, I glanced at my car, now covered in a fine layer of dirt and grime from the road. I ran my hand across the roof, my heart clenching as I remembered how Caleb used to draw pictures on the car whenever we got back from camping, his tiny finger trailing lines through the dust.

"Mommy, look. I drew you a pretty picture."
Sunlight flits through the trees as Caleb smiles up at me with his wide blue eyes,
face sticky from the milkshake he had on the way home.
I tangle my fingers through his hair, place a kiss on the warmth of his forehead.
"It's beautiful, honey."

I shook the image from my mind, pushing away the memories that threatened to flood me and all the emotions I did not have the strength to hold.

Sliding into the driver's seat, I turned the key in the ignition and drove back out onto the safe, enveloping silence of the road.

The sky was a slash of blue against the outline of the Rocky

Mountains towering in the distance. The lush green landscape of forest leveled out to an expanse of prairie as I approached Missoula. The pulse of the highway beneath me seemed to shake loose my tangled thoughts, and I knew it was time to face what I was running from. I pulled off onto the nearest exit, following the curve that hugged the open pastures.

I brought the car to a stop on the side of the road and got out. The warm breeze of an early summer's day blew across me, kissing my skin and teasing my hair. The endless stretch of whispering grass released the tight spaces within me, and for a moment I could breathe again.

Clutching my phone, I took a deep breath, gathered my resolve, and dialed John. He picked up after one ring, his voice strained and harsh.

"Where are you, Lara?"

"I'm okay, John."

"Yes, but *where* are you?" Through his clipped words, a controlled anger radiated through the phone like a palpable force.

I cringed and closed my eyes, trying to still the racing of my heart. "I'm in Montana."

A moment of tense silence echoed on the other end before John finally spoke. "What the *fuck* are you doing in Montana?"

"I think you know the answer to that."

"*No... I'm sorry.* I don't know why you're in *Montana.*" His voice dripped with sarcasm. "You just disappeared in the middle of the night. No note. Nothing."

A trembling sigh escaped my lips. "I'm sorry. I just had to get away."

"Clearly."

The heavy pause between us reminded me of every other time we had attempted to communicate, struggling to pry down the walls of self-preservation we had built around ourselves. We had both stopped trying years ago.

"When are you coming home?"

I stared up into the vast expanse of turquoise sky, watching as a flock of birds ascended from a tree, the graceful arc of their movements like the gentle promise of a freedom calling to me.

"I'm not."

"What the hell do you mean?"

"I'm not coming back."

The sound of rustling on John's end was followed by the loud crash of something breaking. "What the hell are you talking about?'

Tears leaked from my eyes, running a hot trail down my cheeks. "I'm sorry, but I just can't do this anymore."

A long silence followed, and I realized that John had hung up. I sank down onto the grass, allowing the tendrils of grief to slip out of their locked cage for a moment and entwine around me.

At some point, I found myself back in the car, my shaky hands gripping the wheel as I continued down the country road, passing a faded sign that read 'Stevensville.'

I stopped at the first gas station I saw, a tiny pit stop consisting of two pumps and a quaint looking general store. Parking alongside one of the pumps, I filled up the tank and headed over to the store, beelining past the cash register and into the cramped and airless bathroom.

The fluorescent bulb flickered above as my bloodshot eyes stared back at me, blurred by the opaque mirror, my hair tousled and stuck to my cheeks from dried tears. *What was I doing?* I had finally found the strength to rip through the suffocating strands of my marriage, and I was now standing untethered in a landscape foreign and immense. Turning on the tap, I let the cool water run through my cupped palms before splashing it against my face, willing the delicate filaments of my composure to return.

I weaved through the aisles of the store as I headed back to my car, when my gaze fell to a flyer tacked upon a faded wooden bulletin board next to the door.

Seeking live-in equine assistance/light caregiving duties. No experience necessary.

On impulse, I found my fingers plucking free one of the numbers provided on the bottom of the paper.

Sitting amidst the murmur of a small diner, I gazed out at the tall waving grass of the prairie stretched beyond the window. This open countryside was such a soothing contrast to the enclosing density of the Northern California coastal forest. I had spent my whole life among fog and ferns, and I welcomed this change in scenery. There were no edges to bump into, only limitless beckoning space.

I leaned back against the worn booth, the material cracked and faded from years of bodies moving over the vinyl surface. My hands curled around a cup of coffee as I waited for someone named Miriam. The cheerful voice I had spoken with over the phone an hour ago in response to the ad had requested we meet here.

Why I had been compelled to call that number on the paper eluded me. I had no experience working with horses, and the only caregiving I had done was sitting beside a bed, holding my mother's hand within the bare, white walls of a nursing home. But I felt a pull to explore the possibility of this place, and the thought of something so vastly different from the life I had been living was strangely comforting.

I glanced over at the customers who sat around me. Salt of the earth people, with dusty boots and worn cowboy hats. The jingle of the door drew my attention to a tall woman walking in. Her dark brown hair, accentuated by strands of grey that caught the light, was twisted into a loose braid slung over her shoulder. She immediately strode toward me, her gait long and purposeful.

"I'm Miriam, and you must be Lara?" She thrust her hand out and enfolded mine in a strong grip, her eyes twinkling as she smiled down at me. I imagined she was the type who laughed loudly and often.

"How did you know it was me?"

Miriam chuckled as she slid into the booth across from me and signaled to the waitress for a cup of coffee. "It's a small town, hun. A new face sticks out around here."

I nodded with a smile that felt strained.

"So, what brings you to Montana, if you don't mind my asking?"

Shrugging, I gazed down at my coffee for a moment as if the dark contents of the liquid held the answers. "I guess I'm looking for a fresh start." I nodded toward the view. "It's so peaceful here."

"Yes, it is." Miriam sighed, looking out the window. "This place can shake your soul free."

I sighed and folded my arms on the table, leaning in closer to her. "I could benefit from some soul shaking right now."

Miriam regarded me with a warmth in her eyes. "Well, you've come to the right place, then."

I gripped my coffee as sunlight filtered in through the window, exposing the harsh state of my nails, which had been worn down to painful slivers by my excessive picking. I quickly hid them in my lap as a plump older woman with a ruddy complexion breezed by our table, sliding a cup of coffee over to Miriam.

"Thanks, Mary," Miriam said with a wink, before her gaze fell back on me. "So, let me tell you a little about the position. It's on my brother's property. He's disabled and will need some mild assistance, mainly help with grocery shopping. He also owns horses, so the bulk of your duties would involve helping him out in the barn with basic grooming and maintenance, nothing you need too much experience for. In exchange, you'll be provided the cottage on the property to stay in." She raised her eyebrow at me as she leaned back against the booth, appearing to take me in for a moment. "Is this something you think you'd be interested in?"

"Yes, I think so." A glimmer of hope fluttered inside me, pushing through the snarled, bleak footpath of my mind.

"Great." Miriam said, flashing me a big smile. "I just got married, and we'll be moving to the East Coast by the end of August. I'm hoping to get all this squared away before then. But the cottage is available now if you want it. All I'm really going to require from you is a background check."

"That sounds good. I'm able to start anytime." The words tumbled from my mouth without hesitation. I had some money stashed away in savings, and the idea of my own quiet place amidst the backdrop of mountains and prairie tugged at me with a convincing force.

"Well, if you're free right now, I can take you on over to my brother's property. It's just a few miles down the road. I can show you around, and you can meet Peter."

"Okay." I shifted in my seat to grab my purse when Miriam's hand fell on mine.

"I have a good feeling about you, Lara, and I think the two of you will get along well. Peter can be a little moody at times, but underneath it all, he's such a gentle soul." Her eyes grew sorrowful. "Things have just been really hard for him, ever since his accident."

"His accident?" I posed my question hesitantly, not wanting to come across as prying.

Miriam squeezed my hand briefly before letting go. "Yes. Peter lost his sight about five years ago."

"Oh... I'm so sorry to hear that." I was all too familiar with the swift change of course that loss could bring, and a swell of empathy rose up.

Miriam waved her hand in the air, as if dismissing my concern. "He doesn't take too well to sympathy, and he is extremely independent, so he won't need much from you, really." She paused, taking a deep breath. "I think this arrangement is more for me. I've been the one staying with him for the past four years, and I just want to make sure someone is looking out for him when I'm gone. He tends to isolate."

I nodded, while a voice in the back of my mind wondered how much help I could possibly be to anyone, given my current emotional state. *Was this really a good idea?* But I had relinquished the oars to my boat when I left California, and I was now adrift in unknown waters, leaving me with a strange feeling of buoyancy.

With a smile, Miriam pulled out some bills from her back pocket and set down on the table. "Shall we head out, then?"

I stood from the booth to follow her as she sauntered out of the diner, throwing friendly comments to the locals as she passed. The small-town jocularity that surrounded the restaurant reminded me of an odd assortment of family all gathered for the holidays. It filled me with longing as I realized how isolated I had become in my own life. *What would it feel like to be a part of something again? To belong to a community that welcomed you with the ease of collective familiarity.*

Settling back into my car, the breeze from the open window blew against my skin like a warm caress as I tailed Miriam's truck. Fields painted in sepia glided past my view while we drove down the quiet stretch of sun-baked road, the imposing mountain range cradling the horizon, beckoning me toward something new and undefined.

Chapter Two

Wheels hit the dirt road, jostling me in my seat while the tires from Miriam's truck kicked up a plume of dust and gravel behind her. I followed her around a bend and past a thick grove of aspen trees, their leaves shimmering against a backdrop of sprawling hills and bright sky. Ahead of me, a single-story farmhouse with a wide front porch came into view, and beyond that lay a small cottage nestled snugly between two giant sycamore trees.

I parked beside Miriam and got out of the car, taking in the vista. Beyond the farmhouse stood a faded red barn and a wooden fence bordering a lush, rolling pasture. The silhouette of horses grazing among the grass completed the idyllic scene before me.

Miriam stepped out of her truck, closing the door softly behind her. "Pretty nice out here, isn't it?"

I turned to her. "It's beautiful." My heart stilled and loosened an emotion I could not quite place. It was a yearning mixed with déjà vu, as if I had stumbled upon a memory I never knew I had until now.

Miriam motioned for me to follow her. "Peter should be somewhere around here."

A large black lab appeared from around the house, tail wagging in enthusiastic circles as it jumped all over Miriam. "Okay, Dusty. Down, boy." Miriam bent to scratch behind his ears before he proceeded over to me, flopping himself onto the ground in the hope that I would rub his belly.

"As you can see, he's not much of a guard dog," Miriam said with a laugh. "But he's been an amazing service dog for Peter. I found him at a shelter last year in Missoula. Though he's not trained to be a seeing-eye dog, it was like he just instinctively knew Peter didn't have his eyesight." Miriam stroked her hand over the top of his head. "Animals can be so amazing like that."

"Yes, they are incredible."

Running my fingers through Dusty's sleek coat, I recalled all those months that our German Shepherd, Zeke, had sat diligently by the side of the bed with imploring eyes and a cold nose pressed up against my hand, willing me to get up. When we buried him last year in the woods, it felt as if the last fragment of who I was had been laid beneath the earth alongside him. Disjointed emotion scrambled to the surface, and I hastily wiped a tear from my cheek, hoping Miriam did not notice.

"Dusty," Miriam said with a click of her tongue, "go find Daddy."

Dusty jumped to his feet in full attention and ran up the stairs of the porch, nudging open the screen door with his nose and slipping himself inside.

"Well then, I guess Peter's inside." Miriam tilted her head at me in a motion to follow as she bounded up the porch and into the house. "Hey, Peter! Will ya come on out here? I have someone I'd like you to meet."

I stopped at the door when I heard the deep tone of a male voice from somewhere within the living room.

"Jesus Christ, Miriam. I thought we talked about this."

Miriam lowered her voice in reply, and I couldn't make out what she said. As their hushed conversation continued, I slowly backed down the porch steps.

I shouldn't be here.

I hastily retreated back to the safety of the car, feeling foolish for thinking this was a good idea. As I frantically searched for my keys within the depths of my purse, the screen door slammed, and Miriam's voice rang out.

"Lara! Where are you going?"

I whipped around to face her, shaking my head. "I should probably go. I really don't want to be intruding on anyone."

She flashed me a warm smile, dismissing my concern with a quick wave of her hand. "Oh, don't worry, it's fine. He wants to meet you." She gestured for me to come inside, holding the screen door open.

I tentatively approached the porch once more, my words coming out uncertain. "Are you sure?"

Miriam placed her hand on my shoulder, giving it a quick squeeze. "Yes, I'm sure. Come on in. He's all bark and no bite. I promise." She shot me a playful wink as I stepped through the doorway and into the dimly lit living room.

I didn't really know what I was expecting when I saw Peter. I suppose I had envisioned a frail, older looking man, with the cloudy eyes of someone with cataracts. But the attractive, towering man that stood in the middle of the room was quite robust and appeared to be somewhere in his late thirties; his face framed by a well-trimmed beard that matched the dark waves of thick hair that fell across his forehead.

"Lara, this is my brother, Peter."

Peter stepped forward, extending his hand in my direction, his gaze fixed somewhere above my head. "Lara, nice to meet you." His handshake was firm, and his large, calloused hand engulfed mine.

"You too. You have a very beautiful place out here."

A tentative smile flickered across Peter's face, showing faint laugh lines against tanned skin. His eyes were surprisingly clear, and in the dim light of the room, appeared to be a deep green color. "Thank you. Miriam says you're new in town?"

"Yes, I'm currently in a transitional period of sorts." I shot him a smile, but then quickly remembered that he couldn't see it.

An uncomfortable pause infused the space between us before Peter spoke again. "Well, I'll just need help with the horses. You don't have to bother yourself with much else around here."

"Peter?" Miriam drew out his name like a long question.

"Despite what my sister may think, I'm perfectly capable of taking care of myself." He swiveled his head in Miriam's general direction, a look of frustration flashing momentarily across his face. "Miriam says the cottage out back is all cleaned out. So, if you're interested, you can start as soon as you'd like."

"Well, I don't want to impose on you at all."

"Good. Then I think this arrangement will work out just fine. Now, if you'll excuse me, I have some work to do." Peter's voice was brusque as he nodded curtly in my direction before turning and walking down the hall, Dusty trailing dutifully behind him.

A wave of awkwardness clawed at me. This man clearly did not seem pleased with me showing up like this. My mind began to scramble for a way to gracefully back out of this situation when Miriam touched my arm with a reassuring smile. "He'll warm up to you in time, don't worry. Come on, I'll show you around the place, and you can get yourself all settled in."

I hesitated in the doorway. "But you haven't even run a background check on me yet."

She waved her hand in the air as if brushing away a fly. "Oh, I will for formality's sake, but like I said at the diner, I have a good feeling about you, Lara. And my gut has yet to steer me wrong."

I followed Miriam along the wide pathway that separated us from the barn, dry earth retaining impressions of our feet as we walked. Through the slats in the fence, sunlight merged with dancing shadows against the ankle high grass of the pasture. The quiet that permeated was comforting and seemed to scoop out all the noise in my mind.

Miriam pushed open the door to the cottage. The place was bright and cheery inside. Gauzy curtains danced against open, white-framed windows, and a galley kitchen lay to the left, adorned with various cooking implements and cast-iron pots hung neatly upon the light oak walls. A wooden table and two chairs sat beside a large window with a wide view of the pasture.

I walked through the living room, which was sparsely furnished with a couch and a coffee table, and into the bedroom which held a wrought iron bed with a colorful checkered quilt in pastel tones. I peeked inside the bathroom to find a claw-foot tub in the corner; the wallpaper sprayed with delicate tendrils of vine laden with purple flowers.

"It ain't much, but it's homey. And it's served me well these past few years," Miriam spoke from behind me.

I turned to her with a smile that felt genuine as a tiny bud of promise hesitantly pressed through the surface. "I think it's perfect."

I sat on the edge of the bed with my meager belongings spread out over the quilt, holding a framed photo of Caleb and me that John had taken years ago. We stood together beside the serpentine shimmer of the Smith River, the towering redwoods off in the distance. The golden light of the sun glinted off our blonde hair as I laughed behind Caleb, my hands on his shoulders as he held out the large fish he had caught, a big grin splashed across his face.

"Alright you guys, smile."
John's voice calls out,

his words dancing in between the playful gurgle of the river behind us.
Sunlight is warm on my skin.
Caleb nestled against me.
"Oh, wait. I think that was a video."
Laughter tumbles from my lips.
"You're never going to figure that camera out, are you?"
A wide smile stretches across John's face.
"Got it."

I placed the photo on the small nightstand beside the bed, running my fingers along the grooved etchings of the frame. That had been our last picture taken together. A brief moment of happiness captured like a bittersweet reminder of who we used to be.

My phone rang from somewhere beneath my clothes, and I fished it out to see my brother's name on the screen. I took a deep breath and braced myself for the onslaught of questioning.

"Hi, Mitch."

"Lara. *Thank God* you answered. I've been trying to reach you for days." In the background, I could hear the girls, their sharp laughter followed by the thumping of feet across his wooden floor. "So, John just called me. Care to tell me what you're doing out in Montana?"

I absentmindedly picked at the stitching on the quilt. "I needed to get away."

"You know you could've stayed with us if you needed some space. You're always welcome here."

"I know, I just can't right now." How could I explain to my brother that the idea of staying with him and his family filled me with the kind of heartache that sucked the air out of my lungs? It was a constant, painful reminder of something I no longer had.

"Listen, Lara. I understand that things have been strained between you two for a while now, considering all that you have been through. But don't you think it's worth it to at least try and get past this?"

"I don't think you *really* understand, Mitch." My words came out tense. "There's no getting past this, and we were having issues before…" I trailed off, letting the silence speak for me.

"So, that's it then, huh? Are you talking about divorce?"

"I don't know. What did John say?"

"Nothing much. He just said that you had left him and were somewhere in Montana."

I let out a lingering sigh. John's complete lack of emotion was a bitter reminder of why I had left. I had grown so tired of living with loneliness; the silence between us like a mute cry. He had shut down so long ago, leaving me to carry the burden of our collective pain alone.

"Lara, I'm really worried about you."

"I'm fine." I got up from the bed and walked over to the window. The sun had begun to sink low against the mountains, cradling the pasture in rippling shadows. A cool breeze slipped in through the screen, ruffling the curtains. "I just found a work trade position as a caretaker, and I have this cute little cottage to stay in. It's beautiful here, and quiet. I really need this right now."

"Are you sure? You're just so far away, and what about the plans we had to come and visit this summer?"

My gut lurched at the thought of my nieces with their wide brown eyes and joyful laughter. "I know, I'm sorry. Will you tell the girls I'll make it up to them?"

"Of course."

"Don't worry about me, Mitch, okay? I'll talk to you soon."

I ended the call and wandered into the kitchen, where a stack of papers lay on the table. Miriam had outlined the day-to-day details for me, including weekly shopping lists for Peter. On the top page, scrawled in big bold marker, was Miriam's number. She had told me to reach out to her any time, for any reason. I flipped through the pages of writing and then glanced out the window to see the sky unveiling the colors of evening; pink and orange tufts of clouds settling against a backdrop of deepening blue.

Pulling on a light sweater, I walked out through the pasture, catching the outline of Peter from beyond the farmhouse, his shrill whistle piercing through the air as he called the horses back to the barn.

The sound of the wind rustling through the aspen trees soothed me like a lullaby, and for a moment all my thoughts fell away, leaving nothing but the gentle reprieve of stillness behind.

Chapter Three

I awoke to a firm knock on the door. Hesitant early morning sunlight filtered in through the curtains as I sat up in momentary confusion, my mind scrambling to orient itself. Bleary-eyed, I padded over to the front door and opened it to find Peter standing there with a cup of coffee in his hand.

"Good morning," I said, as Peter thrust the cup in my direction. I reached for it, wrapping my hands around its warmth as Dusty sat beside him, his tail thumping against the porch. "Oh, this is for me?"

Peter ran his fingers through his hair. "I don't know how you like it, so it's just black."

I looked down at the cup in my hands. "Black is fine, thank you."

"If you're not already dressed, I suggest you go get ready. We're heading on out to the barn."

"Okay, just give me a minute."

I threw some clothes on, pulled my hair into a messy bun, and met Peter out on the porch with the cup of coffee in hand. Following him over to the fence line, he glided his hand over the top of the wooden posts until he found the gate and swung it open for me. The hinges squeaked in protest as we walked through and cut across the pasture toward the barn, my shoes squishing against the soft ground. Peter seemed to navigate himself with an ease while Dusty walked close beside him, occasionally nudging his leg as if steering him forward.

"Do you have any experience with horses?" Peter asked as

we approached the barn. He felt around for the handle and then slid open the large wooden door.

The sharp smell of manure and hay overwhelmed me as I stepped inside. "No, but I've always wanted to work with them."

"Well, enthusiasm's a start." He slowly ran his fingers along the rows of tools hanging up on the wall behind us and took down a pitchfork, holding it out for me to take. "We're mucking today."

"Mucking?"

"Removing the old bedding out of the stalls and replacing it with fresh straw. Do you think you can handle that?"

"Yes. I think I can." I wrapped my hand around the worn wood of the handle, attempting to sound more self-assured than I felt. I needed a challenge, a distraction from the constant noise of my mind, and I only hoped that the force of physical work could purge me.

"Good." Peter brushed past me and felt his way into a stall. "There are some old boots of Miriam's somewhere round here you can use."

Glancing around the barn, I spotted a pair of black rubber boots sitting in the far corner. Setting my now empty coffee cup down beside the door, I slipped them on, feeling the coolness against my socks. They were much too big, and my feet slid around in them as I walked over to the stalls.

We worked in silence for a while, the systematic scrape of our pitchforks against the floor the only sound. Streams of morning sunlight leaked through the rafters of the barn, catching the dust in shimmering beams that hovered in the air.

My arms began to burn from exertion, and I paused for a minute, looking over at him. "So, what is it that you do, besides work with horses?" I asked, breaking the silence between us.

Peter stopped shoveling and glanced over in the direction of my voice. "You wondering what a blind man does with his time?"

My cheeks burned. "No, I didn't mean it like that. I'm sorry. I wasn't trying to pry or anything."

Peter wiped away a bead of sweat trickling down his temple and then continued shoveling the old straw into the wheelbarrow between us. "What is it that *you* do, besides aimlessly pass through small Montana towns?"

An uneasy breath caught in my throat as I struggled for an answer.

"See? Sometimes questions like that can be quite loaded." A faint smile crept across his face for a moment, diffusing the tension. "Are you afraid of heights, Lara?"

I looked over at him. "What do you mean?"

He cocked his thumb toward the ceiling. "I'm gonna need you to climb up to those rafters and throw me down some straw bales."

I looked up into the high loft where an old rickety wooden ladder leaned against the frame. I was in fact terrified of heights, but did not feel compelled to admit that to him.

"Sure, I'll get some down for you, no problem." Feigning confidence, I took a deep breath and headed over to the ladder.

Peter came up from behind, close enough that I could detect the faint woodsy smell of whatever soap he had used that morning. "Here, I'll hold it for you. It can be a bit wobbly."

Taking slow, cautious steps, I ascended the ladder, careful not to look down. I kept my eyes fixed on the next rung in front of me until I reached the top and scrambled my body over in relief. The wooden boards creaked beneath my feet as I made my way to where the straw bales were stacked against the far wall.

"Just roll them on over to the edge and drop 'em. We'll need about three."

My arms strained from the weight, the sharp fibers of the straw digging into my skin as I rolled them across the loft, the barn filling with plumes of dust as the bales crashed to the floor below. "Okay, I'm coming down now," I called out to Peter, who remained standing by the ladder, waiting for me. When I reached the last rung, Peter's hand grazed across my arm.

"You're shaking?" His voice grew soft, and his fingers lingered on my skin for a moment before pulling away. "Are you afraid of heights?"

I chuckled nervously, glad to be on solid ground once more. "A little, but it's good to face your fears, right?"

"That's what they say, I suppose." He stepped back and ran his hand along the stable door, retrieving his pitchfork. "Why don't you take a little break? I've worked you hard enough for one morning."

Picking straw out of my hair, I tried to regain my composure. "No, it's okay. I'm fine."

"Tell you what." He turned toward me. "Why don't we both take a break? I figure you don't have much in the way of food over at the cottage right now, and I was going to cook up some breakfast. Why don't you join me?"

The invitation threw me off guard. "Okay, that sounds nice. Thank you."

I followed him out of the barn with Dusty plodding beside us. The sun had risen above the trees, gaining strength as it bathed the pasture in a warm, hazy glow and spread across the peaks of the mountains like golden brushstrokes of paint. A feeling of peace washed over me, reminding me of the long walks I used to take in the redwoods, with nothing but my thoughts and the movement of the trees as they bowed their ancient branches to the wind.

"God, it's so beautiful here." My words came out breathless as we made our way up to the porch.

Peter paused to hold the door open for me with a nod. "It is, isn't it?" He turned his head in the direction of the pasture. "Some things you don't need to see, you just feel em. Early mornings have always been my favorite."

I stepped into the house as Peter closed the door behind him. "Make yourself comfortable. I'll be in the kitchen."

"Would you like me to help with anything? I asked, feeling a sudden awkwardness as I stood there in his entryway with nothing to occupy my hands.

"No thanks, I got it."

I watched him as he made his way across the living room, hands trailing over the furniture and walls. There was a fluid grace to his movements that reminded me of someone suspended in water. I tried to imagine what it would be like to live in a state of perpetual darkness, the kind that encompassed you, forcing you to slow down.

I glanced around the room, the colors around me all in muted tones of grey and brown. Oil paintings lined the walls, various renditions of the Montana mountains depicted in exquisite detail. There were a few of horses as well, their manes flying behind them as they ran through a landscape of open wilderness. Whoever the artist was had managed to capture the wild beauty of freedom which spilled from their dark eyes.

The stone fireplace was the focal point of the room, taking up almost the entirety of the front wall. To one side stood a shelf filled with music albums and an old record player nestled between the stacks. I crouched down and scanned the impressive collection neatly arranged before me.

"How do you like your eggs?" Peter's voice drifted from the kitchen.

I stood and peered around the doorway to find him cracking eggs into a cast iron pan on the stove. "Any way is fine."

"Okay, I'm making them over-easy then."

"Good. That's my favorite."

A smile played on his lips as he flipped over the bacon, which had begun to sizzle in the pan beside him. I leaned against the counter, watching his hands deftly navigate around the gas stove. "Are you sure you don't need help with anything?"

Peter pushed back a lock of dark hair from his eyes. "I know how to make breakfast, Lara, but you can grab some plates from the cupboard, if ya want."

I opened the cupboard only to realize that the plates were resting on the very top shelf. "Um, I'm afraid I can't quite reach the plates," I replied sheepishly.

"Hmmm." Peter leaned across me and grabbed two plates, setting them down on the counter. "I had a feeling you were a petite one."

"And how would you know that?"

He shrugged, and I noticed a slight twinkle gather behind his eyes. "I have my ways. But there is something about your voice. There's a softness to it."

I found my cheeks warming for some reason and nervously began to fiddle with the dish towel that lay next to me. "You can tell I'm short just by my voice?"

Peter clicked off the burners and turned in my direction, motioning to the plates beside me. "There's a lot I can tell by your voice."

I handed a plate to him, suddenly emboldened by my own curiosity. "Really? Like what?"

"Well, you're very introverted, aren't you?"

His response caught me off guard, and I bit my lip, looking out toward the window as a loneliness swept through me. "I didn't use to be."

"There's nothing wrong with being introverted, Lara," he said with a gentle smile.

We sat together at his kitchen table. Dusty curled underneath Peter's chair, his tail a constant thump against the linoleum, hoping for a handout. I didn't realize how hungry I was and found myself enjoying the food with an enthusiasm I had not felt in a long time.

"So, I'm curious." Peter had stopped eating and appeared to regard me from across the table, his gaze shifting slightly above my head. "What exactly drew you to this place?"

I set my fork down and glanced out the window. "I guess it's all the wide-open space. There's something so soothing about it for me. I can't really put my finger on it, but it feels really peaceful here."

Peter nodded. "I know what you mean. I fell in love with this land about ten years ago. So, I bought it, fixed up the farmhouse and built the cottage out back."

I looked at him in surprise. "Oh wow, you built the cottage yourself?"

"Yep, I used to run my own construction business. That was, of course, before my accident." He ran his hand across the table and found his glass of water, lifting it to his lips. "I had to sell it a few years ago. It's given me a financial cushion, but I miss the work."

"I'm sorry to hear that. You seem to get around pretty well though." I inwardly cringed as the words came out of my mouth.

Peter only smiled, tapping his finger against his temple. "Everything is all mapped out up here. I know this place like the back of my hand, and there is always Dusty to help keep me on course." At the sound of his name, Dusty got up and stood beside Peter expectantly, his brown eyes watching him. Peter reached down to stroke Dusty with an absentminded tenderness before standing up and making his way over to the sink with his dish. "I'm going to go finish up in the barn."

"Well, thanks so much for breakfast," I said, grabbing my empty plate. "I'm ready to go whenever you are."

"No need. Why don't you use this time to get settled in," Peter suggested with a sharp nod as he turned and made his way to the door, his hand resting on the knob for a moment. "You can let yourself out whenever you're ready."

I watched as he slipped himself out the back door with Dusty, leaving me sitting alone in the kitchen with my thoughts as an unsettled silence pressed against my skin. My hands, nervous and unsure, traced over the grooves in the dark wood of the table, acutely aware of how much I feared my own idle time.

"What are you doing?"
John's eyes are blank as he surveys the flour strewn across the counter,
lumps of dough rising in bread pans.
"I'm baking."
"Why?"
I push a strand of hair away from my face, hands like hardened, cracked clay.
"My therapist said it would be a good idea to pick up a hobby."
"We're not going to eat all this."
His brow furrows as he sweeps past me and into the living room.
"Just make sure you clean this mess up when you're done."
My hands tremble as I dig into the dough.
Hot anger like bile coating my tongue.
Ripping apart the pieces, I throw them in the trash.

Standing, I brought my dish over to the sink and turned on the tap, allowing the hot water to run over the pots and pans as I began to clean and stack them neatly on the drying rack that sat on the counter. I stared as if in a daze at the swirls of steam which rose around me, obscuring my vision, and blanketing my thoughts which hung like dark clouds above; tense and full of all the things I was reluctant to sit beside.

Chapter Four

Staring at my phone, I debated whether I should call John. He had not reached out to me since our conversation three days ago, and a part of me was deeply saddened by this. Ten years together and in the end, he couldn't even be bothered to fight for us. I knew he was angry that I left the way I did. I had not handled myself with grace. But there was nothing graceful left in our marriage. It had been tattered and broken for so long now, I had forgotten who we were before the damage. And I wondered if there was even anything left of us to fight for.

Sighing, I began to pick at my nails, falling into the comforting feeling of ripping away at something, the sting of tender exposed skin creating a buffer between my emotions.

From where I sat at the kitchen table of the cottage, I could see Peter walking through the pasture with Dusty. We had not spoken since our breakfast together the day before. All I got from him was a brief nod in greeting when I had passed by on my way back from the store, my arms full of groceries. There was a hesitancy between us. I could feel it like a guarded creature lingering in the shadows. But I felt compelled to push past it. I didn't want to spend my free time hiding away in the cottage. The stillness fell too heavy on me, I needed movement.

The creak of the pasture gate as I opened it alerted him to my presence, and he turned in my direction, raising his hand in a silent greeting.

"Hey there, Peter." My voice came out tentative as I approached him.

He gave me a nod as he slid his hands into his pockets, his gaze slanting off into the distance behind me. The glare of the mid-afternoon sun hit him, illuminating streaks of auburn hidden within the strands of his dark hair. "Are you settling in alright?"

"Yes, I am. I went to go get some groceries yesterday, and it's a really cute little town."

He only smiled, and I nervously twined my hands together as we stood there in silence for a moment. Peter's eyes flickered around, as if trying to gauge my intentions, and I suddenly felt foolish for approaching him like this. "Well, I was just going to go take a little walk…"

"Would you like to meet the horses, Lara?"

A large smile spread across my face, grateful for his invitation. "I would love to."

Peter gave a sharp whistle, and the three horses appeared from the far edge of the pasture. They trotted toward us, their sleek and powerful muscles contracting against the dappled sunlight. I had never been this close to a horse before, and the sheer size of them filled me with a sense of awe.

"Just hold out your hand to them," he said.

The chocolate-colored one stepped closer to me and swept the soft velvet of its nose against my fingers, nudging my palm with a sudden burst of warm breath. Peter ran his hand across its back. "This one's Penny." He then moved to trail his hand through the thick mane of the ebony horse standing beside him. "This guy's Spirit, and Ginger is probably being shy somewhere out there in the pasture," he said with a faint chuckle.

The chestnut mare watched us from a distance, appearing to be in a state of agitated indecision as she tossed her head back and forth.

"How are you able to tell them apart?"

"Oh, that's easy. They each have their own unique personalities. I've had Penny and Spirit for almost ten years now. Ginger over there is Penny's yearling. She's still learning and can be quite skittish at times." Peter clicked his tongue, and Ginger began to take small, cautious steps closer to us. "Penny is the big lover around here and is always the first one to say hi." He chuckled as Penny nudged against the both of us, looking for a handout. "While Spirit is more stoic. He prefers his solitude."

Pulling out a slice of apple from his pocket, he gestured for me to take it. "Would you like to feed her?"

"Sure." I reached for the apple and held it out to Penny.

"Just keep your hand open with your fingers flat."

Penny took the apple gently between her teeth, her whiskers tickling my palm. I ran my fingers over her shiny coat, which was sleek and warmed from the sun, her back rippling like water beneath my touch. I stepped closer, breathing in her rich, earthy scent. "They're so beautiful." A sudden reverence overcame me as I stood beside Penny and looked into the depths of her soft eyes.

"Some of the most intelligent and intuitive animals I have ever known. They have saved me in so many ways." He looked wistful as he spoke, and for the first time, I noticed the startling brilliance of color within his eyes as the light caught them; swirling, ethereal flecks of blue and brown against green. I lost myself in them for a moment before my cheeks began to flush, and I forced myself to look away, feeling like a voyeur.

"And do you still ride them?"

"I do." Peter stroked the length of Spirit's back. "It's a dance of trust, one in which they become my eyes. It's incredibly freeing for me to relinquish my control over to an animal."

"I've never ridden a horse before."

Peter cocked his head, a look of amusement hovering in his eyes. "Is that so?"

"Yeah. I've always wanted to; I just never got the chance, I guess." Standing beside him, I realized how vastly different my life was from his. Peter was open meadows and tall grass, while I was dense forest and scattered sunlight.

"Well, I think we should change that. Don't you?" A wide smile spread across his face. "I could take you riding sometime, if you'd like."

His offer drew forth a swell of interest which burst through the low-lying fog of my emotions. "I'd like that."

He nodded, looking thoughtful. "I used to lead therapy rides for people. A lot of them were troubled youth or those overcoming addiction or depression. We'd spend a few days up in the mountains, camping under the stars with no distractions, just stillness and sky."

"That sounds really nice." This knowledge of him softened me. He understood fragility, and the stumbling steps we took to find ourselves again. I sighed and looked up at the delicate wisps of clouds which hung above like spun sugar. The sun on my skin was a blanket of heat enfolding me as the horses grazed between us. There was something comforting in his presence, and it quieted the space inside me. "I think I could use some of that right now."

"Couldn't we all." There was a flash of something sorrowful within the depths of Peter's eyes, and for a moment, it felt as if he could see me.

The days of summer passed before me. The optimism of July had given way to a languid August, and I fell into an easy rhythm of working with the horses alongside Peter. His moods were much like the weather, at times animated and light, other times brooding, his silence infusing the space between us.

Every few days I would drive into town and stock up on provisions, running through the shopping list that Miriam had outlined for me, our correspondence punctuated by brief checkups through text. I had a lot of free time as well, and at first, the discomfort of my thoughts weighed heavily on me. The unspoken words between me and John. The damage we couldn't erase. And all the prowling memories which wanted to rush in with their sharp claws, tearing away at the tender layers of my skin. I would find myself restlessly pacing the cottage, trying to push back the tide of emotions that threatened to consume me. But then I would step outside and breathe in the air which smelled of grass and earth, watching the gentle sway of the aspen trees that grew beside the pasture like a consoling whisper against the unbroken blue of the sky, and everything in my mind would grow quiet.

Dusk had fallen in soft colors that spilled through the window as I curled up on the couch with a glass of wine in my hand, the phone cradled against my ear like a lifeline. I had finally made contact with Sasha, the one person who still managed to anchor me.

"I'm *so* sorry I haven't been available to talk. I had absolutely no cell reception at that two-week dance retreat up in the mountains. So, what's going on, Lara?" Sasha's words were thick with concern.

"I left him."

There was a pause on the other end as Sasha let out a long exhale. "Well, it's about time."

Sasha did not mince her words; we had been friends since grade school, and she had always been unflinchingly honest. It was one of the many things I loved about her. Though she was far away in New York teaching dance, the distance never affected the closeness between us. Her voice was a comfort that filled the room, as if she were sitting on the couch beside me.

"I know."

"So, what happened?"

I took a deep breath as memories from that night rushed forward. "I panicked. I woke up from a dream, and I knew that I had to get out of there, that if I didn't leave at that moment, I might never find the strength to do it."

"Wow." Sasha paused for a moment. "I know how hard that must have been for you to do, but I gotta say, I'm really proud of you for doing it. Have you guys talked since you left?"

"Just once, about two weeks ago, when I first got into Montana. He was pretty pissed, and then he hung up on me." I shifted my legs up onto the couch and took a large gulp of wine, letting the warm burn settle in my stomach.

"What an asshole." Sasha's words fell heavy on me. I knew she had never been terribly fond of John. She had told me once how he *stifled my energy*. But I had been pregnant and hopeful when we got married, and I believed that becoming a dad would relax his constant need to control everything in his life. And it did, for a while.

I blinked back the tears that threatened to surface. "Was it stupid of me to hope that leaving would... I don't know, wake him up?"

"No, honey, not at all." Her voice grew soft. "But you know that he's been checked out for years."

"I just wonder how much of that is my fault?" I began to pull at the tassels on one of the couch cushions. "I've been angry with him for so long."

"And you have every right to be, Lara. Honestly, I am shocked that you stayed with him as long as you did."

"I know." My words hung like a heavy sigh as I glanced out the window to see Dusty running through the pasture, with

Peter off in the distance. The visual was a comforting contrast against the press of my melancholy thoughts.

As if she could feel the weight on my end, Sasha shifted the topic. "So, you're in Montana, huh? What's it like out there? Tell me all about it."

With a sigh, I sunk back into the couch. "It's so peaceful. I *really* like it here. I'm staying in this cute little cottage on this guy Peter's property in exchange for work. He's blind, so I've been helping him out with his horses and doing grocery runs every few days. But for the most part, I have a lot of free time."

"That sounds nice." There was a pause, and the distant sound of traffic filtered in through the phone. I knew she was sitting on the open window ledge of her apartment, her favorite place to perch and watch the city down below. "Okay, so... tell me a little bit about this guy Peter?"

"Well, he's around my age, I think. He's interesting... a bit closed off sometimes, but then other times he can be really sweet." As I spoke, I realized that even though I didn't know much about him, there was some unspoken current between us, and I had a mild curiosity to explore the boundaries of what that could be.

"Lara?" Sasha's voice grew playful, and I could envision that slow, teasing smile of hers. "Are you attracted to this guy?"

Heat rose to my cheeks like a flush of shame, and I tried to push the feeling away as I fiddled with the stem of my wine glass. "No, what makes you say that?"

Sasha chuckled. "Because I *know* you, and when your voice gets all wistful like that, it can only mean one thing."

"Well, he *is* attractive, but I'm in absolutely no state of mind right now to entertain thoughts like that."

"And why not? In a way, you're free now. Don't completely close yourself off to the possibility of something new. You and John both left your marriage a long time ago. I mean, you guys haven't even been intimate in over three years. That makes me really sad. I can't imagine going that long without being touched."

Squeezing my eyes closed for a moment, I tried to remember what my own desire felt like before it had become nothing more than another casualty of loss.

"Sasha, this is just a work trade arrangement until I can figure out my next step."

"And do you have any idea what that next step is?"

I sighed and finished off my glass of wine with a quick tilt of my head. "I have no clue."

Chapter Five

The morning breeze fluttered the curtains as I lay underneath the blankets. Today was one of those days where I couldn't seem to get out of bed. I curled into myself, draping the thin cotton sheet over my head, the world around me becoming white like the stillness of snow.

"Caleb, look. It's snow."
I place his mittened hand in the deep white powder, watching as his eyes grow wide with wonder.
Evergreens tower above us.
The mountains whispering silent secrets, tucked away within the folds of winter's sleep.
He tumbles onto the soft ground with an exalted smile, his giggles like light dancing against my heart.
"Can we live here, forever, Mommy?"

A soft rap on the door startled me, and I pulled the sheet from my face, debating whether I should answer. With a reluctant sigh, I tossed the covers back and forced myself out of bed. Shuffling over to the door, I opened it to find Peter standing there.

"Morning, Lara." He sounded chipper, and there was a glint of enthusiasm in his eyes. "I'm thinking today would be a good day to teach you how to ride a horse."

A part of me just wanted to crawl back into bed. A dull ache pressed against the back of my head, and I realized I may have drunk too much wine the night before.

"Um." I furrowed my brow. "Can you give me a minute?"

Peter tilted his head, a look of concern flickering across his face. "Rough night?"

I sighed. "Something like that."

"Well, I guess I came at a perfect time, then. Nothing like riding to get you out of a funk." A smile tugged at the corners of his lips. "Tell you what, why don't you meet me in the barn in an hour?"

I found Peter standing in the barn, adjusting the saddle on Penny with a long length of rope coiled over his shoulder. He turned when he heard me approach. "You ready?"

"Yes, let's do this."

With a chuckle, he led the horses out into the pasture. Morning sunlight spilled across the field, illuminating the dew on the grass as Dusty loped ahead of us. Peter gestured for me to come closer. "You'll be riding Penny today. She's great with beginners."

I placed my hand on her side, running my fingers over her coat. She let out a soft nicker and turned her head to gently nudge my arm.

"Hey there, sweetie," I cooed, looking into her gentle brown eyes.

Peter spoke from behind. "We're going to start with a mount. You want to place your left foot into the stirrup and grab hold of the pommel of the saddle with your right hand."

"The pommel?"

Peter's hand reached out and felt around until he took hold of the leather rise in front of the saddle. "This right here."

"Okay, got it." I took a deep breath and placed my foot in the stirrup. Penny shifted her weight slightly, causing me to momentarily lose my footing. Peter's hands landed on my waist, steadying me, his touch causing my pulse to suddenly accelerate. He was close enough that his breath grazed delicately against the back of my neck as he spoke.

"I got you. I'm gonna give you a boost up, okay?"

He lifted me up as I threw my other leg over and perched atop the saddle, grasping the pommel with both hands.

"Are you settled in?"

"Yes." I took a deep breath, acclimating to the feel of Penny beneath me.

"I want you to get used to her movements for a bit. Then when you're ready, you can grab onto the reins lightly for support." As Peter spoke, he began to thread the rope from around his shoulder onto Penny's halter.

My legs gripped tightly against Penny, causing her to sidestep for a moment. Peter's hand rested on her neck, his touch stilling her movements. "I'll be guiding you here, so just sit back and try to relax. Horses are very sensitive to our body language. If you tense up, it'll give Penny conflicting messages."

Shifting myself more comfortably onto the saddle, I felt the power of Penny's muscles flexing beneath my thighs. I reached over and grabbed the reins, careful not to tug on them. "Okay, I have the reins."

"Great, we're going to start moving now." Peter began to walk slowly in front of Penny, guiding her with the rope. My body tilted awkwardly to the side as I tried to adjust myself to her undulating stride.

"The first thing when learning to ride a horse, is settling into the gait." Peter's voice was soft as he walked the horse through the pasture. "You need to learn to match the movements of the horse, so you don't get bounced around. This can be tricky at first, but the secret is in letting go, and allowing the horse to move for you. In time, you'll find a rhythm together."

I closed my eyes and let myself sink into the movement of Penny beneath me. Eventually, I fell into a relaxed sway, and a large smile spread across my face. "I think I got it, Peter," I called down to him excitedly.

"That's good. It appears you may be a natural, Lara." He let out a soft whistle, and Spirit appeared alongside us. Without breaking Penny's leisurely stride, Peter mounted the black horse in one fluid motion, his hand on the rope tethering us together.

"How did you do that?" I asked incredulously.

He turned his head in my direction, shooting me a sly grin. "*Years* of practice."

Peter settled into a trot beside me as we made our way around the perimeter of the pasture. The wind lifted my hair and blew it against my back as a calmness swept over me. The only sounds were the crunch of the horses' hooves upon the grass, the twitter of birds in the distance, and the soft rush of Penny's breath. My mind grew light, and the nagging emptiness clawing inside stilled for a moment. "I can see how this is therapeutic," I said, breaking the comfortable quiet that had settled over us.

He turned his head in my direction. "Yes. There is nothing more peaceful for me than being on a horse. They remind me to find my center."

The look on his face was one of openness, as if he were unlatching a door and letting me in for a moment. This growing closeness between us was comforting.

The sun had risen higher in the sky and beat down upon me as we approached the barn. Peter dismounted and stood below, extending his hand with a playful smile. "Do you feel like going on a real ride?"

"What do you mean?"

"Would you like me to show you?"

"Um... okay." I navigated myself off Penny, feeling the warmth of Peter's hands on me as he helped me down. He clicked his tongue, and Spirit sauntered closer to us, standing patiently while Peter threw his leg over and hoisted himself up.

"I'm going to help you onto Spirit, alright? Just use my foot as leverage and grab my hand."

I hesitated for a moment, unsure if I would be able to stay upright without a saddle to anchor me. Seeming to sense my unease, he tilted his head downward. "Don't worry, I won't let you fall. I promise."

Even though he couldn't see, his calm confidence made me feel surprisingly safe. Placing my foot atop his, I grabbed his hand and lifted myself onto Spirit.

I settled in behind him as Peter took the reins. "You'll have to hold on to me tight."

Tentatively, I wrapped my arms around his waist, breathing in his earthy scent. The feel of him so close caused a flicker of heat to sweep through me.

"Are you ready?"

"I think so."

Spirit began to move at a gentle trot, forcing me to slide closer to Peter, my hands tightly curling around the well-defined muscles of his abdomen.

"Just try to move with me." Peter instructed as we lurched forward, gradually picking up speed as Spirit's trot turned into a steady gallop. My heart leapt, hammering in my chest as the pounding of Spirit's hooves against the ground surged through my body like a drumbeat. The wind whipped loudly in my ears and brought tears to my eyes. I clung tightly to Peter, elation coursing through my veins as the pasture flowed by us in a dreamlike blur of weightlessness. I closed my eyes, the sheer velocity liberating me, and for one brief moment, I felt so alive.

We slowed as we approached the barn once more, easing

back into a trot before coming to a full stop. I was breathing hard as Peter dismounted and placed his hands on either side of my waist, guiding me back down to the ground.

"Oh my god. *That* was amazing." My words came out in a breathless pant.

"Thought you'd like that." He grinned. "I didn't take you as fast as Spirit usually likes to go. But it's the closest thing to flying you'll ever feel without leaving the ground."

My body hummed with adrenaline as I followed him back into the barn. I stood in the doorway and watched as he efficiently moved around the horses, removing Penny's saddle and bridle, and placing them on hooks beside the stalls. "Would you like to help me brush down the horses?"

"Sure." I watched as he moved to a small table in the far corner of the barn and felt around for the two brushes sitting there. Retrieving them, he held one out for me to take. "Why do we brush them like this?" I asked as I walked over to where Penny stood beside her stall.

"Well, it's important to always brush em down after a run. It removes all the sweat and debris that can irritate their skin and helps keep their coat healthy." Peter ran his brush down Spirit in long, gentle strokes as he spoke. "And it also feels good."

"Oh, really?" I looked over at Penny, who was swishing her tail back and forth as I moved the bristles down the length of her back.

"Yep, it's like a relaxing massage for them."

I observed him for a moment. There was a deep tenderness there in the way he spoke and interacted with the horses. John had never been too fond of animals. Our dog, Zeke, was only a reluctant compromise gifted to me on my birthday.

"So, I was going to light up the barbeque tonight. Would you care to join?" Peter's voice stirred me from my thoughts.

"For dinner?"

A faint smile played upon his lips as his voice became low and vaguely intimate. "Yes, for dinner."

My skin prickled with warmth as I ran the brush through Penny's mane. His invitation felt cloaked in something beyond a friendly offer, but I wasn't quite sure; he was so hard to read sometimes.

"Yes, I'd love to join you for dinner."

Peter turned in my direction, his gaze hovering above my head. "Okay, how does around six sound?"

"That works for me."

Placing his brush back down on the table, he let out a short whistle, and Dusty materialized from one of the stalls, shaking out straw from his fur. "Great, I'll see you then." With a nod, he slipped past me and made his way out of the barn, the sunlight hitting his back in a soft silhouette as Dusty followed dutifully beside him.

Chapter Six

The last of the day's sunlight swept through the cottage, bathing the walls in rich tones of amber as I stood in front of the mirror. My fingers ran through the loose strands of my hair as I glanced back at my reflection, wondering how Peter perceived me in his mind. Most of my life, I had relied on my appearance to dominate how others saw me. The full lips and flirty smile, clothes that hugged my curves. These traits, which I thought had always defined me, did not apply when I was around Peter. The realization hit me like a burst of freedom. Liberated from the constraints of my physical facade, I no longer needed to concern myself with these habitual expectations of beauty, the ones that had molded and warped my self-worth for so many years. Small breasts I wished were bigger, a stomach that could be flatter. For the first time, none of it mattered anymore.

I headed into the kitchen and dug through the cupboards, looking for the bottle of wine I had stashed. With the bottle of Cabernet in hand, I walked down the dirt path that hugged the fence line, the smell of charcoal and wood smoke wafting through the air as I approached the porch. Dusty pushed open the screen door and ran over to me in an enthusiastic greeting, his thick tail whipping against my legs.

"Come on in, Lara," Peter called from somewhere within the house.

I found him in the kitchen, standing at the counter chopping vegetables. "Hey, there. I brought some wine."

Peter set down the knife and reached out his hand to take the bottle. His fingers wound momentarily around mine, and a soft tingle of electricity spread across my skin.

"Thanks. Red or white?"

"Red."

Peter nodded. "This will go great with the steaks then. You do eat steak, right?"

"Yes, I do." I tried to push away the growing feeling of giddiness that rose inside. I knew it was only my loneliness breathing convincing stories in my ear.

"Oh, thank god." Peter flashed a smile.

"Can I help you with anything?"

He resumed chopping. "Nope, just make yourself comfortable. I'm gonna throw all this on the grill in a sec."

I nervously watched him slice through a potato. "Aren't you afraid you're going to cut yourself?"

Peter chuckled. "Oh, I've cut myself plenty. But after a while, I've learned to perceive things in grids. I map out the length of something and determine how many cuts I need to make. Kinda like a mathematical equation."

"That's interesting." I watched as he continued to chop the vegetables, noticing how even the pieces were, his motions smooth and precise. "Is that what makes it easier for you to get around? I noticed that you don't use a cane or anything."

He nodded with a slight chuckle. "Well, part of that is just sheer stubbornness, honestly. But yes, once I'm able to map out the dimensions of what is around me, I can navigate it a lot easier." He opened a drawer with one hand, felt around inside, and retrieved a bottle opener, placing it on the counter. "Here, you can open the wine if you'd like."

"I want to thank you for taking me riding today." I twisted the opener through the cork, removed it with a loud pop, and grabbed two glasses from the cupboard. "It really did help get me out of my funk."

Peter threw the remainder of the vegetables into a large bowl. "I'm glad to hear that. Any time you want to get back on a horse, just let me know." With a small smile, he slid past me and out the back door.

Following him outside with my glass of wine, I gazed out at the long shadows of early evening which spread across the pasture. "You know, I could really get used to this."

"Having a man cook you dinner?" Peter grinned as he placed the steaks on the grill with a loud sizzle.

"No. I mean all this open space." I turned to him with a playful smile. "Though a man cooking me dinner definitely adds to the view."

A deep laugh resonated from low in his throat. "Well, I'm so glad I can add to the view."

We sat at the picnic table beneath the large sycamore tree, wine glasses resting on the cloth Peter had laid out, while a gentle breeze ruffled through our hair. We ate in a comfortable silence for a while as shadows from the leaves overhead cast soft patterns across the table. I had learned that Peter didn't care much for small talk, and I found that refreshing. So much of my relationship with John had consisted of me nodding while he rambled on unaware, entertained by the sound of his own voice. But there was a stillness between Peter and I that did not need words to fill the space. Our legs occasionally brushed up against each other under the table, and something about it felt natural and intimate.

"You know, Peter, when I first met you, I figured you were going to be a tough nut to crack."

He cocked his head to the side, his fork paused in mid-air. "What do you mean?"

"Well, you didn't seem very pleased with me when I showed up that day with Miriam, and she did warn me that you could be a bit bristly at times."

Peter chuckled at that, his hand skimming along the tablecloth to find his wine glass. "She did, did she?"

I leaned toward him, my elbows resting on the table. "But you have been *surprisingly* hospitable."

He shrugged. "What can I say? I enjoy your company, Lara."

A warmth rose to my cheeks. "And why is that?" I found myself boldly asking.

His eyes drifted to a point beyond me. "There's a quietness about you."

"A quietness?" I furrowed my brows.

"Yes, your energy is calming."

"Really?"

A slow smile spread over Peter's face as his voice grew soft. "Really." I watched him as he resumed eating, his candid words settling around me like a quiet invitation.

The sun shifted its soft light across the pasture as we finished our meal and poured the last of the wine into our glasses. "That was really a good dinner, Peter."

"I'm glad you liked it."

Standing up, I stretched out my limbs and grabbed my empty plate from the table. "Do you mind if I use your bathroom?"

He nodded. "Sure thing, it's the first door down the hall."

I made my way into the house and down the hallway. Opening the first door I came to, I stepped into a room that was clearly not the bathroom. A large table in the corner contained brushes and oil paints scattered across the worn wooden surface. Beside the window sat an easel with a half-finished painting of a mountain range, streaks of violet and crimson splashed across the sky. I stepped closer to study it, noticing the thick layer of dust on the canvas.

Glancing around, I realized that everything was covered in dust, as if Peter had not been in this room for years. Quietly closing the door, I found the bathroom and flicked on the light, a tight feeling of sadness overcoming me as I tried to imagine how it must feel for him to be an artist and then lose his sight. I was familiar with the feeling of life pushing you away from the things that mattered most.

> *"Lara, are you sure this is what you want to do? You can take an extended leave of*
> *absence. Your job will always be here when you're ready to come back."*
> *The muffled sounds of children laughing on the playground filters in through the open window,*
> *cutting me like a knife.*
> *I choke back the tears, my words coming out in a trembling rush.*
> *"I don't know if I'm ever going to be ready to come back."*

Returning to the kitchen, I found Peter washing the dishes. I leaned against the doorframe, watching him. His sleeves were rolled up, showing the muscular definition of his arms, his skin a golden brown from the sun.

"I didn't know those paintings in the living room were yours."

The sound of my voice caused him to abruptly turn around. "How did you know those paintings were mine?" His words came out clipped.

"I just saw the art room."

"What were you doing in my art room?" Peter's face grew tense.

"I'm sorry." I bit my lip, a feeling of mild discomfort washing over me. "I wasn't trying to snoop or anything. I just accidentally opened the wrong door."

He let out a deep sigh, and a sorrow seemed to sweep through him as he spoke. "Yes, I *used* to be a painter, Lara."

"Well, they're really beautiful." My words came out cautious as I realized I had broached a topic he was clearly sensitive about.

He moved closer to me, his eyes abruptly flashing with a sharp intensity. "So, now that you seem to know about all the things *I* used to do, I think it's your turn."

"What do you mean?" I stared at him, a flicker of tension curling around me.

"What's your story? I may be blind, but I can clearly see that you're running from something."

My heart pounded, and an emotion akin to anger stirred inside. "That's none of your business."

"You're right. It is none of my *business*." He threw the words back at me like a challenge.

I sucked in a breath. "You know, I think I'm going to call it a night, Peter. Thank you for dinner."

"Lara, wait." He reached out to me, his hand lightly touching my arm as his eyes softened. "I'm sorry. I didn't mean to-"

"I'll see you tomorrow, okay." I abruptly pulled away, leaving him standing there in the kitchen with his face furrowed.

The sun had sunk below the ridge of the mountains, washing the sky in a bright pink glow as I walked back to the cottage. My heart was a stone tumbling around in my chest, as if all my pain had solidified into a substance that left me inert, so terrified of what would spill out if I opened my mouth.

Opening the cottage door, I walked into the kitchen, my eyes falling to the blinking light coming from my phone on the counter. My breath caught within my throat as I read the message from John that flashed across my screen.

Please call me. We need to talk.

Chapter Seven

Sitting on the couch, I held the phone. My thumb hovered indecisively over John's number before pressing the call button.

He answered on the second ring. "Lara."

"Hi, John." I leaned back against the cushions and closed my eyes. The headache that had been threatening me all day suddenly burst through and settled around my temples.

"I think it's time we talked about some things." John's voice fell deep and somber against my ear, causing a weight to settle in my chest.

I yanked a throw pillow onto my lap and frantically picked at the threads as if I could unravel the snarled reality of what we had become. "Yes, I agree. We do need to talk."

"I need the address of wherever you are staying."

"Why?"

"So, I can send you the divorce papers."

He spat his words out, and my heart stilled, a bleak emptiness overcoming me. "I thought you wanted to talk?"

"Yes, I want to *talk* about getting a divorce."

A sharp anger rushed out unrestrained. "Jesus, John. You can be so *fucking* cold sometimes."

"Oh, *I'm* fucking cold? You're the one who left this marriage, Lara." His voice turned icy. "What do you want me to do? Come chasing after you?"

I bit my lip as the sudden sting of tears clouded my vision. "I don't know. I just really didn't want us to end like this."

"Well, you should have thought about that before you left." John let out a heavy sigh. "We also need to discuss the house."

Eight years we had spent within those walls of knotted oak, nestled among the thick undergrowth of the forest. I remembered the day we bought it. John had ushered me excitedly through the door, his deep brown eyes twinkling with joy while I cradled the growing life inside me. So many memories were held inside that house. Caleb's birth; years of laughter and growth. Then the darkness that followed. A haunted silence and a suffocating pain that twisted around us until we could no longer breathe in the same room together.

Tears slipped down my cheeks in warm rivulets. "You can have the house, John. I don't want it."

Late morning sunshine blanketed the field in a glaring brightness that did not match my current state of emotions. I longed for moody grey skies that made me want to curl up in a blanket with the soft steady patter of rain upon the roof, drowning out all the noise in my mind.

Walking over to the barn, I found Peter inside, brushing down Spirit. His gentle rhythmic movements stopped as he heard me approach, and he tilted his head in my direction.

"Afternoon, Lara."

"Hey... I was going to make a grocery run in town today. Is there anything you want besides the usual?"

Peter set the brush aside and turned toward me. "Actually, I do need to grab a few things at the hardware store. I was hoping I could tag along?"

"Sure, that's fine." I glanced down and noticed I was picking at my nails again, not realizing how painful and raw the skin around them had become. "I'm going to head out in a bit."

Something must have wavered in my voice, because Peter took a step toward me, his face flashing with concern. "Lara, are you okay?"

"Yeah. I'm okay." I tried to lighten my tone, hoping he wouldn't be able to sense the myriad of emotions churning within me. "I just had a little trouble sleeping last night."

"I'm sorry to hear that. I hope it didn't have anything to do with me."

"No, not at all."

He stood there as if waiting for me to share more while I absentmindedly scuffed the straw around on the floor with my feet. "How about we meet by the car in twenty minutes?"

Peter nodded. "Sounds good."

I watched him as he resumed brushing Spirit and took the opportunity to make a quick retreat out of the barn, back to the safety of my solitude, where the only questions plaguing me were my own.

Peter sat beside me in the front seat as we took the twenty-five-minute drive into town. I enjoyed the fresh air from the open windows as it hit my face, clearing my head from the night before.

"Lara," Peter gazed straight ahead as he spoke, "I want you to know that I feel really bad about how things ended last night."

I let out a sigh. "I told you, it's fine."

"No, it's not. I shouldn't have reacted the way I did." His voice grew soft. "I like you, Lara, and I really want you to feel comfortable around me."

There was something acutely tender in his words, and I

glanced over at him, taking in his profile; the trimmed beard against a strong jawline, and his thick dark hair, which I had the sudden urge to run my fingers through. "Don't worry, I do." I reached over and placed my hand on Peter's arm briefly. His muscles twitched from the contact, and he turned towards me, seemingly startled by my touch. Heat bloomed across my skin as I wondered why I had just done that. I pulled away, gripping the steering wheel.

"Okay, good." Peter flashed a warm smile as he settled back into the seat, allowing the wind to fill the space between us.

We arrived in Stevensville. The backdrop of the mountains rose in the distance, framing the small, quaint shops that lined the sidewalks, the buildings reminiscent of days long ago.

Peter stepped out of the car and leaned up against the door, his head tilted toward the sky with a pensive look on his face, reminding me of some brooding cowboy, with his fitted denim jeans and worn boots. "Little trivia for you. Did you know that this town was the very first settlement in the state of Montana?"

I glanced around, taking in the old buildings, their unspoken history embedded in the silence of the faded red brick. "No. I didn't know that."

"Yep. It was founded by a group of Jesuit missionaries who came here in an attempt to proselytize the Salish tribes of this area." His voice was tinged with disapproval as he spoke.

I rested against the car beside him, the warmth from the door radiating against my back as I squinted off into the distance, trying to imagine this place before buildings and roads. "And did they succeed?'

Peter turned to me as the sun hit him, illuminating the green within his eyes. "What do you think?" He motioned his hand out to the street. "There's a little museum down the road from here, holding various artifacts from the Salish tribes that lived on this land peacefully for hundreds of years. I find it so ironic, that we swoop in, destroy their culture and then commemorate the remains." Peter gestured toward the sidewalk. "Do you mind walking me over to the hardware store?"

"No, of course not."

Peter placed his hand tentatively on my arm as I walked him down the street, his touch causing something to stir within like tiny embers I thought had been long extinguished. So many years I had spent recoiling from John's touch, as if the very act of intimacy had become a sin.

John's hands reach for me in the darkness, trailing over my skin.
The press of his arousal against me like a demand.
Sucking in a sharp breath, I pull away from him, inching further toward the edge of the bed.
"Lara."
"Please, John. I can't."
"I need to feel something else right now. Let me feel something else."
His voice is pleading, his hands grasping at me.
I grit my teeth,
his touch like sandpaper against an open wound, my words fragmented and torn
"What about what I need?"
The blankets are tossed aside, the weight of him beside me lifts as he stalks out of the room,
the slamming of cupboards ringing through the empty house.

"I think we may have passed it, Lara."

"What?" Peter's voice roused me from my thoughts. "Oh, right. Sorry." My cheeks flushed as I pivoted on my heels and turned around, walking back the way we came. "Looks like I make a pretty lousy navigator."

He chuckled as I stopped at the entrance to the hardware store, his hand sliding from my arm and feeling for the handle to the door of the shop. "Guess we have something in common, then."

"Wait." I looked back at the way we had just come. "How were you able to tell that we passed it?"

He gestured up at a large awning which hung ahead of us. "When the sun is out, I can always tell that I've gone too far when I hit the shadows." Peter flashed me a smile before disappearing into the store.

I ducked into the market down the street, where I loaded my cart with various items from Miriam's list. My hands ran over the produce as my mind wandered back to Peter. There was a softness there between us that I wanted to rest against. Though my marriage was ending, I felt a sense of calm for the first time in years, and beneath that, the stirring of something new. I melted into this new feeling, as if a layer of myself was slowly peeling away.

Placing the groceries in the back seat of the car, I headed over to the hardware store. The bells on the door jingled as I entered. Large antlers hung against the walls, and a hodgepodge of assorted objects crowded the shop, ranging from boots and hats to farm equipment. I saw Peter at the counter, chatting with an old man who was ringing up items at the register, his long white beard hanging well past his chest.

"Afternoon, Miss," the man said, nodding to me with a smile.

Peter turned around. "That you, Lara?"

"Yeah, it's me." I walked up and stood beside Peter, my hands running over some embroidered leather pouches displayed on the counter.

"Lara, this is Mike." Peter gestured to the man, who leaned over to firmly shake my hand.

"Pleasure, Lara. Peter says you've been helping him out on his property."

"I have, yes."

"Well, it's nice to see him in such lovely company." Mike shot me a wink as he bagged up the rest of Peter's purchase.

Peter leaned in close to me. "So, Mike was just telling me about a really great band that's playing over at the saloon tomorrow night." A playful grin spread across his face. "Feel like getting a taste of some good ol' Montana culture?"

The idea of breaking the monotony of my quiet nights sparked an unexpected eagerness, and I found myself smiling. "You know, I think I would."

The blue sky had given way to scattered streaks of gold as we arrived back at the house, the sound of crickets filtering through the air as I cut the engine.

"I just love that sound," I said with a sigh.

Peter turned toward me, the glow from the setting sun bathing his skin in a golden hue. "Me too. It always reminds me of my childhood."

There was a tension that pulled between us, and for a moment, neither of us moved to break it.

"Well, thanks for the ride to town," Peter finally said, stepping out of the car and opening the back door to grab the two bags from the seat.

"Here, let me help you with those," I said, moving to open my door.

"No, I got it." He shot me a smile. "Have a good night, Lara."

I watched him as he walked toward the house, his pace plodding and cautious as he navigated up the steps. I had a sudden urge to call out to him, to say something, but I couldn't find the words; they were locked inside. My longing was a hesitant child, uncertain of her own thoughts.

Making my way to the cottage, I reflected on the feeling of emptiness inside me. It prickled and stung, like nerves waking up after a prolonged sleep, and it left me with a strange sense of hope. I still had life inside, waiting patiently to be let out. The empty shell I thought I had become was only a mask slipped over my heart, and I could feel the cracks forming.

> *I lie in bed, the sheets in a tangle around my inert limbs.*
> *Lost in the desolate vacuum of my thoughts.*
> *Outside the window, the hours blend into days.*
> *Sunlight trapping itself between the branches of the redwoods, and then fading to the dusk of nightfall.*
> *John appears beside the bed, his face contorted in a hostile sorrow.*
> *"Get up, Lara."*
> *My mouth moves, but no sound comes out. I close my eyes, blocking out his gaze.*
> *"God damn it!"*
> *The door slams shut, rattling the windows like an earthquake that only the two of us can feel.*

As I walked into the cottage, the last rays of the day threw soft light across the carpet and suffused the room in a rich, comforting glow. The grip of exhaustion settled over me, and deciding to forgo dinner, I retreated into the bedroom. Slipping on my nightgown, I climbed beneath the sheets. The feel of loose cotton against my skin was a comforting caress, and I closed my eyes, awaiting the soft dance of dreams to carry me away.

I awoke with a jolt. I had been dreaming of Caleb, hazy images I desperately wanted to cling to, but were already fading from me like mist rising off water, leaving my hands grasping at nothing but air.

Moonlight flooded my bedroom in distorted shadows as the sound of rustling and muffled footsteps broke the silence within the cottage. An icy chill sliced through me, and I sat upright in bed, clutching the sheets, my heart a frantic rhythm in my chest.

Off in the distance, I heard Dusty barking.

"Who's there!" My voice came out shaky as my eyes adjusted to the darkness, and that's when I saw the shadowed outline of a man beyond my doorway, standing in the living room.

Chapter Eight

The man swayed on his feet and then stumbled and lurched toward the bedroom.

A shrill scream burst from my mouth.

"Hey, hey, hey now." The man's words were slurred and drawn out as he raised his hands up in the air. "I ain't gonna hurt you." He lost his balance for a moment, and gripped the door frame for support, peering into the room.

I slid my body up against the headboard. Cool metal pressed against the thin fabric of my nightgown. My pulse pounded in my ears. Here I was, staring at every woman's fear. The shadow in the night. The monster beside the bed.

"Get the hell out of here!" I tried to sound strong and assertive, but my voice came out choked, cracking around the edges.

"Calm down, calm down. I just…" But before he could finish his sentence, the front door burst open. There was a flurry of movement as Peter rushed into the house with Dusty at his heels. Peter's arms reached out wildly until he made contact with the man and threw him to the ground.

The man gave out a muffled groan, then a chuckle escaped from him. "It's good to see you again too, Peter."

Peter sat on top of the man, pinning his wrists to the floor, his voice sharp. "What the fuck are you doing here, Greg?"

My grip on the bed sheets loosened as a wave of relief flooded me. Peter clearly knew this person. I moved to the far side of the bed and flicked the lamp on, flooding the room with light.

Greg grimaced and squinted up at Peter. "I was just looking for a place to crash, man. I didn't think anyone would be here."

"I thought I told you never to set foot on my property again."

Greg's head lolled to the side, dark sweaty hair plastered against his face, his eyes trailing over me. "Where d'ya manage to find this pretty lady?"

Peter's hand found Greg's face, and gripping it tightly, yanked his gaze away from me. His voice came out in a low growl. "You need... to shut... the fuck up. *Now*." Peter's eyes flashed with a hot anger as he turned in my direction. "Lara, could you please do me a favor and call the Sheriff's Office? I want to make sure that my brother gets a proper escort back home."

I fumbled for my phone on the nightstand, my hands trembling as I dialed the number that Peter gave me.

Lights flashed through the windows of the cottage, bathing the living room in blue and red as Peter's brother was led away by the tall, imposing sheriff, who apparently was quite familiar with Greg.

"All right, Greg. Let's get you on home so you can sleep it off, okay?"

Dressed in nothing but jeans, Peter sat stiffly on the couch. The muscles of his bare chest rippled with tension, and I could make out patches of mud smeared on his knees as if he had fallen. The thought caused my throat to tighten.

"Hey, Pete, do you want to file a report?" the sheriff asked as he stood in the doorway with his hand clamped down tightly on Greg's shoulder. "This is breaking and entering, you know."

Peter shook his head. "No, just get him out of here."

The sheriff nodded and closed the door behind him, leaving the room infused with a heavy silence.

Standing, Peter ran his fingers roughly through his hair. "I'm *so* sorry about all that, Lara. Greg has *never* showed up like this before." He took a step in my general direction, seeking me out, his face etched with worry. "Are you okay?"

I folded my arms around myself, a slight tremor taking hold as the adrenaline subsided and replaced itself with the grip of exhaustion. "Yes, I'm okay. Just a little shaken up."

The cold press of Dusty's nose nudged against my hand, and I leaned down to pet him. "Looks like Dusty is a pretty decent guard dog, after all."

"Yes. He was going nuts in the house, so I went outside to see what was going on. Then I heard you scream." Peter's eyes grew dark. "I don't remember the last time I ran that fast." He let out a long sigh, his face contorted with a mixture of emotions I could not read. "Are you sure you're alright?"

I placed my hand on his arm. "I'm sure. I just got startled, that's all." He appeared to stiffen for a moment, then relax against my touch. My eyes momentarily trailed down the length of his chest, taking in the contours of his muscles, before pulling my hand away. "So, you have a brother."

Peter felt his way back over to the couch, sinking down as anger flared in his eyes. He shook his head, his hands sliding up his face. "A worthless drunk of a brother, yes."

"I'm sorry to hear that."

He shrugged. "It is what it is. Miriam and I have tried for years to get him help. He's been in and out of rehab at least a dozen times."

"Did something happen between you two?"

"You don't want to hear about my family drama, Lara."

I stepped closer to him. "Yes, I do. If you feel like talking about it."

With a sigh, Peter leaned back against the couch. "Well, Miriam realized that Greg was stealing money from me, and that's when things really fractured between us. One day, she confronted him. He was drunk as usual, and he hit her."

"Oh my God." My hand rose to my mouth.

"Yeah. I completely lost it on him. It was really ugly, and we haven't spoken since. That is until tonight."

"How long has it been?"

"About a year."

Joining Peter on the couch, I settled into the cushions and curled up my knees, resting my chin against them. "I can't imagine how hard that must be for you."

"Yeah, well, the apple doesn't fall too far from the tree."

I turned to him. "What do you mean?"

He let out another sigh. "We were teenagers when our mother passed away from breast cancer. That's when our father started hitting the bottle pretty hard, and Greg followed shortly after. They enable each other. It's all pretty fucked up."

"Sounds like a mess. I'm sorry."

A morose chuckle spilled from his lips. "We all have our own special brand of family dysfunction. Mine just happens to be sponsored by the liquor corporations."

A feeling of fragile intimacy seemed to settle around us as Peter shared his tangled family history with me. He radiated a loneliness as he sat there with his jaw tightly clenched, confined behind a wall of isolation brought on by the darkness that surrounded his sight. I wanted to reach him, to somehow temper the emotions that I knew were boiling inside, searching for release.

Peter abruptly stood up, passing his fingers vigorously through his hair again. "I'll let you get some sleep." He turned in my direction with a look of intensity. "And I promise you. What happened tonight, will *never* happen again." He ran his hand along the wall as he found his way to the door before stopping, his fingers hovering over the knob. "I'm going to leave Dusty here with you."

Dusty had taken up a spot on the floor beside the couch. Upon hearing his name, he began to thump his tail with enthusiasm.

"Oh, that's not necessary. I'll be fine." I glanced down at my nails, picking at what was left of the edges. "Don't you need him to help you back to the house?"

"Don't worry about me. I'll be okay. I'd prefer he stay with you tonight." A small smile crept over his face, distilling the heaviness that hung in the room. "Besides, Dusty happens to be really great at snuggling."

"Oh, really?" I couldn't help the sudden heat that rose to the surface as I tried to push away the thought of Peter in my bed with his arms enfolding me. I had lived without intimacy for so long, I didn't even remember what it felt like anymore. But there it was, a murmur of longing hiding beneath all the layers of myself.

He nodded, a lightness momentarily gathering in his eyes. "Yes. I promise you won't be disappointed."

"Okay, if you insist." I smiled at him, wishing he could see it, wishing that there weren't so many subtleties lost between us.

"Stay, boy." Peter extended out his hand in a command as he opened the door, pausing for a moment as he stood in the threshold. "Oh, and you might want to get in the habit of locking the door from now on."

"Of course, I didn't even think about that." I flinched, realizing that the remote location had given me a false sense of security.

With a nod, Peter stepped out and closed the door softly behind him.

I shuffled into the bedroom and slid under the covers while Dusty jumped up onto the bed. His warm tongue flicked against my nose before he settled against my side with a contented sigh that stole away the silence in the room. Grateful for Peter's thoughtful gesture, I wrapped my arms around Dusty and nestled my face against his fur, breathing in the clean canine smell, which always reminded me of wind, earth, and grass.

The comforting rise and fall of his breath lulled me into a state of relaxation as my eyelids closed and exhaustion joined me beneath the sheets, leaving impressions of dreams that drifted into the air above me like the gentle hand of a mother, soothing her child to sleep.

Chapter Nine

"So, what happened?" Sasha's voice cut through the receiver as I lay in bed. "I just got your message."

I turned over onto my side, running my fingers through Dusty's coat. "Well, apparently, Peter has a brother with a drinking problem. He showed up at my place in the middle of the night, completely trashed, and scared the crap out of me."

"Jesus, Lara. Are you okay?"

"Yeah. Peter charged in and had him hauled away by the sheriff." Visions from the night before flashed through my mind. The look in Peter's eyes as he grappled with a past that he could not outpace.

Sasha let out a long exhale. "Wow. That sounds intense."

"It was." Morning sunlight streaked across the blankets, washing me in its buttery warmth. "Oh, and John called me."

"Really? And what did he have to say?"

I paused for a moment as the weight of our conversation from a few days ago, gripped me once more. "He wants to send me divorce papers."

"This is what you wanted, right?" Sasha's words came out in a hesitant question. "I mean, you guys have been unhappy for *so* long."

My fingers traced the creases in the sheets, the lines like patterns etched into a surface I could not erase. "I know."

A heavy silence settled over us for a moment, and when Sasha spoke again, her voice was soft with empathy. "So, this is it. This is the end?"

I sat up, glancing out at the view of the aspen trees beyond my window, their limbs like delicate dancers reaching out to the cobalt sky. A deep sorrow cut into me. Our love had never been strong enough to survive losing Caleb. All the years we had spent together, navigating our own private minefields, locked within a grief neither of us knew how to process. And in the end, all it took was a phone call to wipe away our entire history. How fragile and fleeting we had become. Or had we always been that way?

"I guess it is." I sighed as Dusty yawned and shifted his position against me on the bed. "He also wanted to know about the house."

"And?"

"I said he could keep it."

"Why, Lara? That's a really nice house, don't just give it to him."

"Sasha, there are too many bad memories for me there. I can't go back to them."

Her voice grew soft. "I understand, but maybe you guys could agree to sell it and split the money? That would give you a financial cushion."

"I don't know. John wants to keep it."

"Well, screw him. He doesn't get to call all the shots. You know I can hook you up with a really good lawyer-"

"Sasha." I took a deep breath. "I'm sorry, but I don't feel like talking about this anymore, okay? I'm just trying to process the end of my marriage here. The legalities of it are unimportant to me right now."

"I'm just trying to help, Lara."

"I know." I bit my lip, trying to still my swirling thoughts. "I'll figure it out. If anything, he'll probably end up buying me out of the house."

"Well, that would help." She paused for a moment, her voice twinged with sadness. "God, I wish I wasn't so far away."

I let out a long exhale. "Me too."

"Okay, so why don't you tell me a little more about this sexy cowboy of yours who swooped to your rescue last night?" Sasha turned playful, obviously trying to lighten the mood that had settled between us.

The image of Peter standing shirtless in my living room flashed through my mind, and I quickly pushed it away, momentarily flustered. "You know, I need to get out of bed and start my day, I'll call you later."

"Okay." She let out a chuckle. "I love you, Lara."

"Love you, too."

I stood and stretched as Dusty jumped to the floor, his tail smacking against my legs as he circled me. I missed having a dog around. I missed the solid consistency of Zeke's loving brown eyes and the sound of his pattering feet as he followed me loyally throughout the house. Perhaps that had been the last thing tethering me to my life and my marriage, and when he died, there had been nothing left to cling to.

Early afternoon sun danced across my skin as I walked through the pasture with Dusty. Approaching the barn, I spotted Miriam's truck parked in the driveway and could hear the tense hushed tones of her and Peter talking.

"I don't understand what the hell he was doing here. I thought he was living out in Missoula now?" Miriam's voice sounded strained. "Have you talked to Dad?"

"No. I'm not speaking to Dad right now, Miriam."

I stood at the entrance of the barn while Dusty ran to greet Miriam, his tail lashing frantically as he looped around her.

"Lara!" She turned her head in my direction and slipped on a bright smile as she walked over and took my hands in hers. "It's so good to see you. I've been meaning to stop by sooner, but life's been a bit crazy with packing these days. How have you been settling in?" Her voice grew serious as she gave me a gentle squeeze before letting go of my hands. "I'm so sorry about last night. Peter was just telling me what happened."

I looked over at Peter who was shoveling feed into the stalls, his back toward me. "Well, except for the excitement of last night," I shot her a wan smile, "it has been very peaceful out here."

"Oh, good," Miriam said with a sigh. "I was worried you wanted to head for the hills after Greg's little display." Her eyes darted over to Peter. "And what about Peter? Has he been behaving himself?"

He shot his head in the direction of us, letting out a low grunt.

"Yes, he's actually been really nice." For some reason, I found myself blushing as I said this.

Miriam let out a chuckle. "Nice? Really?"

"Miriam, don't you have somewhere to be?" Peter called out gruffly from behind one of the stalls.

"Yes, I do, little brother, and don't you forget about dinner this weekend, okay?"

"I won't." His reply was muffled as Miriam signaled for me to follow her out of the barn.

"Would you like to join us for dinner as well?" she asked as we walked down the driveway to her truck. "My husband and I are having a little get together over here before we leave for New York next week."

"That sounds nice. I'd love to."

"Hey." Miriam touched my arm. "I'm *really* sorry Greg showed up like that and scared you. Peter told me this morning that he's put a restraining order on him. So, he shouldn't be coming around again."

I nodded as the images from last night swept over me once more. "That's good to know." I gazed out to the pasture, watching Peter as he led Spirit out of the barn. He slid onto the saddle and dug his heels against Spirit, bringing him to a fast trot that quickly became a gallop as they raced across the field.

"There he goes again," Miriam said with a long sigh as he sped off to the far edge of the pasture. "That's his therapy, you know."

"Don't you ever worry about him falling off and getting hurt?" I asked.

She nodded. "Oh, I do, but horses are his life. It's the one thing he refused to give up after his accident. He's been working with horses since he was a kid, and he's really amazing with them; he seems to understand them in a way most people don't. Peter may push himself too far at times, but he's not reckless." Miriam turned to me. "When he was a little boy, he wanted to be a race car driver." She shook her head as a smile tugged at her lips. "He's always loved the thrill of speed."

A sudden yearning to reach out and ask more about his accident pulled at me, but I knew it was his story to tell. We both held traumas that defined us, secrets that kept us safe from prying eyes. I knew how hard it was to sit in the middle of a storm while others watched from the safety of dry land.

Miriam opened the door to her truck, leaning against the frame. "So, I'll see you this weekend?"

"Yep, I'll be there." I raised my hand in a wave as Miriam started up the truck and backed down the driveway, leaving plumes of dust rising into the sky.

Dusk gathered around the cottage as I spooned soup into a bowl for dinner. The silence that consumed the room felt like a sharp ache in my gut that I struggled to sit with.

It was moments like this that Caleb crept from the corners of my mind. Bittersweet memories that saturated me with longing and an incredible sorrow. The feel of his silky hair against my lips as I kissed him goodnight. The way he would curl his fingers around mine as we would walk into the forest, looking for gnomes and fairies hidden beneath the dewy ferns. The sound of his laughter like rays of sunshine, showering me with his endless, energetic joy.

"Why can't we see the fairies, Mommy?"
Dappled light dances through the trees as we crouch down among
the wet earth,
our fingers trailing across the ferns.
"Well, because they are made of magic."
I reach out and press my lips against Caleb's forehead. His skin damp
and smelling of forest.
"Magic is not something that you can always see with your eyes,
it's something you feel inside your heart."
Caleb looks up at me,
his eyes bathed with the vibrance of a four-year-old's imagination.
"Like love?"
"Yes, honey. Love is a lot like magic."

A knock on the door tore me from my recollections. "Come in."

Peter popped his head through the doorway before stepping inside. "Lara, I don't suppose you're still up for going out tonight?"

I had completely forgotten about the show, and I stood up from the table, running my fingers through my hair. "Um..."

"Figured you probably weren't after the drama of last night. But I thought I'd check, just in case." Peter stood in the living room with his hands shoved in his pockets, looking faintly sheepish.

"No. I'm okay. I think I could use the distraction. Can you just give me a minute to freshen up?"

Peter nodded, a smile lighting up his face. "Alrighty then. I'll meet you over at the house."

It was dark by the time I headed over to Peter's house. Dusty met me as I got to the porch, running up and nearly knocking me down onto the grass. Laughter tumbled from my lips as I attempted to block his onslaught of kisses. "Did you miss me, boy?"

"Seems he's taken quite a liking to you."

Peter's voice startled me, and I threw my hand to my chest as I saw his shadowed figure sitting on the steps. "Oh, gosh. I didn't see you there."

"Sorry." He stood and walked down the stairs, the light of the moon hitting his face and revealing a playful grin. "One of the many occupational hazards of being blind. I can sometimes be unaware of when I'm lurking around in the dark."

With a laugh, I pulled my keys from my purse. "Well, I guess that means I'm driving again, huh?"

Hes chuckled, his hand falling on my back as I led him over to the car. "Oh, you're funny, Lara." With a smile, I slid into the front seat and saw a slow, teasing look flash within his eyes. "Just don't go and get us lost, now."

"I'll do my best, but I can't promise anything." I responded playfully as I started the car and backed down the driveway.

The lighthearted banter between us faded into a soft silence as we drove down the empty road toward town, the path of scattered stars strewn like a blanket across the sky.

Following Peter's directions through town, I parked the car beside a white and red two-story brick building with a faded sign that read *The Shady Lady Saloon*. People crowded the balcony that jutted out above the door as the sound of laughter and the thumping of an upright bass spilled out into the street.

"Shady Lady, huh?"

He turned to me with a half grin. "Yup, this place used to be a brothel back in the day."

"Oh, *how lovely*."

"Well, lots of people back then sure thought so."

I let out a little snicker as I got out of the car and shut the door.

Peter leaned toward me from across the hood. "I think you'll like it inside. It's nice."

Slinging my purse over my shoulder, I stepped up to the sidewalk beside him. He cocked his elbow out, his voice low. "Would you mind being my eyes for tonight, Lara?"

"No, not at all." A bloom of a smile crept across my face as I took his arm in mine.

Chapter Ten

The hum of conversation and clinking of glasses filled the large, dimly lit room, the warmth from the summer night clinging to the air around us. Intricate swirls of blown-glass light fixtures hung from the ceiling, while in the far back was a stage where the musicians were warming up their instruments and checking the sound on the monitor.

Peter leaned in close to me, his breath a murmur against my ear. "Shall we get something to drink?"

"Yes, that sounds good."

Navigating through the crowd, I led Peter over to the bar. He released his arm from mine as we stood against the antique bar top, its surface stained and scarred from decades of drinks sliding across it. I signaled to the bartender for two beers just as a tall, lanky man wearing a cowboy hat sidled up next to me, leaning in close enough that I could smell the whiskey on his breath.

"Evening there, beautiful," he drawled. "Mind if I buy you a drink?"

I smiled stiffly at him, stepping back to put some space between us and bumping into Peter in the process. "Oh, no thank you. I just ordered something."

"Well..." The man's gaze slithered over me. "How about a dance then?"

"I'm good." I tucked a strand of hair out of my face and kept my focus on the bartender who was retrieving our bottles from the cooler.

The man leaned in closer. "Aw, come on now, just one dance?"

Peter's hand suddenly smacked against the counter, startling me. "Leave her the *hell* alone."

The man raised his hands. "Relax, Peter. I was just being friendly. Didn't know she was with you."

"Whether she's with me or not is irrelevant, Scott," Peter snarled. "She's clearly not interested."

"Well, I'll be on my way then," Scott slurred, tipping his hat to me, and shooting Peter a lingering glare before blending into the crowd.

Our beers arrived, and I reached for them, passing one tentatively to Peter. "You okay there?"

His hand gripped the bottle as he raised it to his lips, taking a long gulp. "Sorry about that." He shook his head, setting the bottle down hard upon the bar. "Scott is a piece of shit who treats women like cattle at an auction." Peter took another swig of his beer. "Can't stand that guy."

Surprised by this sudden shift in his demeanor, I rested my hand on his for a moment, giving it a squeeze. "Thanks for swooping to my rescue again, but you know, I would've been able to handle that situation myself."

Hes gave a strained smile. "I know. I'm sorry, I guess I've been a little on edge since last night."

"Are you sure you want to stay? We can go if you want."

"No, we came here for some music," he said, tilting his head over in the direction of the stage. "Let's enjoy ourselves."

We found a table at the far end of the room, nestled in a corner where I had a good view of the performers, but we could still hear each other talk. I settled in a chair next to Peter, the proximity of him causing a rush of warmth as his arm grazed against mine. "So, what's this band called?"

"Missoula Creek. They're a pretty big act these days, and usually play large sold-out shows, but the fiddle player is from around these parts. So, once a year, they'll do a small show out here."

"Oh, that's cool. So, you've heard them play before?"

He nodded, a smile tugging at the corners of his mouth. "I used to be quite a live show connoisseur back in my day."

"Oh, really." I leaned in close to him. "What's the best show that you've been to?"

"That's hard to say. They've all been good in their own way. You see, music is not so much about personal preference for me, it's more a general appreciation for the craft itself."

"You don't have a favorite band then?" I asked, thinking back to the large record collection in his living room.

Peter shook his head. "Nope, I like all music as long as it makes me feel something."

Our voices were suddenly drowned out by the explosion of clapping and whistles as the mandolin player stepped up to the mic and addressed the crowd.

I sat back and took in the rich melodic harmonies of the band as they began to play. The sorrowful fiddle blended with the energetic tempo of the banjo, and the thump of the upright bass merged seamlessly with the dreamy cadence of the slide guitar and mandolin.

The band was spirited, but at the same time haunting and lyrical, stirring up a faint nostalgia and memories of late summer nights before I had met John. Nothing but freedom and endless possibility as my body swayed to the rhythm of music from an outdoor concert.

Was that person still inside me somewhere? The one that used to laugh loudly and dance without restraint. *How long had it been since I let myself go?*

I glanced over at Peter, who appeared lost to the music, nodding his head to the beat while his boot tapped against the floor. The beer crept through my veins, and my limbs grew languid. I found myself watching him with an unabashed intensity, allowing my gaze to take in his features with a liberty I seldom felt comfortable with.

As if sensing my eyes on him, Peter suddenly turned to me and leaned in with a small smile. "Are you enjoying yourself?"

"Yes, I am." My cheeks warmed as I took a sip of my beer and noticed a few couples gliding onto the dance floor. "Do you dance, Peter?"

He nodded with a playful glint in his eyes. "When the mood suits me, I've been known to dance."

I stood and boldly took his hand in mine. "Then dance with me."

Peter cocked an eyebrow before he stood, allowing me to lead him into the center of the room. He drew me close to him, one hand resting on the small of my back, his other hand clasped over mine.

"Do you know how to do the two-step?"

"No, I'm afraid I don't. I tend to be more freestyle." I laughed nervously as the feel of him against me sent my senses reeling.

"Would you like to learn?" Peter was close enough that his breath was like the whisper of a kiss against my forehead.

"Yes, I would."

"Okay then, just relax and follow my lead. It's pretty simple," a playful smile spread across his face, "I've actually been told I'm a pretty decent dancer."

"Really?" My words came out breathless as I rested my free hand on his shoulder, feeling the heat between us, like sparks of electricity. Sliding his leg in the space between mine, Peter's feet slowly shifted forward and then back before stepping forward again. I looked down, following his feet until I found the rhythm.

Peter's lips drifted close to my ear. "See, you got it."

We fell into a rhythmic sway with the music that seemed to match the steady drum of my heart. Peter's movements were relaxed and graceful, and I was surprised at his ability to navigate me through the room with such ease. It was as if we had merged into one fluid form, guiding each other through the current of bodies around us.

I pressed myself closer against him, breathing in his masculine scent, a mixture of hay and earth that grounded me and enticed my senses at the same time. Lost in the moment, my mouth drifted close to his neck, my words lightly brushing across his skin. "You *are* pretty good at this."

Peter took in a sharp breath and stiffened. Releasing me abruptly, he pulled away to run his fingers through his hair, a sudden unease flickering over his face. "I'm sorry. Do you mind if we step outside for a minute? I think I need some air."

"Okay." Confusion swam in circles as I took Peter's arm and quickly led him through the bar and out into the cool breeze of the evening.

"Are you alright?"

"I'm fine, Lara." His features seemed to loosen a little as he motioned down the street. "Do you feel like taking a little walk?"

"Sure, that sounds nice." I tried to shake off Peter's change in demeanor. I could tell that he was trying to push something away, but I had no idea what it was.

The moon was a crescent hanging above as we walked arm-in-arm down the sidewalk. The sounds of people up on the balcony of the saloon faded into a soft silence as we passed the shops and headed out to where the buildings began to grow sparse, opening into stretches of shadowed pasture. I gazed up at the brilliant burst of stars unfolding across the night sky.

In awe, I took a deep breath. "Wow, the sky is so beautiful. I wish you could see it right now."

"Oh, I've seen it. They don't call Montana 'Big Sky Country' for nothing." Peter had stopped walking and stood beside me. His hands were shoved deep in his pockets, with a look on his face as if he were searching for something.

I tilted my head up to the stars, watching the glimmering magnitude of light, so vast it made me dizzy, the limitlessness a reminder of my own insignificance. I was only a tiny body composed of matter spinning through space, and my spark would fade long before the stars ever did.

I turned toward Peter. "Do you mind me asking what it's like being blind?"

He sighed. "What do you want to know?"

"Well, when we were in town yesterday, you said something about seeing shadows. So, it's not complete darkness for you?"

"No, it's not. I can make out some light and shadows."

"You can?"

He nodded. "Kinda like if you draped a cloth over your eyes, you may not be able to see, but outlines still remain."

I wanted to ask more, but I was reluctant to pry. This growing connection between us felt fragile and hesitant, the boundaries unclear.

A subtle wind picked up, rustling the grass as Peter moved closer to me, his hand touching my arm. He tilted his head toward the range of mountains. "Lara, listen. Do you hear that?"

A long, mournful cry rang out in the distance, followed by another in answer. We stood in stillness, listening to the ethereal melody which pierced the air and brought chills to my skin. The melancholy song spoke of wildness and power, filling me with a yearning that quickened my heart and gently stirred against my soul.

"Are those coyotes?" My voice came out in a whisper.

Peter shook his head. "Nope. Those are wolves."

Chapter Eleven

I sat folding my clothes, warm from the dryer, my phone cradled between my shoulder and ear, listening to the simultaneous chatter of Mitch's daughters on the other end of the line.

"We miss you, Auntie Lara," they chimed in unison.

"I miss you girls, too," I said as a wave of bittersweet emotion hit me. A rustling sound crackled on the other end as they handed the phone over to their dad.

"Hey, Sis. How are you holding up over there?"

"You know, I'm doing good. Montana is really growing on me, and I'm learning to ride a horse."

"Is that so?" Mitch faintly chuckled. "And how's that going?"

"Well, I haven't fallen off yet."

There was a pause, and I took in a deep breath. "Mitch, I've been meaning to ask you, how's Mom doing these days?"

A long sigh filled the receiver. "The same."

Guilt pulled at me. The last few years, Mitch had been the one diligently visiting Mom with the kids, while I found it increasingly difficult to go and see her. It was just too painful to sit beside her, watching as Alzheimer's ravaged her mind, taking her further away from me, until eventually there was nothing left of my mother at all. Only a body that lay motionless in the bed of a nursing home, her eyes vacant to the world around her. It was another crushing reminder of the inherent fragility of life.

"She was having brief periods of lucidity about a month ago, but even those have stopped."

I bit my lip, wishing I could have my mother back. I missed the comfort of her unwavering presence that enfolded me like a warm blanket. I wanted nothing more than to be able to talk to her again, to feel her arms around me, to unburden all the grief and loss of the past three years.

"I'm sorry that I haven't been there."

"It's alright. I know it's been really hard for you since Caleb's death."

My gut lurched as Mitch spoke, his voice growing distant as a visceral ache rushed through me. I realized it had been so long since I had heard his name spoken aloud. John and I had tiptoed around his memory for so long, as if the very sound of his name would destroy whatever remnant of strength we had left in us.

"What are you doing?"
My voice wavers as I stand in the doorway to Caleb's room, watching John place Caleb's clothes and toys into a box.
"I'm taking this stuff to Goodwill."
"No."
I shake my head and drop down on the floor beside the box, grabbing a shirt from his hands.
"You're not giving these away."
"Lara." John's voice comes out measured. His eyes hard.
Tears burn, running a trail down my cheeks as I frantically pull everything out of the box,
clutching clothes against my chest, as if the solidity of them could bring him back.
"They're all I have left."
John heaves a sigh, his face pinched as he stands and stalks out of the room,

leaving me alone with the scattered remnants of a life I no longer have.

"I should probably go, Mitch," I said, feeling the familiar weight of pain settle in my chest like a stone lodged against bone.

Rising from the couch and moving over to the window, I watched the long shadows of early evening ripple across the pasture. "I have this dinner thing tonight, and I should get ready for it."

Mitch let out a long sigh. "Okay, I'll let you go, Lara."

I stood on the porch, hovering outside the door, unsure if I should knock or let myself in. I could hear laughter from inside and the low, deep voice of Peter. Pushing the screen open a crack, I peeked my head through.

"Lara's here!" Miriam called out from the living room, enthusiastically gesturing me inside. "Come on in, love."

Dusty bounded toward me, his tail propelling in a wide circle as he proceeded to lick the entirety of my hand with his large tongue. In the kitchen, I could see Peter leaning against the wall, talking to someone.

"Clive, come over here and meet Lara!" Miriam shouted.

A tall rugged-looking man with salt and pepper hair was suddenly in front of me, shaking my hand.

"Lara, this is my husband, Clive."

"It's nice to meet you, Lara. Miriam has been telling me how grateful she is to have found you." He winked and turned to Miriam with a smile. "I don't think she would've agreed to follow me to New York if you hadn't shown up so serendipitously."

Miriam wrapped her arm around my waist, giving me a

playful squeeze. "Yes, I think it was fate. She has even managed to soften up my brother a bit. What's your secret, Lara?"

"That's enough, Miriam." Peter walked up to us, his hand trailing along the top of the couch. "Lara." With a nod, he held out a glass of red wine in my direction. Our fingers touched as I took the glass, eliciting a current of energy that brought a sudden flush to my cheeks. There had been an awkwardness between us since our night out, as if we were still dancing around something yet to be named.

Miriam raised her eyebrows at me, a look of amusement on her face. I tipped my head down, hoping my hair would obscure my blush, and cleared my throat nervously. "Thanks."

"Well, okay then," she drawled, her voice thick with implication. "Shall we get dinner going? I'm starving."

Peter and Clive went outside to start up the grill, their voices drifting in through the open windows as I flipped through Peter's large record collection, my fingers running along the raised tags that were pasted in the corners.

"Took me over a month to get all those labeled in Braille."

I turned to find Miriam standing beside me. She crouched down to my level. "Whatcha in the mood for?" I held out the record in my hand, and a slow smile crept across her face. "Marvin Gaye, huh?" she asked, nodding. "I could get down with that."

I watched as she slid out the record and placed it on the player, the nostalgic crackle filling the speakers as Marvin Gaye's rich, soulful voice spilled out. Miriam stood and swayed her hips rhythmically as she moved around the living room. I envied her ease; she seemed so comfortable in her own skin.

"So, I heard you managed to get Peter out of the house and to a show the other day."

I settled onto the couch, leaning against the cool leather. "Well, that was actually his idea."

"That's interesting." Miriam's eyes grew wide. "He hasn't gone out to a show in years."

I shrugged. "I haven't gone out to a show in a long time myself."

Miriam stopped dancing and sat down next to me. "Do you think you're gonna stick around for a while?" Her hand squeezed my knee. "I really hope you do."

I smiled at her. "I'd like to think I will." Though what that meant, I had no idea. I was still in a state of suspended animation, bobbing motionless in a silent sea with no direction.

Clive's voice called in through the window. "Dinnertime, gals!"

A light breeze stirred the leaves on the tree as I followed Miriam outside.

"So, Lara," she said, flashing me a broad smile as she picked up a stack of plates on the picnic table. "I'm very curious about you. You're a little enigma. Tell me all about what you were doing before you ended up here in Montana."

I bit my lip as a sour taste rose in my mouth. The uncomfortable silence that overcame me whispered of all the things I did not have the fortitude to speak aloud.

"Miriam, will you *please* stop prying." Peter's voice startled me from behind.

Miriam waved away his words. "Simmer down. I was just trying to make friendly conversation." Miriam breezed by Peter as she headed back into the house, her hand reaching out to ruffle his hair playfully, causing him to flinch.

"Sorry about that," Peter said, "my sister can be a bit nosey."

"No, it's fine. I like her, she's really nice."

"Oh, I heard that..." Miriam called, coming back out with two bottles of wine in her hand and a large grin on her face. "See, she likes me, Peter."

"Of course, she does," Peter replied sarcastically. "You're a relentless people pleaser, Miriam."

She raised her eyebrow at me as she chuckled at his off-handed comment. "Do you see what I have had to put up with all these years?"

We sat around the table, cheeks flushed from wine, our empty plates stacked to one side. Night had fallen, and the flames from the votive candles Miriam had lit cast flickering patterns across our faces. Peter sat beside me, close enough that I could feel him every time he shifted his body. A subtle graze of his arm against my skin that teased my senses.

"So, where are you from originally, Lara?" Clive sat across from me, with Miriam snuggled against him.

"Northern California."

"Oh, like by the Redwoods?" Miriam asked.

I nodded. "Yeah. We actually lived right down the road from them." I realized the *We* had slipped out unintentionally, my tongue growing loose from my fourth glass of wine.

Peter turned in my direction, appearing to take note of my plural reference. His face was full of questions I didn't want to answer.

"Oh, I've always wanted to see the Redwoods," Miriam said wistfully. "And the ocean... it's been so long since I've seen the ocean." Miriam leaned across the table and pointed to Peter. "Did you know that Peter has never been to the ocean?"

"Seriously?" I turned to him in surprise.

He nodded his head, wisps of hair falling against his temples. "I'm afraid so."

"Though we did go to this lake once, outside of Kalispell. Peter was around five." Miriam's eyes flashed with amusement. "Do you remember this, Peter? You were so convinced that we were at the ocean, and when we told you that it was in fact a lake, oh, you got so angry. You stomped your feet and stormed off, calling us all a bunch of liars." Miriam laughed loudly, slapping her hand against her knee. "God, you were such a little hothead back then."

I glanced at Peter, watching as a faint grin crept over his face. "You know, Miriam, life is all about perspective. You could've just let me believe it was the ocean."

"Oh, but what would have been the fun in that? You know how much I loved getting you riled up."

Peter only grunted in response, draining his glass of wine.

Miriam and Clive gathered the plates from the table, chuckling as they went into the house.

"Have you lived in Montana your whole life, Peter?"

"Yep. Never felt the need to leave, I guess."

"That's too bad. I mean, there is so much to see out there."

The sudden look of sadness on Peter's face made me wince.

"Shit. I'm sorry." My fingers fiddled with the stem of my wine glass. "You know what I mean."

He leaned in close to me, his hand sliding over the table until it found mine. "It's okay, Lara. I do." Peter's thumb brushed across my skin, his touch like a burst of heat. My heart accelerated as his breath lingered close to my ear like a caress.

"Hey, you guys. We're gonna head on out. It's getting pretty late."

Miriam's voice startled me, and we both jerked away from each other. Peter drew back his hand as he stood up from the table and retreated into the house, leaving me alone. I took a deep breath and waited for the gentle thrum of my heart to settle back into its normal rhythm as I scrambled to comprehend the visceral effect Peter's presence had on me.

With a sigh, I stood and walked inside, where I found Miriam out on the front porch with Peter and Clive. She moved toward me and wrapped me up in a crushing hug. "Take care of my little brother for me," she whispered into my hair.

"I'll do my best," I said with a smile. "And have fun out there in New York."

She squeezed my shoulder for a moment, her voice candid. "You know, I can't really explain it, but I feel like you were meant to be here, Lara."

I gazed out into the evening, the comforting stillness like a blanket unraveling across the pasture. "I think you might be right."

"And hey, you're kinda a part of this rag-tag group of ours now." Miriam chuckled as she shot me a playful wink.

Unexpected emotion welled up within me, and I found myself stifling back tears. "That means a lot to me, Miriam."

She nodded and gave me a quick kiss on my cheek. "We'll keep in touch."

I leaned against the porch railing and watched as Peter walked with Miriam and Clive to the truck, their voices merging with the chorus of crickets as their silhouettes faded into the night.

Chapter Twelve

Sweat trickled down my chest as I heaved the final pile of straw into the wheelbarrow.

"Is this the last of it, Lara?"

"Yep." I took a deep breath and wiped my forehead, longing for a shower.

The sound of tires on the gravel driveway caused Peter to raise his head and turn toward the door before abruptly striding out of the barn. I followed behind him as he crossed the pasture. "Can I help you with something?" he called out brusquely as a short man in a pressed suit stepped out of his car with a folder tucked under his arm.

"I'm looking for a Lara Peterson?" the man squinted in my direction.

"That's me," I said, brushing the straw out of my hair.

Peter squared his shoulders, appearing to tense up as the man stepped closer to me, his polished shoes crunching on the gravel beneath him. "This is for you."

I reached for the envelope, noticing the familiar address of John's law firm stamped across the upper left corner. The man thrust a clipboard in front of me. "I just need you to sign here, please." He stood beside me in silence as I shakily signed my name upon the *Acceptance of service* line.

"Have a nice day, Miss." He nodded curtly and quickly retreated back into his sleek air-conditioned car, the chrome and steel like a misplaced artifact among all the rugged beauty.

"Who was that?" Peter asked.

I stared down at the envelope in my hand. "Oh, just some delivery guy." I tried to mask the strain in my voice as a feeling of discomposure rushed in and a heaviness settled in my gut. "Hey, if we are all done in the barn, I think I'm going to go take a break."

Peter nodded, his face flashing with momentary concern as I turned from him and headed toward the cottage.

I sat at the kitchen table, staring at the divorce papers. There had been no additional correspondence from John within the thick manilla envelope. Only the terms of our agreement outlined, and a series of red sticky arrows pasted throughout with *SIGN HERE* typed in bold block lettering.

This is it. This is the end. The corpse of my marriage sat beside me with smirking, lifeless eyes.

"I promise I will always love you, Lara."
John lowers his knee in the sand, the waves crashing behind us.
I run my hands across the swell of my belly,
buoyed by his fervent promise;
by the possibility of a life with him and this growing child inside.

It was a promise neither of us had been able to keep. My mouth felt dry as I pressed the pen against the paper, my signature flowing out onto the page like a permanent stain of finality.

Everything from the life we had built for ourselves was gone. There was nothing left.

Waves of heat flooded me, my heart pounding like a desperate drum in my ears as I shoved the papers aside and stood up. I needed to get out. I needed to move, to breathe.

Leaving the cottage, I ran through the pasture, my gaze fixed on the enclosing safety of the aspen grove.

My head swam and the magnitude of all the loss held within the past three years pressed against my chest. I gasped for air, my legs shaking as I collapsed beneath a tree, knees sinking into the earth. I allowed the familiar wave of panic to consume me. It had been so long since I had been gripped by an attack; I thought I had left that broken piece of myself behind in California, but of course it had followed me. I could not outrun this snarling beast. It clawed at my insides, demanding attention.

I squeezed my eyes shut, rocking back and forth as the heaviness of dread crushed my chest, sucking the air out of me. My hands raked the earth, and my breath came out in labored pants as I desperately tried to anchor myself to the solid reality around me. But the swirling darkness only wrenched me further away from myself.

Time moved in distorted fragments as iterations of the same thought tore into my mind. *It's over. It's really over.* My last connection to Caleb was gone.

I don't know how long I sat there as the relentless, violent pull of anxiety tossed me around, but eventually my heart rate slowed, the piercing panic softening to a dull hum as the world around me came back into focus.

I leaned my head back and watched the sway of the aspen trees against a backdrop of blue, their leaves like a sigh of comfort, stilling the trembling inside. Pulling myself off the ground, I walked toward the horses in the pasture, their flicking tails swaying in the breeze.

My mind was washed out like bleached paper, and I needed something solid and breathing to cling to. As I came closer, Penny lifted her head, her ears swiveling in my direction. I clicked my tongue as I had seen Peter do so many times, and she sauntered over, her head bobbing with each fluid step.

Running my fingers over her coat, I felt her breath tickling my skin, the softness of her muzzle against my hand. Tears pricked my eyes as I rested my head against the warmth of her side and allowed the rhythmic movement of her breath to lull me back to myself.

I heard the faint rustling of grass from behind and felt the lurch of Penny moving away from where I stood beside her. I turned to see Peter approaching from across the pasture with a bucket in his hand, a whistle drifting past his lips. The horses encircled him as he began to feed them bits of vegetables out of the bucket. I stood there in silence, observing his gentle, intimate interaction with them. I thought I had gone unnoticed when Peter suddenly paused. "Lara?" He tilted his head in my direction, his intuitive senses picking up on my presence.

"Yes. It's me." I tried to hide the shakiness in my words as I moved closer to him.

"Whatcha doing lurking out here?" His voice was playful and light as he spoke, and a large grin stretched across his face, accentuating his laugh lines and instantly soothing my battered mind.

I sighed. "Oh, I was just visiting with the horses."

Peter nodded. "You want to help me feed them?"

He held out a carrot in his palm, and I reached for it as Ginger hesitantly crept close to me and nudged my hand, her lips quickly reaching out to pluck the carrot away. "Peter," I said in a whisper, "Ginger just came up to me."

"She must like you. She's never let anyone other than me get close to her." Peter winked as he held out another carrot. "Perhaps you two have something to learn from each other."

Ginger stood only a few feet away, her hesitant brown eyes resting on me, seeming to reach into my soul.

"What do you mean?"

"Well, horses are drawn to certain people, while shying away from others. They are an incredible judge of character and will tend to gravitate toward someone who matches their own energy."

"What? Like shy and skittish?"

A teasing smile played across his face. "You said it, not me."

"You think I'm shy and skittish?" My tone grew serious as I realized he was right. The timing of this moment suddenly felt so meaningful as I stood there, my body still trembling; my mind stretched and worn from my own silent battle among the aspen grove. *I am so much like Ginger,* a jumpy colt, so terrified of my own emotions that I have allowed them to grow into apparitions that I was constantly running from.

Peter placed the pail on the ground, closing the space between us. His face was full of a tenderness that made me want to sink into the solid safety of him. "I think you are wary, Lara."

My breath came out in a long, shuddering sigh. "You're right. I am wary."

Peter held his hand out, and my fingers rose and curled around his invitation. His grip engulfing mine was so comforting that tears sprung to my eyes again, my scattered sense of self finding a safe place with him.

He gave my hand a squeeze before letting go. "Looks like we are just two peas in a pod over here."

I chuckled, wiping away the tears as I followed Peter back through the pasture, allowing the stillness between us to settle like delicate leaves falling from a great height.

Morning light woke me. My body tired and my mind bruised from the events of the day before. I stumbled into the shower, feeling the cascading heat seeping deep into my muscles as I tried to shake away the sluggish, dreamlike state that always cloaked me after an attack.

I remember my therapist explaining it to me. *"Disassociation is a common side effect of anxiety, and it can last for days after a panic episode."* I had been sitting on her couch, nervously picking at my fingernails as the indecisive sunlight hovered through the trees of her office windows. *"This is your body trying to process the trauma of loss, Lara."*

I went to the bedroom closet and grabbed my duffle bag. Rooting through the contents inside, I pulled out a faded teddy bear with patches worn from Caleb, running his thumb repeatedly against it at bedtime. He would drag the bear with him everywhere, calling it his "Stinky Bear." Over the years, it had grown so tattered that we could no longer wash it. Breathing in these memories, I pressed my face up against the bear, which still held traces of Caleb within the fabric. Smudges and stains from his fingers, the blurred black ink on its face from when he had tried to draw in the missing eye. I clung to these physical remnants like a lifeline.

The grip of exhaustion settled over my body, and I retreated back to the bed, burrowing underneath the covers, grateful that Peter had said he didn't need my help out in the barn today. With Caleb's bear in my arms, I willed sleep to take me away. I wanted nothing more than to slip back into the depths of dreams, to find the places where Caleb would be waiting for me with his arms outstretched, and his blue eyes holding all the love I had left in me.

Chapter Thirteen

Summer had begun her slow waltz with autumn, and a blush tentatively spread across the hills, peppering the landscape in color. I had always loved fall the most. The crisp mornings that whispered of a winter to come. The somber call of geese high above, like notes of nostalgia clinging to the filaments of a vague memory.

I stood beside the window, my hands wrapped around my cup of coffee, breathing in the steam that floated softly to my lips. My mind drifted as I watched the morning sun collide with the mist that rose off the pasture, showering the air with ethereal light.

The sound of my phone ringing from the table beside me jostled me from my thoughts.

"Morning, gorgeous!" Sasha's exuberance rang out from across the line, and I smiled, her voice like a comforting balm.

I puttered around the kitchen while Sasha regaled me with stories from the latest misadventures of her dating life. It was a pleasant distraction from my own mind, which vacillated like the weather.

"Can you freaking believe that? He wanted to use a surgical glove!" She cackled on the other end. "Oh my God, Lara. You'd think in a city with eight million people I would be able to find at least one sane guy." She let out a sigh, like an abbreviated pause. "I'm sorry, enough about me. How are you doing, sweetie?"

I grimaced. "Well, I guess I'm officially a divorcée now."

"Oh, honey," Sasha's voice grew soft.

"Yep, signed the papers a few weeks ago and sent them out. John agreed to buy me out of the house, and provide me with alimony on top of that, which I honestly wasn't expecting and didn't even want from him." I paused, reaching into the fridge. "But the reality is, I could sure use it right now while I try to figure things out. I don't have much left in my savings."

"Wow. Well, *that's* good. At least he's being generous in that department."

"That's one thing John has always been good for, right? He loves to flaunt his money around."

"And how are you doing with all this?"

I bit my lip as I began to slice tomatoes for a sandwich. "I have my good days, and then I have my bad ones."

"How has your anxiety been lately?" Sasha asked, a deep wave of concern filtering through her words.

"Well, I actually had an attack after I signed the divorce papers. The first one I've had in a while."

"I suppose that's not terribly surprising. I'm so sorry, love. You know, I have always been convinced that John is a huge trigger for you."

"You're probably right."

My fingers traced the rim of my coffee cup, noticing the hairline fractures within the surface of the glaze. Trapped in the heavy inertia of grief, the last three years with John had been the loneliest years of my life. The strained silence between us was a suffocating weight that clamped itself tightly around my chest; all those days I had spent in bed, unable to move, while John crept around me with anger in his eyes, as if the very sight of my pain enraged him. "*You need to pull yourself together,*" he would hiss.

A trembling exhale escaped me. "The strange thing is, I actually feel less alone out here in Montana."

"Really? So does that mean that you're going to be bunking down for the winter out there?"

I moved over to the window once again, my free hand moving to rub the tight knots in my neck. "I think so. I'm kinda looking forward to being somewhere where there will actually be snow in the winter."

"Oh, you and snow," she chuckled. "I *just* don't get it; I can't stand the stuff. I don't know what I was thinking moving to the East Coast."

I let out a little laugh. "Because if you lived on a tropical island, you would have nothing to complain about."

Sasha snorted. "Touché."

I padded back into the kitchen and began to wrap the sandwiches, placing them into a paper bag.

"So..." Sasha dragged out her words, "what are you up to today?"

"Well, Peter is actually going to take me on a trail ride in a bit. Apparently, there's a place he wants to show me. He told me that I should pack a little picnic and wear something warm."

"Really?" Sasha's voice was tinged with a teasing curiosity. "Sounds like a date to me."

"I don't know what it is, Sasha. I just really like being around him. He makes me feel settled somehow. It's like everything gets a little quieter when I'm with him."

Sasha let out a wistful breath. "Oh, that sounds nice."

"Yeah. It is." A smile crept across my lips as I glanced out the window and across the field to the barn, where I knew Peter was with the horses, waiting for me.

Penny and Spirit stood saddled up in the barn beside Peter, their hooves impatiently pawing at the ground.

Peter tilted his head in my direction as he heard me approach. "You ready, Lara?"

"Yep, and I brought sandwiches."

"Oh, good, I'll pack them up for us." He reached his hand out for the food and tucked it into the leather saddle bag that hung against the side of Spirit. "Got a sweater too? This time of year, it can get a bit windy up where we're going."

"I do. Though I think I need to go into town in the next few days to find some more clothes. I didn't exactly pack for cold weather when I left California."

Peter turned to me with a lazy smile. "So, does this mean I get you all to myself for the winter?"

There was something intimate in the rich softness of his words that caused my body to surge with heat as sensual thoughts rose to the surface.

"Um, I guess it does." I laughed nervously, trying to push away the sensations that dislodged my composure, leaving me shaky and ungrounded.

"Well," he continued, "there's a great department store over in Missoula; you should check it out sometime."

Clicking his tongue, Peter led the horses past me and out of the barn. The warmth of the sun drifted against me like a teasing caress as I followed him out into the pasture. A hint of a breeze ruffled the hair around my face, while the crisp smell of turning leaves lingered in the air. Peter stood beside Penny, holding her steady while I hoisted myself up onto the saddle.

"Are you going to tell me where we're going?" I asked, watching as he threw his leg up and over, quickly mounting Spirit.

He pulled his reins in, trotting Spirit in a circle and brushing up against Penny. The wind played with the dark strands of his hair as a grin spread over his face, the sunlight catching the dizzying depths of his eyes. "You'll just have to wait and find out."

Peter settled Spirit into a trot beside me as we traversed the field and through the grove of aspen trees, fragmented shadows spilling through the honey-colored canopy. Over the past few weeks, I had grown comfortable riding Penny, the soothing sway of her gait lulling me into a state of stillness. There was also a power I felt when riding. While my life swirled around me in a jumble of uncertainty, being able to connect with the silent wildness of a horse brought a feeling of strength to my soul.

We slipped through the trees, following a worn trail that wove up a gentle slope and ascended over a hill. Pastures dotted the landscape before me like a patchwork quilt, stretching out until it met the base of the mountain range.

"There should be a bluff straight ahead." Peter sidled up next to me as he reached out toward the mountains, gesturing to a large outcropping of rocks in the distance.

I turned to him. "How are you able to tell where we're going?"

"These horses have taken this route hundreds of times with me. They know where they're going." Peter guided Spirit forward, and I followed behind him as we descended the hill and made our way across the valley.

We came to a thicket of trees that wound their way up the mountain. Knotty pines and dried grass speckled the landscape as the horses plodded upward. The temperature slowly dropped as we made our way up the mountain. The trail had changed into a narrow switchback, snaking through tall ponderosa flecked with sunlight that filtered through the branches. The wind picked up, and the smell of earth and dried leaves wafted around me as we climbed higher, the low notes of Peter's whistled tune drifting through the air.

The horses came to a stop, tossing their heads before veering off the path and through the trees, which opened to a wide ledge. The view below us stretched out like a breathtaking painting, with mottled brushstrokes of color speckled across the valley.

Peter dismounted and moved over to Penny, his hands gently grasping my waist and guiding me down off the horse.

"What do you think?" His words were a shiver against my skin as his hands lingered briefly upon my back. "Beautiful, isn't it?"

We sat together on the Mexican blanket that Peter brought, finishing up the sandwiches and oranges I had packed, rivulets of sweet sticky juice staining my fingers.

"Thank you for bringing me up here. This view is amazing."

Peter leaned back on the blanket, propping himself up on his elbows. "Yep, it's pretty stunning, ain't it?" Peter's words came out in a slow drawl, something I noticed he did when he was feeling relaxed. "I found this spot years ago, back when I first bought the farmhouse. It's off the beaten trail, so no one really knows about it. This is the best time of year to be up here, in my opinion. I used to spend hours sitting here, just taking in the beauty and quiet."

I gazed over the brilliance of color that stretched out before me. The sun rested low in the sky, grazing the tips of the mountains as the wind blew around us, lifting my hair and teasing my skin with its refreshing chill. Peter was giving me a glimpse into his own private world. The fact that he wanted to share this place with me, even though he was no longer able to appreciate the full beauty of it, was a gesture that enveloped me in a warm affection. It made me want to share myself with him, and something loosened inside my chest, overcome with a sudden and sharp longing to unburden my story.

"You asked me before what it is I used to do."

Peter turned his head in my direction, his eyes almost appearing to catch mine for a moment. "Yes?"

I took a deep breath, mustering courage, my heart pumping wildly as the weight of all my locked-up words tumbled out. "I used to be a teacher." A pause filled the space between us before I continued. "I used to be a wife." My breath caught in my throat, and my voice wavered with all the unspent emotion that charged to the surface. "And... I used to be a mother."

I glanced over at Peter, who sat up with a look of confusion. "What do you mean?"

"I had a son, Caleb. He would've been eight this year."

"Lara." Peter's voice came out in a whisper, his eyes wide.

I threaded my fingers together, trying to still the tremor in my hands. "We lived in this really beautiful house out in the woods, built by some fancy architect from San Francisco. It had these walls of windows surrounded by redwood trees. It felt like you were living in a treehouse. But it was so close to the highway. That road always made me nervous. All the twists and turns... the semi-trucks rushing by... I never let Caleb play outside unless one of us was watching him."

I paused and drew in a shaky breath as the memories rushed at me. "One day, I had to run to the store. I remember, we were out of milk. John, my husband, was at home working. He had a deadline at his law firm and was stressing out about it." I took another deep breath, staring out at the horizon as if it could anchor me. "I was only gone for twenty minutes. Caleb must have gone outside without John noticing."

Peter sat beside me while my words spilled out, ugly and broken. His body was still, eyes full of a quiet sadness, holding space for me within the hurricane of my recollections.

"We had just gotten this little tabby cat. Caleb was so in love with it. He followed that cat around everywhere. It must have run out the door and toward the road." My voice came out choked as I fumbled for words, my heart constricting around the tight band in my chest. "John said he was in his office when he heard the squealing of tires and the blaring horn of the semi-truck."

The images tore into me like a vivid nightmare I could never escape. The ominous flashing of lights along the road as I approached the house. The sickening grip within my chest, lungs grappling for air. Caleb's tiny lifeless body on the asphalt covered by a blanket, paramedics swarming all around. And then the sound of my frantic screams, my nails clawing at John, digging deep into his flesh as he gripped his arms around me, dragging me away.

"He never let me see Caleb," I whispered. "I needed to see my son. But he wouldn't let me. I never got to say goodbye." My hands clenched into tight fists, my knuckles turning white. "The paramedics said Caleb's death was instantaneous, that he most likely felt no pain. One minute he was there, right beside me in the kitchen, begging me to get him a toy at the store... and then he was gone."

Tears slipped down my cheeks, obscuring my vision. "I blamed John for his death. I blamed him for everything. I couldn't look at him for months; I was so angry." I shook my head, the heaviness of it all washing over me. "No wonder he shut down. What else could he do?"

Peter finally spoke, his face etched in sorrow. "We all grieve in different ways, Lara, and I can't imagine how hard it would be to try and save a marriage after something like that." Peter's hand searched across the blanket, tenderly curling his fingers around mine. "I'm so sorry you lost your child. Though I know there are no words I can say that can take away that kind of pain."

I wrenched my hand away from his and abruptly stood up, moving over to the rock ledge and looking down at the yawning space below. How many times had I thought about ending it all. How many moments had there been when the strength to carry on was nothing but a dim ember inside me, and all I longed for was to join Caleb in that delicate place between dreams.

"There is *just* so much *fucking pain*. It's been suffocating me for years, eating away at me, and I don't know what to do with it all, anymore. I don't know where to put it." I turned to face Peter, who had stood, his arms hovering at his sides. *"Where do I put it?"*

"Lara." His voice was soothing and quiet, his eyes full of sadness, scanning the horizon as if searching for me. "Please come here."

I hesitated as my entire body trembled from the bite of the wind and all the emotions I had just allowed to churn to the surface. Peter stood facing me, his words like a soft plea. "Lara, please."

I moved to him, closing the space between us, and then his arms were around me, wrapping me up in his warmth and pressing me against his chest.

I sunk into the sturdiness of him, the feel of his heartbeat against my ear. It had been so long since I had been held like this. A loud choking sob erupted from me as the floodgates opened. In the comfort of Peter's tender hold, thick and brutal tears poured out. I allowed this relentless grief that had lain dormant for so long to pull me under like a tidal wave. I knew I could no longer run from it.

My legs gave way, and I crumpled to the ground as Peter followed, buffering my fall and holding me tighter against him while I wailed into his chest, tears pouring down my face, soaking his shirt.

Peter didn't say a word, he just let the clawing animal of grief take hold of me. His silence was a drink of cool water after years of thirst. There was no grappling for words of wisdom from him, those empty hushed promises that it will all be okay one day, because it wouldn't be. *It never would be,* and he seemed to understand that. My child had been violently yanked from me, and the vastitude of my pain was an endless canyon.

I don't know how long we sat on the rocky ground as I clung to him, cocooned in his embrace, releasing so many years of anguish into the arms of a man whom I had only begun to know. Eventually, my sobbing subsided, the well of grief diminished, leaving nothing but a soft, hollowed-out space inside.

As I came back to myself, a wave of embarrassment rose to the surface. I pulled away from him, frantically trying to wipe at the mess I had left on his shirt. "I'm *so* sorry. I just completely lost it on you there, and I think I messed up your shirt."

"It's just a shirt, Lara." Peter's eyes seemed to shimmer with emotion as his hands rested on my arms. "And don't ever apologize for sharing yourself like that."

A stillness settled against me as I looked up at him. There was no pity there, only a gentle compassion that filled me with gratitude. "Thank you."

Peter slowly moved his hand up my arm, his fingers tentatively touching my cheek, wiping away the remainder of my tears. "Anytime." His hand lingered against my skin, and my breath hitched in my throat as his thumb briefly swept over my bottom lip before pulling away. He tilted his head up to the sky. "We should probably head on back before it gets too dark."

I watched as he carefully moved over to the tree where the horses were tethered while I quickly gathered up the blanket and food. Peter took Penny's reins and tied them onto Spirit's saddle bag before hoisting himself up onto Spirit and holding his hand out. "Why don't you ride down with me."

I grasped his hand, inserted my foot into the stirrup, and allowed him to lift me up; my limbs shaking as I settled in front of him.

"You're shivering." He removed his jacket and handed it to me. "Here, put this on."

"Thanks." I slid my arms through the sleeves, traces of his earthy scent enveloping me as I rested against him, the warmth of his chest radiating against my back. Peter wrapped one arm around me, while his other hand took the reins, guiding us down the mountain as streaks of color spilled across the sky, bathing the landscape in a dim, rosy glow.

My body was spent and sore as I leaned into the comforting feel of Peter's arm around my waist like a tether, drawing me safely back to land. Evening had already crept into the forest, surrounding us in a blue dusk as the rhythmic sway of the horses lured me into a state of relaxation.

I must have drifted off, for the jolt of Penny coming to a stop startled me. Peter's voice was soft in my ear, his hair brushing my cheek as he drew me from of the fragments of sleep. "We're back, Lara."

We were in front of the cottage, the glow from the porch light illuminating the night around us. I found it hard to extract myself from the warmth of him.

Peter helped me down off the horse, his hands slipping from my waist and reaching up to lightly run a strand of my hair between his fingers. The tender gesture caused a sudden ache to rise up, and a part of me wanted to invite him inside, to curl up in my bed with him. But I couldn't find the words, there were none; I was caught between yearning and exhaustion.

"I'll let you get some rest." His hand lingered close to my cheek for a moment before he turned and hoisted himself back up onto Spirit. I stood there with my arms clasped around my chest, watching the shadowed outline of Peter and the horses as they disappeared into the darkness.

Chapter Fourteen

Morning sun kissed my eyelids, and I rolled over in bed; the day before staring at me from across the pillow. I was surprised to find that my sleep had been deep and restful, as if baring my soul up on the bluff had released something. There had been no haunted dreams prying me awake, only tender, hazy images of Peter which floated through my mind like fragrant memories. His hand running up the length of my arm, his lips so close to mine. My eyes fluttered shut, willing the visuals to sharpen until I found my longing stir and quietly coil around me.

An ache began to press tightly against my core, and I found myself slowly slipping my hand down past my stomach. My fingers tentatively brushed against the folds of my sex, drawing out a warm rush of arousal that begged for more.

Taking a shuddering breath, I abruptly withdrew my hand and sat up, feeling flushed and vaguely ashamed. I had not touched myself in so long, it felt like I was trying to seduce a hesitant stranger. *How long had it been since I allowed myself to feel pleasure?* I had shut that door so many years ago.

I slid out of bed, hoping a shower would wash away the tangled guilt that had grown thorns around my desire. A desire that was suddenly unraveled and demanding my attention.

Finding Peter out in the barn, I lingered in the doorway until

Dusty gave me away. The sound of his tail as it excitedly thumped against the floor caused Peter to turn in my direction.

"Hey, Lara." He walked out from one of the stalls, his hands lightly trailing along the wall as he made his way over to the open door. "How are you feeling this morning?"

"I'm okay." There was a softness in his eyes as he approached, an intimacy I was unaccustomed to seeing in him. I knew something had shifted between us after I poured my heart out yesterday, a closeness that was unspoken but deeply felt. But at the same time, it left me with a feeling of vulnerability. The safety of my walls had crumbled, leaving me with shattered pieces I did not know how to rearrange.

Dusty's nose nudged against my hand. "Hey, buddy," I said, crouching down for a moment to run my fingers through his fur.

Peter chuckled. "He sure did pout up a storm when I got back last night."

I looked up at him. "Why didn't you take him with us?"

"Because that dog has a weakness for squirrels," he said with a half-smile. "I would have spent the entire time out in the woods searching for that damn mutt."

"As opposed to holding some sobbing, broken mess in your arms?" My tone was light as I tried to dampen the intensity of yesterday with some humor. But the look on his face grew somber.

"*Lara.*"

"What?" My voice cracked as I stared up into his eyes, vibrant colors that changed with the light but could never look back at me.

"Please don't feel bad for what happened yesterday."

I sighed. "I don't, I just wasn't planning on dumping all that on you."

Peter stepped closer to me, and I breathed in the familiar

earthy scent of him that I had begun to find so comforting. "Do we ever plan these kinds of things?"

"I guess not." My hands absentmindedly moved to my fingernails, lightly picking before I stopped myself.

"Hey, I'm pretty squared away here. Why don't you take a few days off for yourself?"

I glanced around the barn. I always looked forward to our days together, the relaxing distraction of physical work, the quiet moments between us that seemed to soak up all the emptiness inside.

"But there's one condition," a tentative but playful smile spread across his face, "you let me take you out to dinner tonight."

My heart lurched in my chest, and a giddy rush tumbled through me.

"There's this great restaurant in town. They have some of the best steaks this side of Montana."

"Is this a date?" I replied boldly, feeling my pulse accelerate.

Peter's voice became low, the deep seductive green within his eyes pulling me in. "Do you want it to be?"

Tendrils of heat licked across my skin, and I found myself breaking out into a wide grin that I was thankful Peter could not see. "Maybe I do."

A smile played on the edges of his lips. "Well, I guess that makes two of us then."

Closing the door to the cottage, I wrapped my sweater around me and stepped out into the chill of the night. A cool breeze drifted through the aspen trees, the leaves rustling like paper as I skirted along the fence line toward Peter's house.

Anticipation trickled through me. I had no idea what was happening between us, but being with him felt good, like sinking into a warm bath that took away all the ache, and I wanted more of this feeling.

Peter stood out on the porch, wearing a black button-down dress shirt. His hair, usually in a state of rumpled dishevelment that I found charming, had now been brushed back; though a few loose strands escaped, falling against his brow. "You clean up well." He smelled faintly of cologne as I walked up the steps toward him.

He dipped his head down. In the glow of the porch light, his eyes appeared to twinkle. "Wish I could say the same for you. But I wouldn't know, now would I?"

I let out a small laugh. "Don't worry, I put something nice on." I touched the cuff of his shirt. "How do you know what to wear?"

Peter smirked. "My sister. She got a braille tagging machine a few years back and went a little crazy."

"Yes, I saw your records."

Peter put his hands up in mock defense. "The record collection. Now *that* was essential. My clothing, on the other hand, I couldn't care less about. Don't usually have much of a reason to dress up these days."

"Well, you look really nice."

"Why thank you." His voice dropped an octave, provoking a flutter inside me. Stepping closer to me, his hand swept down my arm, his fingers grazing the fabric of my sweater. "And what is it that *you're* wearing?"

A blush crept across my face. There was something sensual in the way he asked, and it caused my core to tighten as a whisper of arousal bloomed within me. "I'm wearing a black dress, and a blue cardigan."

Peter's eyes flickered back and forth as if he were painting a picture of me in his mind. He reached out and found my hair, fingering the loose waves that fell against my shoulders. "I've always wondered what the color of your hair was?"

"It's a dark blonde." My words came out breathless as his fingers slipped through my strands.

"And your eyes?"

"They're blue."

"What kind of blue?"

"I guess, they're a light blue."

"Like the sky," he smiled, "you sound beautiful, Lara." He moved closer to me, and I felt a ripple of heat pass between us that left me lightheaded. Peter motioned down the stairs with a sweep of his hand, breaking the concentrated moment. "Shall we hit the road, then?"

My legs shook as we walked to the car. The idea of exploring this growing intimacy between us filled me with an elation that boldly peppered the landscape of my mind with a burst of optimism.

The stars illuminated the night, dancing over the sky as we drove through the dark. My body buzzed with energy as Peter sat close beside me, the air around us like an electrical current. I watched him fiddle with the radio until he found a jazz station, and a languid smile teased the corners of his mouth as he leaned back in his seat. His fingers rested against his knees as he tapped along to the textured, upbeat rhythm drifting through the speakers, and I tried to push away the distracting thoughts of his hands on me.

We drove down the quiet streets of Stevensville while Peter gave me directions to the far end of town. Silence enveloped us as we stepped out of the car, the sound of our closing doors echoing off into the distance.

Peter cocked his elbow out with a lighthearted smile, and I wrapped my arm around his as we made our way into the restaurant.

We entered a room bathed in candlelight; a few couples sparsely populated throughout. On an elevated platform in the far corner sat a man at a piano, silky notes drifting through his fingertips. A waiter came over with a huge smile that spread across his lined face, the light reflecting off his glasses. "Peter, what a pleasant surprise." The waiter clasped his hand in Peter's, giving him a firm, enthusiastic shake. "It's *so* nice to see you. My god, how long has it been?"

"Too long." Peter motioned to me. "Lara, this is Chuck. He's been running this joint since I was a kid."

Chuck tipped his head at me. "Pleasure, Lara. Will it just be the two of you tonight?"

Peter nodded as Chuck led us over to a table draped in white linen. I settled into the seat across from Peter, picking up the napkin which had been neatly folded into the shape of a swan. "This place sure is fancy."

Peter chuckled. "Yes, it is. Chuck is a pretentious old geezer. Why he insists on a fine dining restaurant out in the middle of nowhere I will never know, but he's an old family friend of ours, and I try and stop by on occasion to support him. Plus, the food is amazing," he said with a wink.

The glow of the candle flame danced between us while the music from the piano drifted around the room. I had grown flushed from the wine and rich food. The flavors danced across my palate, and I settled into a state of sated contentment. I could not recall the last time food had tasted this good. For so many years, eating had been nothing more than an obligatory activity to me, and I reveled in this new feeling of tactile enjoyment, as if I were slowly awakening from a long sleep.

Chuck breezed by, clearing our empty plates from the table. "It appears you two enjoyed your meal."

I looked up at him with a smile. "We did. It was really delicious."

Peter swept his fingers against my arm. "Are you in the mood for dessert, Lara?"

"I really don't think I have any room left."

Chuck laughed, nodding to us before disappearing back into the kitchen.

"So, you used to be a teacher, huh?" Peter's arms rested on the table as he leaned in close, the light catching his face, accentuating the curve of his cheekbones.

"I was." I bit my lip, staring into the flame of the candle beside us. "I taught first grade."

"Is that something you always wanted to do?"

"Yes." I fiddled with my napkin, folding it into neat creases. "I've always loved working with kids."

I sat back in my chair, evoking memories of my classroom; the walls that hung with vibrant colored drawings, the chatter of children's voices. Their eyes, so open and filled with wonder as I watched them grow throughout the year, bursting forth like beautiful flowers.

"But after Caleb died, I just couldn't do it anymore. It was too hard to be around kids. I was such a mess." I sighed as I recalled that first week back. The crippling anxiety attacks in the bathroom, the false smile I stretched across my face like a mask that I feared would crack at any minute, and then the grappling with a new kind of loss that overcame me when I finally resigned. What had once been my joy had become another source of pain.

Peter's eyes grew soft as his hand reached across the table in search of mine. I wove my fingers through his, the comfort of his touch stilling my tangled thoughts. "I'm sorry, Lara. We don't have to go down this road again if you don't want to."

"No, it's okay." I sighed, looking at our hands entwined against the table. "You know, it actually feels really good to talk about all this. To talk about Caleb. It feels like I'm honoring him, somehow."

Peter nodded, giving my hand a gentle squeeze. "I take it you and your husband never spoke of him much after the accident?"

I looked up at him. "No. We didn't."

Peter released his hand from mine, leaning back in his chair. "After my mom died, our dad never let us talk about her around him. Like her death was some dirty secret we had to tiptoe around."

"How old were you when she died?"

Peter ran his hand through his hair. "I was thirteen. Just a scrawny little kid who didn't know what the hell was going on and had no one to talk to about it. Miriam was in college, and Greg had just got his license and would disappear for days on end." He paused, his brow furrowing. "Not a moment goes by that I don't think about her, Lara. We have to be able to talk about those we lose, otherwise it will eat us up inside. Like it did with Greg, and my father."

I watched Peter as he sat there, his hair once again tousled and falling into his eyes. His loneliness was a tangible force that encompassed him. It was the same kind that followed me. Perhaps that was why I felt so safe with him. We understood each other.

Chuck appeared at the table with the check, interrupting the moment between us. "Thanks for coming in tonight."

With a nod, Peter retrieved his wallet from his back pocket and handed Chuck a card. "Don't take too much now," he said with a wink as Chuck laughed and disappeared around the corner.

Returning with the receipt, Chuck leaned down and gave Peter's shoulder a squeeze that seemed to speak of a fatherly affection. "You two have a wonderful evening, and Peter, don't you be a stranger," Chuck playfully scolded.

"I won't, Chuck, I promise." With a smile, Peter stood and extended his arm out to me. I took his hand, interlacing my fingers through his as I wove us between the tables and out into the cool of the evening.

My phone rang as we pulled into the driveway. I cut the engine and glanced down at Mitch's name lighting up the screen. I hastily muted it, wondering why he was calling so late.

Peter got out of the car and walked around to my side, opening my door with a playful flourish, his hand outstretched. "Would you like me to walk you to the cottage, Lara?"

"Yes, I would like that very much."

With a smile, I took his hand and allowed him to help me out of the car. Peter's face was so close to mine, I could feel his breath on my skin, the energy hovering between us like a heavy blanket that made my limbs weak. My eyes fell to the fullness of his lips, and I was overcome with an acute desire to feel them against mine.

The harsh ring of my phone sounded once more within my purse.

"You should probably get that." His voice was throaty as he stood beside me, his eyes full of a smoldering heat that made me woozy.

I fumbled around in my purse for my phone, Mitch's name flashing across the screen once more.

"Lara." Mitch sounded strained and garbled on the other end.

"What's up, Mitch?" I moved away from Peter, pressing my finger against my ear to hear him better.

"It's Mom... she's in the hospital."

Chapter Fifteen

I stared out the window of the plane as it descended into the lush valley of Humboldt County, the ocean like a slip of unbroken blue silk.

It was only this morning that I had stood in the driveway with Peter. His hands had been thrust in his pockets; a look of concern etched across his face as I loaded my bag into the car.

"I don't know how long I'll be gone. But I'll keep you posted, okay?" He had only nodded, uncertainty flashing in his eyes, almost as if he wondered if I would even return at all.

The plane touched down on the tarmac, the forceful rush of the brakes causing me to grip the armrests. The whine of the engine faded to a dull hum, and I quickly gathered my bag and filed out, taking the narrow steps down the ramp and onto the asphalt. Cold wind whipped at me, tugging my clothes while I slung my bag over my shoulder and made my way into the tiny airport of McKinleyville, breathing in the familiar smell of ocean and forest.

Pulling the rental car out of the parking lot and onto the highway, I drove south toward Arcata. *A stroke*, Mitch had said. My mother was on life support. This reality settled into my gut with a sickening grip as the lush greenery rolled past, contrasting the inky grey of the sky. Guilt tore at me as I realized I had not seen her in almost four months. The last time I had gone to visit, she had been asleep, her long hair splayed out across the pillow. She had looked so peaceful, happy even, and I always wondered if her dreams were still vivid and clear, despite the rest of her being so far away.

It was a quick drive from the airport, and I soon found myself staring up at the peach-colored stucco building of the community hospital. Taking a deep breath, I clutched my purse tightly as the double doors slid open with a hiss, my footsteps echoing along the shiny linoleum floors as I walked over to the reception area.

The lady at the front desk directed me to the intensive care unit, and I followed the narrow white hallway until I located the correct room. Pausing at the door, I peered through the window to see Mitch inside, sitting in a chair next to Mom's bed, his hands clasped together as if in prayer. He looked up as I entered, tension etched across his soft features.

"Lara, you made it." He stood and crossed the room, wrapping me up in his arms. He smelled of Cheerios and coffee.

"Where are the girls?"

"They're back at the motel with Steven." Mitch ran his hand through his closely cropped blond hair, his eyes rimmed with red.

"You look exhausted, Mitch. Have you gotten any sleep?" My eyes flickered over to the bed, where our mom lay surrounded by blinking machines, a ventilator assisting each rise and fall of her breath.

"No, not really. We flew in last night." His hand rested on my arm as I stood there, staring at Mom.

"She looks like a ghost," I whispered, a ripple of anxiety sweeping over me as I took in her pale, paper-thin skin, veins like tiny rivers threading up her arms. Everything around me appeared hazy and distorted as I walked over to the bed and sat in the chair beside her. I took her hand cautiously in mine, afraid she would break apart at any moment. "Hi, Momma." My voice wavered as I leaned over and placed my lips against her forehead, breathing in the unfamiliar scent of her, a mixture of disinfectant and emptiness. Whatever fragments that had been left of my mom were now completely erased.

"The doctors say she has no detectable brain activity, but there's still a very small chance that she could be in a coma state and regain some function." Mitch stood by the door, his arms crossed around himself.

"What are you saying, Mitch?" The long pause that followed seemed to stretch across the room and suck the air out of me.

"We have to decide what we're going to do."

I turned to him, taking a deep breath. "I think we *both* know what we need to do."

Mitch sighed and began to pace the room, rubbing his hands furiously through his hair. "I know. But there's still a very slim chance she could recover enough to get off life support."

"A slim chance. And then what?" I stood from the bed and walked over to him. "She's been gone for years, you know that." Tears formed in the corners of my eyes, blurring my vision. "She's been trapped in that body for so long. Do you think she would have wanted this?"

Mitch furiously shook his head, resignation clouding his face. "No, she never wanted any of this."

A memory flashed through me.

Sunlight glinting off the trees, my mother's laughter. The tinkling of ice in our cups. It was her fifty-fifth birthday, two years after dad died. She had already begun to show the subtle signs of Alzheimer's, but at the time we didn't recognize them. Her memory loss was only something we lightly chuckled over, like an amusing quirk, nothing more.

I sat in one of the lounge chairs beside John, my hands resting against the rise of my belly, Van Morrison drifting through the speakers from inside while Mitch and Steven lay in the hammock, arms wrapped around each other, their love as fresh and new as the life growing inside of me. Everything seemed so complete in that moment. So tender, simple, and still. My mother, her silky dark hair dusted with only faint strands of grey, was on the porch dancing, her long skirt ruffling in the wind. I watched her as she swayed to the music, lost in her own private world, her wild beauty untouched by age.

That evening, I had stood beside the sink in her kitchen washing dishes when she came over to me, gripping my arm tightly, her face serious. "Lara," she said, her dark eyes piercing mine. "Promise me something, okay? Promise me that if anything ever happens to me, you will let me go."

I brushed her away in jest, but a feeling of foreboding tugged at me. "Getting dark on me, Mom? I know it's your birthday and all..."

"I'm serious, Lara." She had stood there, holding her glass of gin. "I love you guys, I love the life I have with you in it, but I miss your father. And there will come a day when I'm going to be ready to join him, and you need to let me do that."

Tears ran down my face, and I wiped them away as the recollection faded back into the neat little compartments of the past.

"We need to let her go, Mitch. You know she wants to be with Dad."

He nodded, sorrow swimming in the blue of his eyes. "I know."

Mitch and I sat at the chipped formica table of the hospital cafeteria, our hands gripping cups of lukewarm coffee.

"I'll have the girls stop by this evening to say goodbye."

Mitch's eyes were downcast, staring into the depths of his cup as if the murky darkness held something there he could hold on to.

I pulled out my phone, realizing it had been off since this morning. A lump rose in my throat as I struggled with the words. "I know how much Mom hated funerals, but I would like to do some kind of ceremony for her."

Mitch smiled, his eyes filling with warmth. "Me too... She always loved the ocean."

I reached over and squeezed his hand, a silence settling over us as we each slipped into our own private thoughts of Mom; the Mom we knew before the disease had crept in and ravaged her mind, stealing her memories and slowly ripping her away from us. All her vibrancy and joy that had surrounded us as children; her songs and laughter, the delicate little slivers of wisdom she would bestow upon us in the form of bedtime stories, with the soothing tone of her voice like a light within the darkness of the room. I had been grieving the loss of her for so long it had become an intrinsic part of me.

The harsh ping of my phone sounded on the table beside me, and I released my hand from Mitch's, looking down to find three missed calls from John. A mixture of anxiety and anger curled around in my gut. "Mitch. Do you have any idea why John is calling me?"

He grimaced. "I may have mentioned that you would be in town when I talked to him last night."

"Why?"

"It just came out, Lara. You know that we've been close since college, and we still talk often."

I waved my hand in the air. "I know. But why is he calling me?"

He sighed. "He's been having a really hard time lately."

"What do you mean?"

"Ever since you sent back the divorce papers. I think the reality of it all has finally hit him."

"It's about fucking time," I mumbled under my breath, shoving my phone into my purse.

"Lara," Mitch said, grabbing hold of my hand. "You know how John is. I really think he just sent you those papers because he was angry and hurt. Underneath all that though, I know he still loves you. He always has."

I yanked my hand away, confusion and frustration pulling at the corners of my mind, threatening my resolve. "I really don't want to talk about John right now."

Mitch walked me to my car in silence. A light drizzle fell around us, coating our hair in a thin layer of mist. He drew me in for a long hug. "I'll see you tonight."

I nodded, my words feeling trapped in my mouth like a flightless bird as I watched him walk across the parking lot, hands shoved deep in his pockets, the wind blowing against his coat like a sorrowful farewell.

My bag made a hollow sound as it hit the floor of the cheap motel I had checked into across the street from the hospital. Here I was again, that familiar state of limbo creeping into the cracks as I sat down on the stiff bed and stared up at a faded painting of the ocean hanging on the wall.

I didn't want to be here. I wanted to be back in Montana with a longing so sharp it wrenched at me. I wanted to curl up in the cottage with the crisp white sheets that reminded me of snow, and the aspen trees gently waving to me from outside the window against all the sky and light. I wanted Peter's smile, like a warm caress, brightening all the dark places inside me.

I found myself wondering what would have happened if Mitch had not called last night. Would Peter have walked me back to the cottage and placed his lips against mine? Would I have invited him inside and allowed his hands to trace over my skin? The heat of arousal washed over me at the thought of Peter's touch. It had been so long since I had experienced desire. It beckoned me with its silky, seductive hum, like a siren's song, stirring something within me I had not felt in years.

I pushed away the thoughts that left me feeling breathless and guilty, as if my desire were a misplaced emotion, inappropriate and crass beside the inevitability of what this evening would bring. I couldn't escape from this reality as the four walls of the motel room seemed to close in on me. I couldn't run away this time. I was here, back in California, and I had to say goodbye to my mother.

Chapter Sixteen

I sat beside the hospital bed, my throat dry and constricted as I held my mother's hand. Despite my sweater, a chill permeated through me, causing me to shiver. The steady beeping of the heart monitor and the drone of the machines pumping artificial life into her filled the room. The last remnants of her clinging to the wires and tubes.

The door opened, and Mitch's twin girls filed in, wide eyed and solemn, their faces lighting up when they saw me.

"Auntie Lara," they cried out as they ran over to me, their tiny arms wrapping around my neck and waist. I pulled them close, breathing in the soothing, fruity scent of shampoo lingering in their hair that was still damp from the bath.

"Evie, Josie. I've missed you girls *so* much." My words came out choked. I had not seen them in almost a year. "Let me look at you." I ran my hands through their dark hair, which fell to their shoulders in ringlets. "You've both gotten so big." I gave them a teasing smile, fighting back the tears that wanted to rise to the surface. "How old are you now?"

They both raised a hand, all five fingers splayed out in pride. I looked over to see Steven standing in the doorway with his arm around Mitch. He gave me a nod, his dark eyes full of sadness as he crossed the room and enfolded me in a gripping hug. "It's really good to see you, Lara."

"You too." I clung to him for a moment before letting go.

The girls cautiously stood beside the bed as Steven crouched behind them, his arms around their shoulders, his voice low and filled with sorrow. "We're going to say goodbye to Grandma tonight."

The room began to close in on me, the finality of this moment like a weight I could not remove. I turned to Mitch. "I think I need to get some air." My sweaty hand clawed at the door as I slipped out and walked down the long hallway.

The wind slapped against me as I stepped outside, bringing with it the briny scent of the ocean. I leaned against the prickly stucco wall of the hospital, picking at my nails as the nauseating grip of anxiety pulsed within like frantic moths tapping against a porch light.

"You're still doing that?" Mitch had followed me outside, his hand falling on mine in an attempt to calm my nerves.

I recalled one summer, shortly after Caleb died, when Mitch had come to visit with Steven and the girls. My fingers had been so bad at the time that they had begun to bleed. The girls had enthusiastically played nurse, sitting beside me on the couch, taping up all my fingers with Winnie the Pooh Band-Aids they had brought from home. *"Pooh Pooh, heals boo boos,"* they had told me in their cheerful lilt. *"You all better now."*

How I wished it were that easy, that all I needed was a magic band-aid and the confidence of a child's loving touch to heal the wounds inside me.

The hospital doors slid open with a shudder and Steven walked out, Josie held curled in his arms, Evie's small hand wrapped in his. "I'm going to put the girls to bed. Lara, would you be able to bring Mitch back to the motel tonight?"

I nodded. "Of course."

Steven placed his forehead against Mitch's, sorrow outlining his dark features. He whispered something to Mitch in the quiet, intimate language shared between them. Watching them together always made me emotional. Eight years and two kids later, their love had only grown stronger, like the roots of a tree entwining beneath the earth. I was happy my brother had found someone who completed him so effortlessly.

I tried to remember if I had ever felt that way with John.

Mitch and I sat beside Mom, waiting for the doctor to arrive. "I just wish we didn't have to make this decision for her," Mitch said as he wove his hands together. "She never signed a DNR or anything."

"I know." I slowly ran my hand through her hair, the strands like silk against my fingers. I had always loved my mother's hair, and though it had gone almost completely grey over the years, it never lost its softness. "She always lived in the moment. I guess she never thought about things like this until it was too late."

The sound of the door opening sent a rush of anxiety coursing through me, and my heart began to pound. I clasped Mitch's hand in mine as the doctor walked in and stood beside us, a look of stoic empathy etched across his face. *This was it; this would be the last moment with my mother.*

"Are you two ready?" the doctor asked, moving over to stand by the machine.

Mitch and I both nodded, his hand squeezing mine.

"Okay, I'm going to walk you through this. Once I turn these machines off, she will no longer have any assistance with her breathing. The process will be relatively quick."

"Will she feel any pain?" I asked, my eyes brimming with tears.

The doctor shook his head. "No, your mother is not conscious, so she will not feel any pain."

The sudden quiet that echoed through the room as the machines shut off felt barren, choking the air from my lungs. The doctor pressed a few more buttons, turning off the alarms.

My eyes blurred as I watched the green line on the monitor, the spikes falling further and further apart.

Leaning in close, I took her hand in mine. "You can let go now, Mom," I whispered as a rattled gasp escaped from her lips. Then nothing but silence.

Mitch gripped my arm, and I felt something press against my chest and then release, as if the bright spark that was my mother had finally been liberated.

Tears ran down my cheeks as the doctor's hands felt for her pulse, giving us a somber nod. "Take your time. The staff and I will be in the hall when you're ready to leave," he said, before slipping discreetly out of the room.

I stared down at my mother's pale hand, which I still held tightly. I couldn't bring myself to let go just yet, knowing this would be the last time I would ever touch her. The last time I would ever look upon her face, so beautifully lined from years of laughter, love and fearlessly dancing through life.

My mother had always been my hero, the song I sang to myself when the darkness got too deep. Even when she began to slip away from me, the soft rhythm of her breath had been my anchor, and now she was gone. The delicate ties that connected her had been released, her story now mine to carry.

My voice came out in a tremble as I turned to Mitch, his face streaked with tears. "She's with Dad now."

I don't know how long we sat there together beside the body of our mother, but eventually Mitch took my hand, gently pulling me out of the chair. His eyes were full of an exhausted sorrow, his voice a wounded whisper. "It's time to go, Lara."

I bent down, my tears staining her cheeks as I pressed my lips against her one last time, leaving the tender permanence of goodbye upon her skin.

The whoosh of the door as it clicked shut behind us hit me with an anguished finality. I leaned against Mitch as he wrapped his arm around me and slowly led me down the hall.

I crawled into bed, the motel sheets cold and abrasive against my skin, my body heavy and splintered like tender fragments washed upon the shore.

The phone rang, startling me from the smothering noise of my emotions. I grappled for the phone, pressing it against my ear.

"Lara."

The sound of Peter's voice was like a wave of warmth rushing over me.

"I'm sorry for calling so late. I don't want to bother you, I...." He paused, and I could sense a hesitancy hanging in his words. "I just wanted to see how you're doing."

A long sigh spilled from my lips. "You're not bothering me, Peter. I'm actually really glad you called."

"You are?"

I wrapped the blankets tight around me. "Yes, I am. We had to take my mom off life support tonight."

"*Oh, Lara.* I'm so sorry." His tone was soft and infused with a tenderness I wanted to curl up in.

I let out another shaky breath. "It was really hard... and of course it's bringing up all this stuff, but at the same time, I feel this heaviness lifted off me. She had been suffering for so long. I could always see this sorrow in her eyes, like she was a prisoner in her own body... screaming for escape."

"You did the right thing, Lara. I know it doesn't make it any easier, but you've given her peace."

"I know." I ran my hands along the blanket, tracing the floral pattern with my fingers. "Peter."

"Yes?"

"Thanks for calling."

"No problem. I've been thinking about you."

"You have?" My heart swelled, his words like a quiet

confession, soothing my battered mind and solidifying what was tentatively growing between us.

"Yes, I have. You sound pretty tired, though. I'll let you go."

Though my mind and body were drained, exhaustion seeping through every pore, I didn't want to get off the phone with him. The gentle resonance of his voice was a lifeline, lulling me into a state of solace.

"Peter, could you just talk with me for a while?"

"Of course." There was a sound of rustling on his end, and I wondered if he was lying in bed. "What would you like me to talk about?"

I gripped the phone. "Tell me a story about your childhood."

He chuckled. "Well, I've got plenty of those. Let's see... once, when I was about eight or so, I decided I was going to run away. So, I snuck out late one night while everyone was asleep and took one of our horses from the barn. I was still learning how to saddle up properly and decided to just drag a bucket over and climb onto the horse bareback."

I rolled onto my back, staring up at the ceiling, picturing Peter as a child; dark hair falling into his face, his eyes full of stubborn determination.

"I must have spooked her, because she reared up and sprinted out of the barn, with me hanging on for dear life. There I was, barreling down the road, heading straight into town. The local sheriff had been sitting in his car when he saw me galloping past. He got out and tried to stop the horse, but she was skittish and kept on running."

Peter paused for a moment before continuing, his tone shifting to one of faint amusement. "She took me all the way down Main Street; straight to the edge of town and then kept on going, with me holding on and the sheriff trailing behind in his car."

"Weren't you terrified?"

"You'd think I'd be, right? But according to the sheriff, when he had finally managed to corner the horse and get me off safely, I had a big ol' grin on my face."

I smiled into the phone. "Your sister did mention how you've always loved an adrenaline rush."

He let out a soft laugh. "Oh, she did, did she?"

"Uh-huh." My eyes were growing heavy, my limbs releasing the burden of the day and sinking into the place where dreams lingered.

A long pause filled the receiver as I slowly drifted off, cradled in the comforting blanket of Peter's voice. "Goodnight, Lara," I heard him whisper.

Chapter Seventeen

A piercing sound yanked me from the depths of sleep, and I forced my bleary, swollen eyes open. My phone was beside my head, its shrill, incessant tone ringing in my ear, and I realized I must have fallen asleep with Peter on the line last night. I looked over to see John's name flashing across the screen. I shot my hand out to silence his call before throwing the phone to the foot of the bed and burrowing deep into the covers, my heart pounding. *Why does he keep calling me?* I did not have the strength to deal with him right now.

I eventually dragged myself out of bed, threw on some clothes, and headed to my rental car. Driving through the grey mist of morning, I followed the winding stretch of highway that hugged the ocean. Fog nestled low upon the waves, enclosing the view in a white shroud while delicate beams of sunlight tried to hesitantly press through.

I parked in a sandy turnoff and made my way down the familiar narrow path of worn wooden boards, splintered and half buried in the sand and sea grass. This was the place where so many of my childhood summers lived, nestled within the threads of my memory. Our mom lying out on a blanket reading her latest romance novel, her long dark hair blowing in the wind. Mitch and I exploring the beach, hunting for sea glass among the hot sand. The two of us gazing into murky tidepools in search of crabs and sea stars while we clambered up the sharp rocks that jutted out from the shore, barnacles sharp against our bare feet.

I could feel her here, like an apparition mingling with the tide, teasing the corners of my vision, as if all I had to do was turn around, and she would be beside me.

I stood out on the beach. The roar of the water and the cry of seagulls drowned out all my thoughts as I watched the violent churning of the ocean slam itself into the rocks, the wind pelting me with its icy sting. My breath came out slow, synching with the rhythm of the waves as I sunk down into the cool sand and wrapped my arms around my knees.

My phone sounded again, vibrating urgently in my pocket. Pulling it out, I stared at John's number on the screen before taking a deep breath and answering it.

"Lara." John's voice was heavy with relief.

"What do you want, John?"

"I heard what happened with your mom. I'm *so* sorry."

His empathy felt rehearsed, and I brushed away his condolence. "Why are you calling me?"

"Are you still in town?"

"Why do you want to know?" I plunged my hand deep into the sand, clenching the grains between my fingers.

"Because I really want to talk to you."

"What is there to talk about?" I sighed and gazed out onto the water, watching as a lone seagull dipped among the waves. "I don't think there's anything left for us to say."

"Please, Lara." His voice sounded desperate. "I need to talk to you."

My resolve slowly crumbled. I knew this would be my only opportunity to stop by the house for the few things that I had been wanting, things I had not thought to grab in my frantic haste to leave.

"Well, I do need to swing by the house to pick up some stuff, if that's okay with you?"

"Yes, of course. I'll be here all day, Lara."

"Okay, then."

I hung up the phone and slid it back into my jacket pocket, watching as the wind began to softly lift away the fog, leaving the morning sky awash in pale streaks of blue.

Mammoth evergreens towered above me as I drove up the long, narrow driveway, my heart a rapid thrum in my chest. I pulled up to the house, watching the last shadows of a late afternoon creep through the trees and dance upon the gravel strewn with pine needles. I stepped out of the car, closing the door quietly behind me. The house looked different and unfamiliar, though I knew nothing had visibly changed. My legs felt like weights as I walked up the wooden steps and onto the large, elevated porch. The wind chimes I had hung up by the door so long ago, now faded and cracked with age, still greeted me with their optimistic melody.

The door startled me as it swung open abruptly, and there stood John, his face sullen. "Lara, thanks for coming."

His dark eyes were rimmed with red, and he wore a scruffy five o'clock shadow. He looked like he hadn't been sleeping well. My heart clenched at the sight of his disheveled appearance, his usual polished and put together attire nowhere to be found.

I stepped into the entryway, detecting a faint whiff of whiskey on his breath. "I'm not going to stay very long, okay. I just need to grab a few things."

John nodded to me as I walked past him and opened the door to the closet, retrieving a large suitcase. My hands shook as I walked into what used to be our bedroom. It smelled stale and was freezing cold. Blankets and pillows were strewn haphazardly upon the floor, a nightgown of mine still tossed over a chair, and I wondered if John even slept in here anymore.

Hastily pulling open drawers, I shoved clothes and other

items into the suitcase. I opened the sliding door to our walk-in closet and bent down to retrieve a box tucked away underneath my winter coats. Nestled inside were photos of Caleb, trinkets of his life held together by crayon drawings, baby clothes and snippets of his silky blond hair tied with string. I carried the box to the bed, carefully placing the contents into the suitcase before zipping it shut, the sound like a note of resolution within the stillness of the room.

"I fucked up, Lara." I turned around to find John standing in the doorway, a glass of whisky clenched in his hand. He stepped closer to me, closing the space between us. "I want you to come back."

Sinking down on the bed, I stared up at him, disbelief tugging at me. "Little late for that, don't you think? You were the one who sent me those divorce papers, remember?"

John placed his whiskey on the dresser with a loud thump, running his hands through his hair, which I now noticed had begun to grow long. "I was angry."

I shot him a weary look. "Yeah, well, you could have tried to talk to me." I threw my words at him. "But then again, you've never been good at dealing with your emotions, have you?"

"Oh, and you have?" John spat back at me, pain welling up in his eyes. "Am I the only one to blame here?"

I sighed and glanced out the window. "No, I guess you're not." My words hung between us like a fractured whisper as memories from the night I left flooded over me.

John moved closer, his eyes pleading. "Listen, I know that things have been really bad between us for years. But I need you to come back. We can work these issues out; we can get through this. We *have to*. We've been through so much together." He dropped to his knees in front of me, gripping my arms tightly in his hands. "Lara, I love you." His voice was strained and cracking around the edges as tears pooled and slipped down his cheeks. "I can't live like this... without you."

John buried his head in my lap as a choking sob rushed out of him. "I need you to come back to me. *Please.*"

There he was, on his knees sobbing, his heart flayed out, showing me the emotion that I had been silently screaming for all these years, and yet I suddenly felt nothing but emptiness and sorrow. There had never been enough room to navigate around Caleb's ghost. Every time I looked at him, I was reminded of all that we had lost. Whatever love I had left, I couldn't seem to find anymore. It was gone, swept out to sea among the tangled wreckage of our past.

"I need you, Lara." His voice was a muffled cry in my lap, and I placed my hand impassively on his head, running my fingers through his hair, soothing him as if he were a child. "*I need you.*" He raised his head to mine, his face streaked with tears as his lips fell to my neck.

"John. *Stop.*"

I pulled away from him as he stared at me; his pain replaced with a red-hot anger that flashed through his eyes. "Oh, that's right, Lara. I'm not allowed to touch you. I almost forgot."

I stood up from the bed, but he gripped my arm, yanking me back down, causing a sharp twinge of fear to creep through.

"Do you know how many nights I used to lie beside you, wanting to touch you, but knowing that if I did, you would give me that look, the same look you are giving me right now." His face was so close to mine, contorted in hostility and sorrow. "How do you think that's made me feel all these years? Huh?" As he spoke, spittle flew out of his mouth, landing on my face as his hand clenched tighter around my arm.

"You're drunk," I hissed, wrenching myself away from his grip. I stood and grabbed the suitcase, trying to push past him, but John was suddenly in front of me, blocking the doorway. He backed me up against the wall, his voice low and full of malice. "Mitch mentioned you have been staying out on some blind dude's property. Are you fucking this guy? When our divorce papers aren't even cold yet? Do you get off on *fucking* disabled people, Lara?"

Rage boiled inside me, and the bitter taste of bile rose in my throat. I shoved him hard, watching as he lost his balance and toppled to the floor. I grabbed the suitcase, throwing him a look of loathing, disgust coiling in my veins.

"What I do is no longer any of your fucking business!"

I stormed down the hallway and out onto the porch. My body coursed with adrenaline as hot tears pricked my eyes. I clamored down the stairs, the suitcase thudding behind me.

"Lara, wait!" John yelled. Out of the corner of my eye, I could see him gripping the doorframe as if to steady himself. "I'm sorry. Please don't go. Lara, please. Just talk to me!"

I yanked the car door open, shoving the suitcase into the back seat, and turned to him. "I have nothing more to say to you. You're a fucking mess, John!" I yelled.

"Of course I'm a fucking mess!" He stormed down the stairs with his finger pointed at me like a weapon. "We lost a fucking child, Lara! And you never forgave me for that, did you?"

At the mention of Caleb, something inside of me burst, and I flew at him in a fury, my fists pounding against his chest. "Because you should've been watching him, you asshole! Why didn't you watch him! Your precious fucking job always came first, didn't it?" John gripped my wrists in an attempt to stop my onslaught as tears poured down my face. My throat felt constricted and raw, choking on all the things we never said, all the wasted years between us. The burden of it all washed against me like a tidal wave, and I had no more strength left.

I twisted myself away from his grasp, my voice coming out hoarse. "You never let me say goodbye. I needed to see him, and you wouldn't let me. There's a part of me that will never forgive you for that. *Never.*"

John slowly shook his head, eyes wide and wet with tears, his fists tightly clenched as if he were trying to hold on to something that was no longer there. "What I saw, Lara, it haunts me every... single... day. I couldn't let you see that."

"You didn't give me a choice, though, did you? You never really gave me a choice in anything. It was always about you, wasn't it? Your agenda, your timeline, and how much you loathed weakness in others... and where has all that gotten you?" My words tumbled out, harsh and splintered. "You wouldn't even let me grieve for him in the way I needed to. You couldn't stand the fact that for months I couldn't get out of bed."

A desolate silence overcame us as we stood there in the driveway, used up and frayed, with nothing left to save between us. I wondered what would have happened if we had only reached out to each other all those years ago? Would we have been able to salvage love? Had love even been there in the first place?

I furiously wiped away my tears, my heart like a wound throbbing against my chest. "We died when Caleb did, didn't we? There's nothing left."

He nodded, his limbs giving way as he sunk to the porch steps in crumpled defeat. *"I know."* His eyes lifted to meet mine. So many years of torment locked away inside, the well of his grief just as deep as my own. His pain sliced through me. The broken shards of what was left of us were so crushing and resolute, and there was no way to fix the damage. I only hoped one day he would be able to find his own version of peace amongst the remains.

"I'm sorry, John."

"Me too." He watched me in sorrow as I slid into the front seat of the car and backed down the driveway. His figure caught in my headlights for a moment like a ghostly impression, before fading into darkness.

Chapter Eighteen

We stood beside the tide, the ocean water lapping at our feet and soaking our shoes. But none of us seemed to care. Evie and Josie trailed behind us, following our path of wet footsteps left in the sand. In his hand, Mitch held a silver tin that caught the faint sunlight streaming through the broken clouds.

"Are you ready?" Mitch's words lifted above the crashing of the waves; his eyes full of a stoic sorrow that matched the mood of the sea.

I nodded as he removed the lid off the top of the tin and handed it to me. Inside lay the fragments of what was left of our mother, ashes that were cool and gritty against my fingers. I cupped a handful of them, holding tightly for a moment before releasing them into the wind, watching as her ashes collided against the sky like a plume of smoke before tumbling into the waves.

"Goodbye, Mom," I whispered to the water as my heart stretched to accommodate all the memories of her vibrancy and love, clinging to them like beautiful, waking dreams.

Josie came up to me, slipping her warm hand in mine. "Auntie Lara. Where did Grandma go?"

I crouched down upon the sand, meeting her wide brown eyes. "Grandma is with Grandpa and cousin Caleb now." Tears made my vision waver, and I squeezed her hand gently. "And do you know what they're doing?"

Josie shook her head. "What are they doing?"

"They are dancing and laughing together. They will always have each other now."

"So..." Josie furrowed her brow. "They'll never be lonely?"

"That's right," I said, swallowing the lump that rose within my throat. "They will never be lonely."

Josie smiled, sparks of innocent joy spilling out. "And they get to dance all the time?"

"Yes, Josie. They will always be dancing." My heart clenched with bittersweet sadness as I watched Josie break away from me, running to join her sister along the beach, her arms outstretched like a bird.

Staring out into the incessant churning life of the ocean, I envisioned my mother reaching her arms out to Caleb, all the brilliant light unextinguished in her eyes while she spun him around, their souls entwining. She held him now.

I clung to this image, and a vibrant bud of hope pressed forth from beneath the rubble of my pain like delicate leaves shimmering with the promise of renewal, and a richness I could not quite define yet.

Mitch and Steven wrapped their arms around me, enclosing me in the comforting fold of what was left of our family. The girls ran along the shoreline, chasing the waves and startling the seagulls, who took flight on graceful wings; their mournful cries calling out into the vastness of the sea.

We stood together in the turnoff beside the road, saying our goodbyes. The wind blew our hair wildly around us as I showered the girls with kisses. Their giggles were like sweet honey, filling me with warmth.

"So, what's next for you?" Mitch gave me a look of tenderness and placed his hands on my shoulders, a gesture reminiscent from when we were young, and he wanted to comfort me.

"I'm going to try and start over, I guess."

Mitch nodded, and emotion welled up in his eyes. "You

know, I'm not worried about you anymore. I understand now, that in leaving John, you did what you had to do, and I'm really proud of you for having the strength to do that." He drew me into a tight hug, and my throat constricted as he spoke softly into my hair. "Go find your happiness, Lara."

The plane descended over the rich Montana soil, touching down onto the tarmac. From the window, I could see a dusting of snow upon the peaks of the mountains. Though I was stretched and worn, something had shifted inside me, revealing a lightness that drifted beneath the layers as if I had left something behind in California.

The air was crisp as I descended from the plane. Lazy afternoon sunlight flitted against my skin, and most of the trees had cast off their leaves while I was gone; the wind blowing their song away, leaving bare branches that trembled against the autumn sky.

I drove down the winding stretch of road toward Peter's house. The rippling grass bowing their golden strands against the blue like a familiar acquaintance welcoming me back.

As I pulled into the driveway, I was hit with a sensation of relief and a tentative excitement that flowered inside. Being back here felt like coming home. Dusty ran to greet me from the porch, his paws landing on my chest and forcing me back against the car as his tongue eagerly lapped at my face. I laughed and pushed him off me. "Okay, boy. I missed you, too."

I turned to see Peter walking toward me through the pasture, his dark hair blowing in the wind against the backdrop of mountain and sky. My heart rose at the sight of him. "Peter!" I called out, briskly crossing the driveway, and opening the gate.

Upon hearing my voice, his face instantly relaxed and a wide smile spread across his features.

I met him in the middle of the pasture, with Dusty running joyful loops between us. "You're back."

"I am." I fought the overwhelming urge to embrace him, to sink into the feel of his strong arms enfolding me. "How have things been here without me?"

"Well, Dusty sure missed you," Peter said, chuckling as Dusty began to make his happy little whiny sound, his tail thumping erratically against my legs.

"Really? I hadn't noticed." I bent down to give Dusty a rub. "And what about you?" My voice grew playful. "Did you miss me?"

He tilted his head, a small smile teasing the corners of his mouth. "Maybe I did."

I took in a deep breath, inhaling the refreshing brisk air. "Gosh, it feels so good to be back here."

"I'm glad to hear that." Peter's face suddenly grew serious, and he reached out his hand, his fingers brushing down my arm and grazing against the delicate pulse of my wrist. "How are you doing?"

I sighed as a sudden chorus of geese filled the air, causing me to look up into the receding light, watching the smooth arc of their flight spill across the sky. "You know, I think I'm going to be okay. The trip was long and hard, and painful on so many levels, but at the same time, I feel like I have found a certain kind of closure with things." I watched as the geese faded from view, disappearing over the mountains. "I feel lighter in a way."

Peter nodded, sympathy flickering in his eyes. "Well, I'm really glad you're back, Lara."

"Me too."

Something hung in the quiet that fell between us, a tenuous dance that neither of us seemed to know the steps to. Peter broke the silence, motioning over to the barn. "I was just about to go put the horses in early for the night. I heard some snow may be on the way."

I looked up into the sky, squinting at the wisps of feathery clouds against the deepening blue of the approaching evening. "Really? Isn't it a bit early for snow?"

Peter shrugged. "Not in these parts. We had a big ol' storm come in last September." He smiled at me. "You'll soon find out that Montana can be quite unpredictable." He shoved his hands in his pockets, his voice growing distant. "Well, I'll let you go unpack, I'm sure you must be tired from your flight."

Disappointment pressed against my chest. I didn't know what I was expecting, but a part of me wanted more from him. "Okay," I awkwardly replied, glancing back toward my car where my bags still sat in the back seat. "I guess I'll see you tomorrow then?"

Peter nodded his head. "Yep, I'll see you then."

I watched him head back toward the barn with Dusty, casting long shadows behind them as the mountains swallowed up the last rays of sunlight.

I sat on the bedroom floor of the cottage, folding my clothes, and tucking them neatly away into the dresser drawers that I had left empty until now. There was a sense of permanence and meaning in this act. It was as if in placing my belongings into the drawers for the first time, I was finally accepting this life that had pulled me so far away from the one I had before. I no longer felt haphazardly strewn about, adrift in the vast unknown; I was consciously folding myself into compartments that whispered of possibility.

Movement from the corner of my eye drew my attention to the window. Large flakes of snow struck the glass, slowly slipping down and disappearing into the darkness. I stood and grabbed a jacket from the bed, my heart swelling with childlike anticipation as I stepped outside.

The chill of the night air was a shock to my system as swirling snowflakes like thick cotton spilled from the sky, covering the world in a beautiful, white silence. My breath billowed out in the glow of the porch light as a giddiness rose inside. A new beginning, like a bright flash of promise, bloomed within as I stared up at the dizzying flakes falling soundlessly, bathing me in a peaceful stillness that swept everything else away.

I don't know how long I stood there watching the snow fall but eventually the cold stirred me from my thoughts, pulling me back to the warmth waiting inside. Shaking the snow off my coat, I stepped into the cottage, my hair wet, and my fingers numb as I grabbed a glass and a bottle of wine from the kitchen and retreated into the bathroom.

Turning on the faucet, I poured myself a glass of wine, watching the water eddy against the porcelain as I shed my clothes and sunk into the bath, the steam swirling around me like fog, obscuring the patterned wallpaper. I closed my eyes as the heat coiled itself through me, slipping through the tension and suspending my body in a blissful buoyancy.

The wind picked up outside, rhythmically pelting the glass with snow. Its mournful whine slithered through the cracks of the windows, and I found the sound oddly comforting as I closed my eyes and slipped deeper into the water, reveling in this feeling of contentment. Color flickered beneath my eyelids, and I opened them to see the lights above me grew dim, filling the bathroom with a dusty amber glow before enclosing me in a sudden, jarring darkness.

Chapter Nineteen

I pulled myself out of the tub and fumbled around in the dark for a towel before making my way into the bedroom. My hands searched across the bed until I found my phone. Using the light from the screen, I shuffled into the kitchen, leaving a trail of wet footprints across the floor as I rooted through the cabinets, frantically looking for a flashlight or a candle. Finding nothing, I went into the hallway and dug through the linen closet. Frustration tugged at me as I came up empty once more. I stood there in the darkness of the hallway, listening to the silence that encompasses a room when the steady hum of appliances no longer fills it.

A soft knock startled me, and I stumbled into the living room. Opening the door, I found Peter standing there with a flashlight in his hand, snow covering his hair and coat.

"Thought you might need this," he said, holding out the flashlight as a blast of cold air rushed into the room. "Noticed we lost power when everything got real quiet."

I clicked it on, and a comforting beam of light slanted across the room. "Thanks so much. I haven't been able to find anything in the cottage."

"Figured you wouldn't. Power may be out for a while, though," he said as he closed the door behind him. "Why don't you grab some stuff for the night and head on over to the house with me?"

His invitation provoked a flush of excitement I attempted to brush aside. "Oh, I'm sure I'll be fine. I saw a bunch of extra blankets in the closet."

"Lara. Don't be ridiculous. You'll freeze out here with no heat. I have a nice fire going, and the couch folds out into a pretty comfortable bed."

I wrapped the towel tighter around myself. "Are you sure? I don't want to impose."

"I would hardly consider this an imposition, Lara." Peter's voice grew low, and a smile tugged at the corner of his mouth. "I just don't want to have to come on out here in the morning and defrost you, that's all."

"Okay, fine," I said with a faint chuckle, "let me just get dressed really quick." In the dim light between us, I noticed a flicker of something cross over his face, and a bloom of heat rose in my chest. "I'll be right back."

Peter stood waiting for me in the living room while I hastily threw some clothes on and grabbed my toothbrush from the bathroom, trying not to let the tendrils of anticipation consume me at the thought of spending a night under the same roof as him.

I found myself breathlessly chattering as we followed the fence line and made our way over to his house. Everything now covered in a heavy white blanket that crunched loudly beneath our feet. "God, I just love the snow, the way it seems to silence everything. We never got much of it in California."

Peter grunted stiffly. "Stuff's nothing but a damn nuisance to me."

"Really?' I looked over at him in surprise. "You don't like the snow? But it's so beautiful, and the way it falls from the sky... it's always felt so magical to me."

I caught Peter as he turned his head in my direction with a look that I couldn't quite decipher in the dark.

We dusted the snow off our coats and left our boots by the door as we entered the warm glow of Peter's living room. Dusty lay stretched out by the fire and did not move to greet us, only lifted his head slightly, his brown eyes following our movements.

Peter hung his coat up on a hook by the door, and I removed mine as well, our arms grazing against each other as I draped my coat beside his.

"Well, Dusty sure looks comfortable," I said, glancing over at his immobile figure on the floor.

"Yep, he gets like this when it snows. I think the cold makes his joints ache."

"Aw... you *poor* boy," I cooed, bending down to run my hand along his back. Dusty thumped his tail softly upon the floor in reply.

Peter walked over to the couch, running his fingers along the arm. "Do you mind giving me a hand with this?"

"Sure thing." I stood and grabbed the cushions off the couch, placing them in the corner of the room. Peter stood on the other side and helped me lift the mattress up and out of the couch frame, placing it on the floor.

"I'll go get some sheets for you," he said briskly before disappearing down the hall.

He returned with his arms full of blankets, and I moved to where he was, taking them from him. "I got this. And thanks for putting me up for the night."

Peter nodded stiffly; his face unreadable as he retreated into the kitchen. The sound of cupboards loudly closing drifted into the living room as I tucked the sheets onto the bed, feeling thrown off by this sudden shift in him. He seemed aloof and detached, and I missed the ease and gentle warmth between us. I tried to ignore the sinking feeling inside me that he was pulling away.

I walked into the kitchen and found Peter crouched down, digging through the cupboards for something. I crossed my arms and leaned against the doorway.

"Peter, are you okay?"

"I'm fine."

"Really? Because you seem a little grumpy tonight."

He stood and turned in my direction. In the dimness of the kitchen, I could make out the outline of his face, shrouded in tension. "I'm sorry. It's just bullshit family drama, nothing you need to concern yourself with."

Relief trickled through me, comforted in the knowledge that it wasn't *me* he was trying to erect a wall around. It was his own thoughts.

"Do you want to talk about it?"

Peter ran his hand through his hair and sighed deeply. "Not really, no."

Stepping closer, I peered into the murky darkness of the open cupboards. "What are you looking for, anyway?"

"I thought I had an old bottle of scotch stashed away in here somewhere."

"Scotch huh? Hold on a minute," I said as I retreated into the living room to grab the flashlight.

"Lara, never mind. Don't worry about it." Peter called out from behind me.

"It's okay. Sometimes family drama needs a little alcohol," I replied playfully as the beam of light glanced around the kitchen. I scanned the shelves until my eyes caught on a dusty bottle tucked away in the far back of a lower cupboard. "Is this what you are looking for?" I asked, handing the bottle to him.

"Thanks." He gave me a sheepish grin. "I do hope you know that the irony of reaching for a bottle right now is not lost on me." He let out a wry chuckle as he grabbed a glass and motioned in my direction. "Do you want some?"

"Sure, I would love some." I took the glass Peter poured for me. The rich aroma of spice filled my senses as I took a sip, feeling the warm burn travel down my throat. I placed my hand on his arm, feeling his muscles contract against my touch, his unspoken agitation like a heavy force that I wanted to somehow strip away. "Are you sure you don't want to talk about what's going on? I had some drama of my own back in California. We could commiserate?"

Peter's eyes softened, and his voice grew low as a slow smile slipped past his lips. "You're persistent, aren't you?"

The snow continued to fall outside, flickering against the windows like tiny ghosts. We sat close together on the rug beside the fire, listening to the crackle and hiss of the flames as we leaned our backs against the couch. Sparks of light played upon the walls, bathing the room in dancing shadows.

I watched as Peter swirled his drink, his jaw tightly clenched. I leaned in and clinked my glass lightly against his. "Should I go first?"

"If you want to?"

Dusty settled on the floor beside me, resting his head in my lap. "Well, I saw my ex-husband the other day when I went over to grab some stuff from the house."

"Really?" Peter shifted himself next to me, his voice growing soft. "And how'd that go?"

I sighed and ran my fingers through Dusty's short, wiry coat. "Not so good. He was drunk and wanted to talk. And then things got really ugly, really fast."

The look on Peter's face was one of concern, and then a flash of anger gathered in his eyes, his body growing rigid. "What did he do to you, Lara?"

"Nothing. He didn't do anything." I stared off into the fire, gathering the fragments of my thoughts, knowing they were safe with him. "There's just so much anger and pain between us. So many things we never said. It all came rushing to the surface." I took a long sip of the scotch, the warmth settling in my stomach. "I realize that I am just as much at fault as he is for the disintegration of our marriage. For so many years he shut down on me, and I didn't have the strength to try and get him back. We were both drowning."

Peter's hand reached out in search of me, his fingers gently sweeping across my arm. "I'm really sorry you had to go through all that... on top of the death of your mom." He shook his head. "Makes me feel like such a self-involved prick. Here I am, brooding over my issues, when you are dealing with things much heavier than me right now."

I placed my hand over his, giving it a light squeeze. "This isn't a competition, Peter."

"I know." He furrowed his brow, a silence filling the space between us for a moment as his eyes stared off into his own vast darkness, an isolation only he could see. I watched as the firelight hit his face, illuminating his features in a warm glow, and my heart stirred, drinking him in until his words broke the stillness.

"My brother got arrested and thrown in jail this week."

"What happened?" I leaned closer to him, brushing against his shoulder as I clenched the drink in my hand.

"He got caught robbing a house," he let out a long sigh, "and the stupid asshole had a gun. He now faces charges of first-degree armed robbery." Peter's eyes grew sharp and flashed with an emotion I knew had been festering for years. "I was on the phone with Miriam earlier this evening. She wants to find him a good lawyer, to try and lower his sentence." He stood abruptly and moved closer to the fire, his hands trailing down the brick to the pile of wood stacked below. Throwing a piece onto the flames, sparks shot up like angry insects rushing up the chimney. "Not much good it will do though. It's a pretty open and shut case in my opinion, and with his prior record, he's looking at anywhere between ten to fifteen years in prison."

"Wow. I'm a little surprised that Miriam would want to try and get him a lighter sentence."

Peter sighed. "That's how Miriam is. She forgives. She's forgiven my brother for all the shit he's pulled over the years." He ran his fingers through his hair and settled back onto the floor beside me, resting against the couch and draping his arms loosely over his raised knees. "I, on the other hand, have not. And I don't know if I'll ever be able to."

Peter's expression held a mask of murky confliction. I could tell the tangled story of his family was a weight around his neck, holding him down. But beneath the complexities of his pain, there was a passion and depth that only made him more beautiful.

"Do you believe people can really change?"

I sighed, staring into the embers of the fire. "I don't know. People have to *want* to change, and that takes a certain kind of strength, but it's a strength that not everyone has inside them."

Peter nodded. "Yeah, I think you're right. Miriam thinks Greg can change, that he's still in there somewhere. But I don't know if he is. I feel like I lost my brother so long ago, and the person in his place is just this vacant shell."

I reached over and touched his hand, slowly running my thumb over the weathered skin marked by years of sun. "I'm sorry, Peter."

He turned his head in my direction, and a sudden flash of heat flickered in his eyes. "What is it about you that's so damn comforting?"

His words sent a surge through me. Feeling emboldened by the whiskey, I slid in front of him and positioned myself between his legs, leaning my back against his broad chest. Peter drew in a sharp intake of breath as I settled against him, his warmth radiating around me like a current I wanted to lose myself in.

"Is this okay?" I tentatively asked, setting down my glass on the floor beside us.

Peter dipped his head down, his breath so close to my ear that it sent tantalizing shivers up my neck, his words a silky whisper across my skin.

"Of course it is, Lara."

Chapter Twenty

Resting my head against Peter's chest, his hand curled around mine, the calloused ridges of his fingertips stroking the inside of my palm. His touch was featherlight, the sensation eliciting a rush that built up in my core and cascaded through my entire body, causing my words to come out shaky. "You comfort me too, you know."

Peter ran his hands up my arms. "Really?" His voice was low and husky as his mouth hovered near my neck, causing the fine hairs to raise like a shockwave of electricity.

My pulse accelerated, and I leaned my head to the side, offering myself up to him, longing for the feel of his lips on my skin. His breath grazed against my ear, soft and hesitant, as if waiting for permission, and I reached up and wove my fingers into his thick hair. "Peter..." His name was a sigh which spilled out of me like an invitation, allowing my desire to claim the space between us as I pulled him closer.

Sweeping his hand up my neck, he stroked my cheek, his thumb brushing against my lips as he gently tilted my head toward his. Then his mouth found mine in a soft, warm explosion that made my whole body weak.

His kiss was a delicious slow burn, a languid tease as our lips delicately met in a drawn-out waltz that left me breathless and dizzy. I had never been kissed like this before. Peter was not claiming me, he was savoring me, and it made me feel precious and alive.

An overwhelming ache grew within as I gripped his arms,

stifling back a moan as Peter wound his hand through my hair, his beard tickling my skin as he drew me deeper into his intoxicating kiss, his tongue sweeping against mine and igniting all my senses. I pulled back, flushed, and gasping for air as I turned around to face him, his eyes heavy with longing as he sought me out, his hand trailing down my neck.

"Lara?" My name came out like a question resting on his lips as his hands fell to my waist, delicately inching underneath the fabric of my shirt. I rose onto my knees, needing to feel his skin against mine. Slipping my shirt over my head, I took Peter's hand and placed it on my breast.

He sucked in a breath as his fingers ran across my nipple, tracing circles that awakened my flesh. With a groan, he rose and gripped my waist, pulling me against him. "What are you doing to me?" His voice was an impassioned whisper in my ear as his mouth fell hot and feverish against my neck, engulfing me in a pleasure that left me unsteady as his lips and hands explored every dip and curve of my body, tracing me like a map he wanted to memorize.

"*God*, I don't think I ever want to stop touching you." His words lingered against me like a promise. Closing my eyes, I leaned my head back. All my thoughts lifted away until nothing remained but the exhilarating sensation of Peter's hands on me, unfurling all my desire which had been hidden and bound for so long.

Grabbing the fabric of his shirt, I lifted it over his head. Shadows from the fire danced across his skin as I ran my hands down his chest, tracing the smooth definition of muscle. Peter let out a sharp exhale as my lips met his neck, tasting the salt of him. Then his arms were around me, lifting us effortlessly off the floor, my legs shaking as I wrapped them around his waist.

"You have to tell me where the bed is." His voice was a low growl against my neck.

"It's just a few steps forward."

Peter moved slowly until he hit the side of the bed and leaned down, placing me gently upon the sheets. Pressing myself against him, my tongue glided along his ear while my hands crept down to his pants, eagerly reaching to unbutton them.

"Lara." He drew back for a moment, breath labored, his eyes wild in the firelight. "I want you to know I'm clean, but I don't have anything. It's been a while, and I haven't..."

I placed my fingers against his lips to silence him. "It's okay. I'm clean too, and I'm on birth control." I pulled him close to me again, but he resisted, hovering over me, his face hesitant.

"Are you sure about this?"

"Yes." My words tumbled out in a long sigh as I reached my hand down and felt the strain of his arousal against the fabric of his pants. "I want you to make love to me, Peter."

Suddenly, his mouth was on mine again and we fumbled like greedy teenagers, shedding the rest of our clothes like husks upon the floor. Skin against skin, I explored the feel of him against me while he ran his hand up my thigh, lightly teasing the slickness of my sex. With a moan, I pressed myself against him as he dipped his fingers inside, discovering the places I had not touched in years. A wild burst of heat erupted within, causing me to jerk and grip the sheets as he continued with his caress, his mouth against my neck.

"I need to feel you," I breathed as I pulled him closer and cupped the length of him in my hand. A deep groan rumbled within his chest as I guided him inside me, a gasp of surprise escaping my mouth as he entered, causing Peter to stop.

"Is this too much? Am I hurting you?" His voice was breathy and ragged in my ear as I adjusted to the size of him.

"No, please don't stop... Just be gentle."

"Oh, Lara," He whispered. "I will *always* be gentle with you." His lips tenderly found mine in a long, drawn-out kiss that broke me open, and I arched my back, wanting to feel more of him, all of him. Peter slipped himself in deeper; slow, lingering strokes that caused bursts of pleasure to cascade through my body.

"Oh, God." Peter's voice was gravely against my neck. "You feel *so* good."

His words sent me reeling, and I gripped his lower back, angling my hips and thrusting him in all the way. A jolt of ecstasy so sharp and encompassing ripped through me, causing a loud moan to burst from my lips. Frantic and unbound, I writhed beneath him, completely unhinged and already precariously close to orgasm as he hit a place inside that obliterated all my senses.

"Lara... *slow down*," Peter groaned.

But I was already there, completely lost to the ecstasy building up inside. "I can't..." I gasped, "you're making me come."

I exploded beneath him, uncoiling all of myself into his arms. Through my haze of euphoria, Peter suddenly stiffened and called out my name, holding me tightly against him as he released himself. An eruption of energy I could viscerally feel spread through me like fire as we rode the last delicious wave together; my mind and body like a cocoon split wide open.

Peter dropped his head to my chest, our labored breath entwined.

"Well, gosh, I *was* planning on lasting a bit longer than that." A sheepish look flickered across his face as he rolled onto his back and enfolded me in his arms. "But apparently I have a hard time controlling myself with you."

With a smile, I nestled against him, listening to the rhythm of his heart pounding rapidly in my ear. "I think you might have the same effect on me," I murmured as my fingers trailed across his skin.

An overwhelming feeling of elation mixed with sorrow abruptly rose to the surface, and the sharp sting of tears obscured my vision. I allowed them to leak onto Peter's chest as they ran a trail down my cheeks.

His eyes were draped with concern as he took my face in his hands, his thumb brushing away my tears. "Are you okay?"

"Yes." My words tumbled out, choked and broken as years of pent-up emotion flooded me. "It's just been a really long time... since I have been with someone like this... since I have allowed myself to feel this... *amazing*."

He pulled me close, tenderly stroking my hair as I let go against him. All the loneliness and grief, the tangled guilt and self-neglect. I had locked myself away in darkness, and Peter was like bright sunlight against my skin.

I lay in his arms, allowing myself to unburden the weight which had pressed against me for so long until all that was left was a stillness inside.

"God, how you move me," he sighed as he threaded his hands deeper into my hair.

I lifted my head to find his eyes full of warmth. He reached out to trace my tears, and then his lips were on my cheek, kissing them away.

I let out a faint chuckle, trying to ease the gravity of the moment. "I feel like I'm always losing it on you. You must have a thing for girls who cry."

"No, Lara. I have a thing for *you*." His hand trailed down my back, leaving goosebumps along my skin. "You know, it's been an awfully long time since I've been with someone, too."

"Really?"

"Yes, I've had sex... but not like this."

He stirred against me as he spoke, and a renewed wave of arousal rose up. I pressed myself against him, longing to feel the rush of him again as I ran my lips down his chest. "And what is *this* exactly?"

"Something I haven't felt in a *very* long time."

My heart trembled, and I rose to meet his mouth, falling

against him in a breathless, frantic kiss as I reached down to cup him in my hand, feeling the steady pulse of his desire. He groaned as I positioned myself above him and slid him inside me once more. A fevered need taking over as I rocked against him.

Peter sat up and gripped my thighs, trying to still my urgency. "Lara." He ran his hands through my hair, brushing away the loose strands from my face. "You have no idea how long I have wanted to be with you like this." His lips swept across mine and traveled down my neck. "We have all night, and I want to experience every... single... part of you."

Like a gift, his words broke open something within me, and my fervency was suddenly replaced with a tender, raw intimacy that delicately grew between us.

I slowed my pace, sinking into him as his hands caressed my skin, holding me close against his chest. We began to move together in a rhythm that felt hushed and sacred as everything else fell away. The soft brush of snow against the windows enclosed us in a trembling silence, and all that was left was the blissful perfection of our bodies discovering each other.

Chapter Twenty-One

Peter ran his hand over the curve of my back, pulling me from sleep. Light streamed through the window, washing everything in white. I rolled over to find him dressed and sitting on the edge of the pull-out bed. Peter had stoked up the fire and it roared in the hearth, cracking and hissing behind him.

"Good morning, beautiful."

A languid warmth coursed through my limbs as I sat up. "Morning." I ran my hand up his arm. "How long have you been awake for?"

"About an hour or so." He leaned in close to me, smelling of coffee, and brushed his lips against mine. "Power's still out, but if you're hungry, there's cereal in the kitchen."

I ran my hand down his chest, my voice playful. "Why do you have clothes on right now?"

Peter chuckled. "Because I have to go check on the horses."

I glanced down at my clothes strewn on the floor beside the bed. "Do you want me to come help?"

"No, it's okay. You stay here." His voice was throaty as he traced his fingers down my breast, causing my nipple to stiffen in arousal. "I prefer you this way, naked by the fire."

I pulled him close to me and breathed seductively in his ear. "Why don't you check on the horses later?"

"I can't do that, Lara."

"Why not?" I whispered, pressing my mouth against his neck.

"Because," he groaned, slipping his hand into my hair. "Once I start with you, I'm not gonna be able to stop." Peter drew me into a deep kiss that made my entire body ache before pulling away, a lazy smile drifting over his lips. "I'll be back soon."

I laid back down on the bed and wrapped the blankets around me. Dusty stood at the side of the bed and nudged my hand. I ran my fingers through his coat as I stared into the leaping flames of the fire. Images of the night before floated over me like a lucid, seductive dream, causing my core to tighten. Being with Peter felt like shedding skin that had grown too tight, revealing a body that yearned to dance again.

Hunger tugged at me, and I reluctantly got up, wrapping the sheet around myself as I padded into the kitchen with Dusty following close behind. My thighs ached and my sex felt tender, a delicious soreness born from a night of pleasure. I smiled as I entered the kitchen where I found cereal and milk laid out on the table, with a bowl and spoon placed neatly beside it. This thoughtful gesture filled me with tenderness as I sat down and poured cereal into the bowl, glancing out the window as I ate.

It had stopped snowing sometime during the night, and the pasture had been transformed into a wonderland of undulating white, the aspen trees bowing low against a milky sky. My heart stilled as I let the perfection of this moment settle against me, the beauty of the snow and the crackling of the fire in the living room, but just as soon as the feeling took hold, it was gone, and replaced with a crippling guilt. The incessant claws of my grief tore into me, attempting to shred the happiness that tentatively grew within.

I pressed my hands against my head, trying to push away the sensation, and the tiny voice inside that hissed at me relentlessly, reminding me that Caleb would always be gone, my mother was dead, and that this happiness I was toying with, was only a foolish illusion. I stood from the table, my mouth suddenly dry and bitter tasting. Anxiety squeezed me like a vice as I went into the living room and scrambled for my clothes lying on the floor. I hastily slipped them on and opened the front door to grab my boots from the porch when the back door shut and Peter walked into the room. He crouched down by the fire, warming his hands next to the flames.

"Where are you going, Lara?"

I let the door shut behind me, cold air mixing with the warmth of the room as my boots landed on the floor with a thud. "I don't know." Tears slid down my face as I stood there, caught between the sudden urge to flee and the powerful desire to stay within his comforting shelter.

Peter stood and walked toward me, reaching out his hand until he found my arm, and slowly ran it up to my cheek, his thumb brushing against a tear. "I have a feeling that these aren't happy tears?"

I shook my head. My throat constricted as I tried to grapple with the confusing array of emotions that had abruptly charged to the surface.

Peter's face grew somber, his brow furrowing as his words came out soft and hesitant. "What's going on?"

A trembling breath spilled out of me. "I had such an amazing night with you, Peter." Trepidation flashed across his eyes as I spoke. "But at the same time, I feel so guilty about it."

"Oh, Lara."

He pulled me against him, and I collapsed into his arms. His strength around me like an anchor holding me back from the furious current of my mind.

"It's like... if I allow myself to feel any bit of happiness, that I'm somehow letting go of Caleb, and my mom." My words spilled out in a broken gasp as I buried my face against his chest, remembering the first time I laughed after Caleb died. I had been in the kitchen, and Zeke was hopping on his hind legs, trying to catch a fly. The laughter was unexpected, and quickly followed by a hollow repentance. How could I laugh when my child was dead? How could I ever laugh again?

"I haven't let myself feel good in so long." I looked up at him, wiping the tears from my cheeks. "I don't think I know how anymore."

Peter reached out and ran his fingers through the strands of my hair. "Lara. You do know that it's not your pain that keeps the people you have lost close to you. It's the love you have for them, and nothing's ever going to take that away."

Peter's words grabbed hold of me. I knew he was right, but I had grown so accustomed to the armor of my sorrow, refusing to let go of the weight, for fear that if I did, I would have nothing left.

"You deserve happiness, and I want nothing more than to be able to give that to you, if you'll let me." His voice against my ear was heavy with a tender intimacy that caused my limbs to grow weak and all my conflictions to slip back into the dark corners of my mind.

I pressed my lips to his, pulling him into a deep kiss that answered his question. Sliding my fingers through his hair, I gazed into the wildness of his eyes. "Where did you come from?"

He shrugged as a grin spread across his face like sunshine, thawing all the frozen places inside me. "Nowhere special, just some po-dunk town in Montana." His smile faltered for a moment as he ran his hand delicately along my jaw. "You know, I really thought for a second there, you were gunna run off on me."

In that moment, standing in front of Peter with all his gentle fire that captivated me, I knew that there was nowhere else I wanted to be. "I'm not going anywhere."

Peter rested his fingers on my lips, tracing the upward curve which blossomed beneath his touch. "Is that a smile?"

"Maybe."

"Oh, good." He suddenly lifted me up into his arms. "Because I have plans for you." He playfully growled into my ear. "You just have to tell me where the bed is again."

"You haven't mapped the bed out yet?" I teased as I wrapped my arms tightly around him.

"No, that damn thing is throwing me off my game."

The sound of laughter took flight from my mouth, filling the landscape of my mood with vibrant streaks of color. The remnants of my fractured self momentarily dissipated as I sunk onto the bed with him, his lips falling on mine while his hands ran up my shirt, awakening secrets on my skin that obliterated all my tangled thoughts.

Peter removed my clothes like a slow unveiling before discarding his own upon the floor. He lay beside me, his hands still holding the faint chill of outside as he traced a silent language against the curves of my body, extracting tendrils of longing that made me ache inside.

"God, you *do* something to me."

"Really?" I reached up to run my fingers through his tousled hair, which had fallen into his eyes. "What is it that I do to you?"

He moved to cup my face, his eyes dancing with emotion as he drew me closer to him. His deep, labored breath was like an erotic charge against my skin as his lips traveled sensually down my neck. "Everything about you inebriates me. The way you smell... the way your skin feels, the sound of your voice in my ear." Peter groaned as his hands ran up my thighs, his touch sending spirals of arousal coursing through me. "Do you remember that night we were dancing?"

"Of course." My words came out halted as his fingers teased my inner thighs.

"And you leaned close to me and whispered something against my neck."

He lightly ran his finger along my sex, causing me to buck against him as a sharp blush of pleasure rushed through me. "*Yes.*"

"And then I pulled away from you." He removed his hand, and a teasing smile tugged at his lips.

"Wait a minute..." I grabbed his arm playfully. "Is that what that was?"

He grinned sheepishly. "I'm afraid so, Lara."

"I was wondering." A giggle escaped me as I rolled him onto his back and straddled him. "Well, you probably could have taken me right there on the dance floor and I don't think I would have stopped you."

"Oh *really?*" He entwined his fingers in my hair. "I'll have to keep that in mind next time we go dancing."

Peter flipped me onto my back, his face suddenly serious as he leaned above me. "I want to make you happy, Lara." His lips fell against my ear. "Let me make you happy." He trailed hot kisses down my neck while I opened myself to him and gently guided him inside me.

A moan rushed out, untamed and raw as Peter filled me with his desire, each slow thrust bringing me closer to the edge of something I had never felt before; reaching into places inside I thought had vanished so long ago. Time drifted away, becoming a silent observer as I lost myself and tumbled into the depths with him.

Darkness crept over the house as I placed tea candles in little glass jars throughout the living room. The space around us glowing with a warm light. Peter knelt by the fire, roasting a mixture of potatoes, vegetables, and chopped steak wrapped up in tinfoil. Shadows from the flames wavered across his bare skin, reminding me of something primal and wild. I crouched down behind him, running my hands along his back.

"You look so sexy right now, you know that?"

He chuckled. "Oh, that's right. I forgot you have a thing for men cooking you dinner."

"No..." I said, placing a lingering kiss on his neck, "I have a thing for *you* cooking me dinner."

"Is that so?" He turned around and grabbed me, playfully nibbling at my ear. "I'm just going to have to keep doing that then, aren't I?" His teeth against my skin was a delicious tease arousing my senses. "Unfortunately, until the power comes back on, you're gunna have to make do with my slapped-together concoction over here." Peter winked as he released me and went to pull the food off the grate with a pair of tongs. "A little something I like to call cowboy dinner."

I watched as he carefully placed the wrapped food on the bricks beside the coals. "How are you able to handle the fire like that? I mean, aren't you afraid you're going to hurt yourself, or burn the house down?"

Peter laughed as he replaced the screen against the hearth, securing it in place. "Well, I haven't burned the house down yet," he said with a playful smile. "You worried about me?"

"A little, yes."

He found my shoulders, drawing me close against him and placing a kiss on my forehead. "Well, don't be. I know what I'm doing. I've been tending fires since I was a kid. It's second nature to me, and a lot like a wild animal. If you learn to respect it and give it space, you can live symbiotically together."

We settled ourselves on the fold-out bed beside the fire, eating our food from the tinfoil, aromatic steam rising into our faces. We were cocooned in a world all our own, with nothing but the warmth of the flames and the stillness of the snow outside.

Relaxed and drowsy, I leaned against Peter with a sigh. "A

part of me really doesn't want the power to come back on. I like this. It's so cozy and reminds me of camping."

He stretched out onto the sheets beside me and drew me close. I nestled my back against him as he lazily ran his hand through my hair, twirling the strands in between his fingers. "I have to admit. This is definitely the best power outage I've ever had."

A slow smile spread across my lips. "Me too."

My whole body felt languid, but so alive as Peter's arms encircled me. My eyes shifted over to his paintings hanging on the wall. The wild soul of Montana splashed upon the canvases in vivid oil paint. I tried to envision him painting these, suspended in concentration, eyes full of all the beauty and light he saw. I rolled over to face him, running my hand along his brow, my voice coming out in a hesitant whisper. "Tell me what happened? How did you lose your sight?"

Chapter Twenty-Two

Peter's calm, steady breath stilled for a moment as his face flickered with a vague reluctance.

Rising onto my elbows, I gazed into his eyes. I wanted to sift through all the layers of him. The ones that reached out to me, and the ones that were woven so tight, like a thick tapestry of secrets that only he had access to.

"I want to know your story."

"My story, huh?" Peter took a deep breath, running his fingers through his hair as he got up and moved over to the fireplace. His hands ran across the brick until he located the poker and began to sift through the embers, awakening the flames, which began to leap and curl around the wood.

"There used to be this spot that I would go rock climbing in the summer. Kootenai Canyon it was called, up in the Bitterroot Mountains." He placed another log on the fire, his eyes wistful. "It was always one of my favorite places. It was so beautiful, with these steep canyons and a crystal-clear river that ran through it. Best of all, it was quiet. I hardly ever saw anyone else up there."

He returned to the bed, smelling of woodsmoke as he nestled beside me, his hands delicately resting on the curve of my waist.

"One of my construction buddies from work was supposed to go climbing with me. We were going to do some belaying, which is a way of climbing that ensures tension in the rope between two climbers and avoids a long drop if there is a fall.

But he wasn't feeling well. So, I decided to go alone." He paused; his face awash with sentiment as his eyes flickered to the ceiling. "I can still remember the way the sky looked that day as I was driving up into the mountains, bleached and dry. The heat in the air shimmering like water, and all the colors that surrounded me, blue against greens and greys."

Peter's descriptions tugged at my heart as I listened to him paying homage to those last delicate images he had captured in his mind; details we so often took for granted.

"I'd been climbing for years. I knew what I was doing. But I think I'd gotten a little sloppy in my confidence. I must not have secured my anchor tight enough, or maybe a rock got dislodged. I'm not really sure what happened. All I remember is that I was about forty-five feet up when I felt the line go slack, and the next thing I knew, I was falling."

"*Oh, God.*" I flinched from the image and pulled him closer to me, feeling the tension in his body ripple as he lay there, summoning up his story from the depths of his memory.

"Honestly, I think I might have died out there if some hikers hadn't found me. Unconscious and bleeding. Both my legs busted." His tone dropped to a low whisper as he continued, his eyes shifting to the color of shadows as his gaze danced around the room, searching for a solid form that was not there. "I was in a coma for three months after that. The doctors didn't know if I was going to pull through or not, but when I finally woke up, the whole world was dark." Peter paused, his silence falling like a somber sigh between us. "Traumatic optic neuropathy, they called it."

I rested my head on his chest, feeling the steady rise and fall of his breath, the song of his beating heart like a metronome. How truly fragile everything was. The simplest gifts we are granted in this life can be taken away in an instant.

"So, it was a miracle, in a way? That you even survived."

"It was, but it took me a while to see it that way. I spent the first few years being so angry with everything. All the months of optimistic doctors poking and prodding me, surgeries that failed to restore my sight. Sometimes, having hope and then losing it, can be worse than having none at all." Peter sighed; his jaw clenched. "You don't know how many times I used to replay that damn day in my head, Lara. What I would have done differently. What would have happened if my climbing buddy had been there with me? Or if I'd just not gone at all? If you let it, the mind will gladly torment you forever with all the what-ifs."

"I know," I said softly as I ran my hand down his arm, recalling my own anguished moments of inner questioning. All the weeks I had spent lying in bed, unable to move or sleep. Staring up at the ceiling and asking myself the same things over and over again. *What if I had not gone to the store that day?* And then the biggest one, which haunts me still, pressing against my heart with a sickening weight. *Why didn't I just bring him with me?* And though I had always blamed John for what happened, there was a deeper part of me that blamed myself, and that belief had become too heavy to carry any longer. I knew I had to find a way to let it all go; blame was never going to bring Caleb back.

Peter took my hand, threading his fingers through mine. "Life is just a series of accidents, Lara. Some will break you, and others will make you stronger."

"And which one was it for you?" I asked as he turned his face toward mine, the trembling light in the room reflected in his eyes. Despite his inability to see, the lucidity of them never failed to transfix me.

He sighed. "I think it's a little bit of both for me. I miss being able to watch a sunset. I miss the way the light looks when it hits the aspen trees in the fall. I miss the freedom that sight gives you, and most of all, I miss painting." He pressed his lips against my forehead, his hand trailing up my arm. "But at the same time, I'm able to appreciate the little things so much more now. It's like all my other senses have been heightened, and there's this sharp clarity that I never had before."

"Really?" I ran my fingers across his palm, tracing circles over the places where years of work had worn them into calloused ridges. "Like how?"

He gently rolled me over onto my back, his eyes burning with a sudden desire as his hand stroked the length of my neck. "Like the way your skin feels against mine." He placed his mouth above my collarbone, sending a swell of desire rippling through my core. "The delicious way you smell."

I closed my eyes as the warmth of him washed over me like a strong drink. "And what is it that I smell like?"

"Like sunshine and honey." He nuzzled into my neck, breathing me in as he began to deftly unbutton the shirt I had borrowed from him, a worn flannel that fell almost to my knees and smelled of his soap.

His hands ran across my breasts, his touch tantalizing and slow as I twined my fingers into his hair, feeling myself slip into that ethereal place of pleasure that he so effortlessly drew out of me.

"I wish you could see me," I whispered.

Peter rose to cup my face in his hand, his thumb sweeping across my cheek. "Oh, Lara. I see you." His lips took mine in a tender kiss that filled me with a buoyant lightness.

"I see you." His words danced against my skin like an incantation as his mouth slid down to the rise of my breasts. "*I see you.*"

My eyes filled with the rush of unexpected tears as he trailed kisses down my stomach and slipped my underwear down, his lips brushing lightly against my sex. A tangled cry spilled out, and I gripped the sheets as his mouth consumed me. All my layers dissolved beneath him as my body trembled and quickly released, my vision shattering against my eyelids.

I pulled him to me, breathless, tasting myself on his lips. Overcome by the emotion he evoked within me, my heart stretched and rose, reaching out to him as if longing for flight.

The crackle of music from the record player woke me as I untangled myself from dreams, Robert Plant's smooth, sorrowful voice spilling across the room. Peter's arm was draped across my chest, his face soft with sleep as the early morning sun peeked through the window, showering our skin with fractured light. I ran my hand through his tousled hair as the click of the baseboard heat turned on.

"Led Zeppelin, huh?"

Peter's eyes opened, and a slow smile crept over his face. "I guess the power's back on."

With a sigh, I draped the blanket over our heads, enclosing us in a cocoon of mutual darkness. "Can we just stay like this forever?"

Peter's fingers traced over the curve of my cheek. "God, how I wish we could." His hands encircled my waist and pressed me closer to him. "You know, I could really get used to waking up next to you every morning."

Hope rose inside me, full of a boldness I dared myself to reach for. "Me too."

With a groan, he pressed his lips against my neck. "Are you ready for a real meal?"

"Hmm..." My fingers lazily traveled down his back. "What kind of meal would that be?"

With a chuckle, he pulled the blankets back and sat up. "Well, I know how excited you get when I cook, but if you can *control* yourself, I was going to make us breakfast."

With a laugh, I chucked the pillow at him. "I'll try."

"Hey now." Peter leaned down next to me with a playful smirk. "Don't be throwing pillows at a blind man. That's an unfair advantage."

"My deepest apologies," I breathed, as his lips brushed against mine. "I'll never do it again."

"You better not." With a grin, he reached down to grab his pants off the floor and slipped them on before heading into the kitchen.

Rolling over, I breathed in the scent of him which lingered on the sheets, my heart fluttering as a large smile bloomed within. This feeling was so foreign but filled with a possibility that made me giddy.

Was this happiness?

The smell of coffee drifted through the air as I folded the bed away, placing the cushions neatly back onto the couch. The room suddenly felt large and empty without the tiny island of sheets and blankets, the memories of the last two nights now tucked away like a secret within the fabric of the couch.

I walked over to Peter's record player and flipped absentmindedly through his collection. "Oh, you have Van Morrison," I exclaimed.

Peter poked his head through the doorway of the kitchen, spatula in hand. "Yep, pretty sure I have all his albums in there."

I slid out the album Moondance, my hands trailing over the cover as recollections of my mother swept over me. I hovered the stylus over the vinyl, searching for a specific song, before letting the needle drop down. I stood and walked over to the window as "Into the Mystic" drifted through the speakers, reminding me of summer nights as a child with my parents slow dancing in the living room. Their love had always been the standard I held up to all the relationships in my life. A love that had remained ethereal. And now they were together again, dancing somewhere between my memories.

I gazed out onto the pasture, still covered in thick snow. The trees had shaken themselves loose and now stood like stark etchings against the flecked blue of the sky.

"Breakfast is ready," Peter called out from the kitchen.

"Okay, I'll be there in a minute." I turned my head back toward the window, wanting to stay in the moment a little longer, suspended in the peaceful pause that captured the space within the silence of my mind.

Peter walked into the room. "Whatcha doing?"

I came up to him and took his hand, drawing him close to me. "I'm just looking at the snow."

He encircled his arms around my waist, pressing his lips against my neck. "I take it back, you know."

"Take what back?"

A warm smile spread across his face as he cupped his hand against my cheek, slowly running his thumb along my lips. "I love the snow."

"You do?"

"Yes. It brought you to me."

Chapter Twenty-Three

"Where have you been?"

Sasha's concerned voice rang in my ear, causing me to flinch.

"I'm sorry. I've been meaning to call you back. But things have been a little... crazy lately."

I sat on the couch in the cottage, looking out the window as sunlight streamed in. All that was left of the snow were thin trailing patches of white concealed in shade.

"Yeah, sounds like it." Sasha grew quiet for a moment. "I'm *so* sorry about your mom. You never returned any of my calls after you got back from California, and I've been really worried about you."

I leaned back onto the cushions of the couch and began to spill the contents of the last week to her. A whirlwind of emotions that left me hanging between exhaustion and elation as I tried to compartmentalize the loss of my mother, the blowup with John, and the delicately beautiful connection that had bloomed between Peter and me.

"Wow. So, let me get this straight," Sasha said. "You guys had two nights of mind-blowing sex, and now you're living together?"

"Not exactly. I mean all my stuff is still in the cottage, I just haven't been sleeping here lately."

The night the power had come back on, after the plates had been cleared away from dinner, Peter had silently taken my hand and led me into his bedroom, revealing a room of white walls, down comforters, and large windows that stretched out to an expansive vista of snow-covered mountains. We didn't need words. We didn't need to navigate arrangements and agreements between us. Our bodies just softly articulated what was not spoken aloud; a language of emotion and pleasure that moved through every part of me.

"I don't know what *this* is, Sasha." I sat up, running my fingers through my hair. My face grew warm, and my heart fluttered as I tried to grapple with the scope and intensity of my feelings. "Peter brings me to this place that I honestly have never been before. It's like he's waking up these parts within me that I never knew were there."

"That good, huh? Damn, Lara." Sasha chuckled.

"But it's not just the chemistry between us, there's something deeper there." I glanced out the window, trying to hold back the swell of emotions rising within me. "The other night, he told me that he could *see me*, and I can't explain the way that made me feel. It's like when Peter makes love to me, it's not just my body, it's *me* he's making love to, and I realize that I've never really experienced that with anyone before... even with John."

Sasha let out a deep sigh on the other end. "Well, it sounds like you just found something really special."

"I know." I let out a shaky breath. "And it scares the hell out of me."

"Why is that?"

"I don't know," I said, picking at the lint that nestled between the couch cushions. "I just can't seem to shake the feeling that this won't last. I mean, how can something that feels *this* good be real?"

"Do you want it to be real?"

"Yes." My voice came out in a whisper as I stood perched over the precipice of my feelings, like a nervous fledgling, afraid to fly.

"Then make it real, Lara."

I stood in Peter's kitchen. The comforting aroma of bread warming in the oven, mixed with the enticing concoction of spices, wafted through the room as I ladled soup into our bowls.

"You've got to be fucking kidding me, Miriam!" Peter's voice rose from the other room. "No. Absolutely not."

I placed the food on the table while Dusty's eyes followed my movements, hoping for a handout. My hand reached out to ruffle the top of his head as I walked past him and into the living room. Peter paced beside the window, the phone pressed to his ear, his face rigid. "I know, Miriam. I just don't feel like talking about this right now. Give me some time to think about it."

"Are you okay?" I took a step toward him as he hung up the phone and shoved it into his pocket. Wrapping my arms around his waist, I felt the tension in his body relax.

He leaned against me with a sigh. "I am now." His hands lost themselves in my hair, running his fingers through the strands and placing a kiss on my forehead. "Let's go eat. Whatever you're cooking in there smells amazing."

Taking Peter's hand, I led him into the kitchen. Dusk had settled through the windows, obscuring the view of the mountains in shadow. We sat beside each other at the table, my feet curled against his, the warmth of him radiating against me as we began to eat.

"Miriam wants me to provide a character reference for Greg at his trial," Peter said, breaking the relaxed quiet between us.

I glanced at him, moving to brush back a strand of hair that had fallen into his eyes. He flinched for a moment before shooting me a small smile.

"Really? I didn't know they did things like that for armed robbery cases?"

"They do if the attorney thinks it will help the case. They're trying to take the angle of culpability defense." Peter's brow furrowed as he broke off a piece of bread and dipped it into his soup. "Which pretty much means that he's guilty but suffers from a lack of mental competency, due to substance abuse. If he had an agreement in place to enter a rehab facility when released, they think it'll shorten his sentence if not close the case completely."

"Are you going to do it?"

"I don't know yet." Peter leaned back in his chair, his eyes shifting across the room. "I know I'm supposed to feel some empathy for him, to *want* to help him. He's my blood, my *brother*, and no, I don't want him sitting in jail for years. But what does family really even mean when so much of what's left is broken?" He leaned forward and took my hand, his fingers grazing my skin. "Did you have a happy childhood?"

I paused for a moment as memories of my family filtered through. Realizing that though both of my parents had been taken away too soon, they had given me so much. "I did. I was blessed with two wonderful parents who loved each other. My older brother has always been incredibly supportive and looked out for me when I was a kid. My childhood was full of magical tall trees and endless ocean." I gazed out the window, into the growing darkness of nightfall. "But all of that couldn't keep me safe from pain. It didn't shelter me from the trauma that came later."

Squeezing Peter's hand, I continued. "I think in a way, having all that goodness growing up made it harder to come to terms with loss. I was unaccustomed to feeling so broken inside, and I didn't know what to do when all the grief came for me."

"Does anyone really know what to do with pain, Lara?" Peter trailed off for a moment, a sadness flickering across his face. "Greg. My father... we've had nothing but a toxic relationship for so long. I feel like at some point, you just have to cut the cords that hold you down."

"I know that feeling," I said, pushing my bowl of soup away and resting my arms against the table. "The night I left John; I had a dream where I was being buried alive. I can still vividly remember the sensation of not being able to breathe. I woke up around three in the morning, sweaty and panicked, and I knew I had to leave. I couldn't be in that marriage anymore; it was slowly killing me. It was killing us both. So, I threw some clothes into a bag, and I just started driving, with no idea where I was going."

Peter's face softened, his eyes filled with sympathy as he scooted his chair away from the table and reached for me, drawing me onto his lap. His arms encircled my waist while his lips rested on my neck, his beard leaving a tantalizing tickle across my skin. "Is that how you ended up here in Montana?"

"Yes." I leaned into him, realizing just how seemingly random but consequential life was. Had I not turned off the highway that day and stopped to stand out in that field to call John, I would have never met Peter.

"I guess that makes me incredibly lucky then."

I smiled, turning to brush my lips against his in a kiss that spoke of all the things my heart was afraid to say out loud.

He groaned against me, gripping my hips. "*Jesus*, Lara. When you kiss me like that, I can't think straight." He bent down and playfully nipped at my neck, causing a flush of arousal to wash over me. "And I really need to go put the horses in for the night."

"Okay," I said, as I ran my hand down his chest. "I'll start cleaning up the kitchen." I glanced over at the array of dirty dishes strewn about on the counter and grimaced. "I kinda made a mess of it."

My hands were submerged in soapy water when Peter came back into the house, trailing a blast of brisk air in his wake. He came up to me from behind, slipping his cold hands underneath my shirt, causing me to shriek.

"Jesus, Peter!" I gasped. "Your hands are freezing."

"*Really?*" The coolness of his touch against my skin sent me into a spiral of conflicting sensation that left me lightheaded.

"I have to admit, I really like the fact that you never wear a bra." His voice was raspy as he trailed his fingers across my nipples. "Those things were hard enough to deal with even when I *could* see."

A soft chuckle escaped me. "Well, I don't have much to fill a cup, so I never saw the point."

Peter encircled his hands around my breasts. "You fill my hands perfectly."

"I'm really trying to finish up the dishes here," I breathlessly whispered as I pressed against him, my head falling to his shoulder.

"Oh, I'm sorry." His voice a teasing murmur as his lips ran leisurely up my neck and hovered against my ear. "I'm afraid I just can't help myself... you're *so* warm, Lara." His hand slid down, inching underneath my pants and tracing along my thighs. I moaned, my legs growing weak as he lightly brushed his fingers over my sex. Dropping the sponge, I reached my hand up to curl my fingers into the thickness of his hair as he began to stroke me in achingly slow circles, his breath a teasing caress across my skin.

Peter's arousal surged against me, his hands suddenly

hungry and urgent as he spun me around and slipped my pants down, lifting me up onto the counter. I grasped at him, fumbling for the buttons of his jeans until I felt the heat of him in my hand, and then the blinding rush of him inside as he filled me completely.

Cradling me against him, Peter kissed me with a fervor that stripped away the layers, taking me to a place where nothing else existed except the feel of his body against mine, and an elation so large; it exposed the delicate, trembling pulse of my heart.

That evening, I lay drowsy in Peter's arms, my body and mind fluid. He ran his fingers through my hair, his voice a tender lullaby which fell against my skin. "I can't remember the last time I've slept as good as I do with you."

I smiled playfully as his lips rested against my cheek. "So, that means you're not going to kick me out then?"

He chuckled, pulling me tighter against him. "*Never.*"

With a sigh, my eyes fluttered closed; Peter's arms around me like a refuge as I blissfully sunk into the calm, beckoning depths of dreams.

I stood barefoot in an open field. Sunlight flickered upon my skin. A stampede of wild horses in the distance barreled toward me, their astonishing speed making my pulse race. Hooves pounded against the ground like a heartbeat beneath my feet.

Suddenly, Peter materialized in front of me. His hand outstretched, eyes clear and focused as they locked onto mine with an intensity.

"Lara, it's okay. Don't be scared. They're not going to hurt you."

He took my hand and pulled me into his arms as the horses flew by us like a warm wind, their manes licking against my skin. Full of wildness, fire, and a freedom that stilled my breath.

The resolute grip of winter had finally won over. The pasture now a frozen land of ice that sparkled in the weak sunlight as it filtered through the opaque sky. Our breath hung in the air like smoke as Peter and I stood in the barn together. I slid the brush through Penny's coat as he tended to her hooves beside me, running his hand along the bottom of them, checking for cracks. Spirit and Ginger grazed off in the distance, two dark figures against a canvas of swirling white mist.

"It looks like another storm is on the way tonight." He sidled up close to me with a roguish wink.

"Really?" I reached over to trail my finger flirtatiously down his arm. "Should we pull out the couch bed by the fire again?"

Peter chuckled and grabbed me by the waist, pressing his lips against my ear in a soft growl. "I think we've gotten pretty good at creating our own heat, don't you think?"

Suddenly, a garbled shriek sliced through the air, causing my heart to still.

Chapter Twenty-Four

"What was that, Peter?"

His face grew dark as he released me with a sudden jerk. Dusty began to whine beside us, and Peter threw his hand out in a motion to stay as he exited the barn. I followed him through the pasture, the icy grass crunching beneath my feet as another shrill cry rang out, intermixed with the disjointed neigh of a horse. My eyes scanned the field beyond the fence line, until I saw the faint, dark shape of Spirit on the ground beyond the aspen grove.

"Peter!" I shouted, my heart hammering as I jogged to catch up with him. I grabbed his hand and pulled him toward the tree line. "It's Spirit. He's way over there past the aspen trees. I think he's caught on something."

"God-damn Macready." Peter's jaw tensed, his face flashing with anger as he made a beeline for the grove.

"Who's Macready?" I asked breathlessly, stumbling to keep up with him.

"Lazy, ignorant son of a bitch cattle rancher who borders this property." His words came out like daggers. "I've been telling him for years to get rid of his goddamn barbed wire fencing. He must have left some over by the tree line."

As we approached, I could see Spirit thrashing around on the ground, panting and frothing at the mouth. His eyes were wild with terror as he lay there tangled and bound up in an old broken-down fence that lay half hidden among the bushes. Peter approached him slowly, speaking in soft, soothing tones as he knelt next to him and placed his hands on his side. Peter felt around and grasped at the wire that twisted around Spirit's legs and torso. A large gash had torn open his chest and blood gushed from it like a steady river, soaking the ground beneath us.

"God damn it!" Peter cried out in anguished frustration as he attempted to free Spirit from the wire, but the horse writhed so violently in panic that it only drove the barbs in deeper. His hands were covered in blood, and I could not tell if it was his or Spirit's as he frantically tried to untangle him.

"Lara." His voice came out strained. "How bad is it?"

I crept closer, my legs trembling as I removed my hands, which had been clamped tightly over my mouth. "I don't know. It looks like he's bleeding really bad from his chest."

Peter felt down the length of Spirit's chest until he found the wound and then stood up abruptly. "Damn it! He's hit an artery." His face was rigid with an emotion I could not decipher. "Stay here, Lara. I'll be right back."

I flinched as Peter tripped over a log and then righted himself before making his way through the pasture and back toward the barn. I crouched down beside Spirit, running my hand along his head which had now flopped to the ground in silent defeat; his eyes clouded over with fear and pain.

Seeing him like this made my gut wrench into a sickening knot. I felt so powerless, and the sharp sting of grief sliced through me. "It's okay, buddy. We're going to get you out of here." My voice wavered as I sat beside Spirit, trying as best I could to comfort him.

I heard the snap of twigs and turned around to see Peter walking back, a shotgun in his hand. I scrambled to my feet, my heart racing. "Peter, wait. What are you doing?" My voice came out choked, panic lacing my words as I grabbed his arm. "Isn't there something we can do to help him? Someone we can call?"

He only shook his head, his eyes full of sorrow. "No, he's

bleeding out. By the time someone gets here, it'll be too late. I'm *not* going to let him suffer like this." He bent down next to Spirit, placing his hand on the horse's side, which rose and fell rapidly from his labored breath.

"You need to go now."

"Peter?" I tentatively touched his arm.

"Go!" His voice came out gruff and strangled. "You don't want to see this."

My eyes wavered with tears, and I took a step back, watching as Peter stooped his head down next to Spirit's and spoke something into his ear while he gently stroked him. Turning around, I stumbled through the maze of trees, their bare branches like hands clawing at an empty sky.

When I reached the pasture, I cringed as a loud crack exploded across the hills, leaving a reverberating echo behind. A flock of crows lifted from the aspen trees, their raucous cries like a mournful reply.

I don't know how long I stood there staring into the aspen grove, shaking in silent shock. Snow began to lightly slip down from the sky above, like tiny angels kissing my hair. Finally, I saw Peter materialize through the trees; the gun clenched tightly in his fist, his eyes dark and full of such deep sadness that it tore into me.

"*Peter.*"

I reached out to him as he drew closer, wanting to somehow soothe away his pain, but he recoiled from my touch, shrugging me off. "Please don't. I need to be alone right now." His words struck at me, abrupt and rigid as he brushed past and made his way to the barn.

His dismissal broke the dam inside, and my eyes welled up as I stifled a sob that threatened to tumble out.

I staggered my way into the cottage, tears blinding me as I ripped off my clothes, stained with splotches of Spirit's blood, and balled them up in a corner of the bedroom closet. The bathroom tile was like ice beneath my feet as I stepped into the hot spray of the shower, watching the rivulets of water as they swirled beneath me and vanished down the drain.

The sky had grown dark as I paced around the cottage, unsettled, and filled with a heaviness I could not chase away. I glanced out the window as snow swallowed up the landscape in white. Spirit's wild, fearful eyes and Peter's turmoil haunted me; the vivid images projected relentlessly upon the screen of my mind. The longing to go to him was a sharp ache that pressed against the marrow of myself, but I knew I had to give him the space he asked for.

Curling up in bed, I yanked the covers tightly around me, the sheets cold and lifeless against my skin. The empty, suffocating silence choked the room as my emotions tumbled along a broken shore, helpless against the rush of the tide.

The sudden steady thump of shovel against earth drifted from beyond the aspen grove with an ominous resonance, like the deep and solemn footfalls of death's finality.

I squeezed my eyes shut and burrowed deeper beneath the covers, trying desperately to drown out the sound which carried me back to the day of Caleb's funeral.

The sky had been like slate above me while I watched his unbearably small coffin being lowered into the ground. The sickening sound of shoveling, like a knife, brutal and sharp against my flesh as the wind blew mercilessly around us. I had never wanted him in a box. That had been John's idea. I had wanted him wild and free, like filtered sunlight, birdsong, and trees that whispered ancient secrets. And that is where I would visit him, slipping deep into the woods to release my grief upon the forest floor.

Tears stained the sheets like a silent companion beside me,

until eventually my mind released its hold, and I fell into heavy, fragmented dreams.

Sunlight tapped against my eyelids, and I sat up to find a world encased in a blinding brightness. The storm had been tepid and brief, blowing through quietly during the night, leaving just a thin layer of white upon the ground and the sky an optimistic shade of blue.

I dressed and forced myself to make some toast, though my stomach was knotted and sour. Stepping outside, I buttoned my coat, my eyes falling upon Peter's wind-blown tracks in the snow. They spread out across the pasture, from the aspen trees to the house, stopping outside the cottage and then doubling back, as if he had stood beside my door for a moment, debating with himself.

My footsteps followed his trail, weaving through the trees until I came to the spot where Spirit lay. Blood had seeped through the snow, staining it a bright pink. A tarp now covered Spirit's body, and next to him was a grave partially dug. I ran my fingers through the frozen earth, tears pricking my eyes as I envisioned Peter toiling for hours; driven by something extreme that compelled him forward, almost as if he were carrying out some penance against his own sorrow.

Turning back toward the cottage, my eyes fell to the bloodstains, hardened like syrup against the thin blanket of snow. I bent down, scooping up handfuls of dirt and leaves and spreading them across the ground in a futile attempt to erase the evidence of yesterday.

The day ticked by in silence as I sat in the cottage, suspended in a state of restlessness and indecision, glancing out the window in the hopes of seeing a sign of Peter in the pasture. A gust of wind would occasionally knock a branch against the window and my heart would stir, thinking it was his footsteps by the door.

As darkness approached, resolution beckoned me forward, and I gathered myself and grabbed my coat. The urge to go to him burned in me, like embers of flame licking at my skin. I missed his touch, the comforting feel of him beside me, his steady breath. Being without him felt abrupt and disjointed.

I knew I could no longer wait for him to come to me. To sit and wonder if he would even come at all. Whatever barrier he had thrown up around himself, he wasn't going to let down on his own. And I wanted to be there with him, to somehow help ease the burden of pain he was carrying alone.

My breath curled into the air as I stepped out into the ink of the night and treaded across the frozen pasture to Peter, hoping that his door would be open to me.

Chapter Twenty-Five

The house was dark when I entered. I called out Peter's name into the silence of the kitchen as I fumbled around for the light switch. The clicking of Dusty's nails on the floor greeted me as he nuzzled his nose against the palm of my hand.

"Peter, are you here?"

"I'm in the living room." His voice sounded strained and far away.

I made out the shape of Peter on the couch and walked over to him, crouching down to touch his knee. He leaned forward and slid his hands up my arms, his fingers ghosting over my skin as he tangled them into my hair and gripped lightly, pulled me close to him. My heart fluttered with relief as he rested his forehead against mine, his breath drifting across my cheeks.

"Are you okay?" I ran my hands down the length of his back, feeling his muscles contract. "I didn't know if you still wanted to be alone or not."

"No." He shook his head, his voice barley audible. "I'm glad you're here." He placed a soft, lingering kiss on the top of my head before releasing me and sitting back.

I reached over and switched on the lamp beside the couch, letting out a low gasp. "*Jesus*, Peter. Your hands." I took them carefully in mine; red angry gashes from the barbed wire fence ran along the inside of both his palms, his fingers blistered and raw.

"I'm fine." He jerked his hands away, his expression distant.

"No, you're not. Those cuts already look infected."

Standing, I went into the bathroom to look for bandages and disinfectant. When I returned, I sat beside him on the couch, taking his hands and placing them on my lap. Peter flinched, sucking in a sharp breath as I poured the peroxide over his wounds and gently wrapped the gauze over his hands, securing them with tape. My fingers hovered over his blisters. "Were these from shoveling last night?"

Peter nodded, his face pinched.

"How long were you out there digging?"

He shrugged. "I don't know, six, seven hours, I think. Not a damn bit of good it did though."

With a sigh, I ran my fingers through his tangled hair. "Do you want me to help you finish?"

He shook his head. "I know a guy with a backhoe. He said he can be here in the morning."

Taking his hand up to my mouth, I placed my lips softly against his fingers. His pain was like a dark cloud hovering between us, and my heart cried out, knowing I couldn't take this away, but wanting so badly to try.

"I'm so sorry about Spirit."

He remained silent, his gaze fixed on the wall behind me. I reached up and stroked his cheek. "Peter, talk to me."

He furrowed his brow. "I don't want to talk right now."

"Do you want me to go?" My question came out hesitant. I could feel his distance like a blast of cold air, and I grappled with this shift between us.

"No." He clasped his hand around mine, giving it a light squeeze. "Stay with me."

He stood from the couch and extended his hand out, leading me into the bedroom. The moon had risen, and the round orb washed our bodies in blue light.

I undressed him in silence, his clothes falling to the floor and joining mine. I drew him close to me, running my hands down his back. Peter's breath accelerated, and he gripped me tightly against him, burying his face into my neck.

"*Lara.*"

He spoke my name like a strangled plea against my skin, and I walked us toward the bed, drawing him down upon the sheets. Despite the sorrow that hung thick in the air, my body cried out for his touch. I needed to obliterate this sudden expanse of space between us. It was a weight against my chest, sucking the oxygen out of my lungs.

I positioned myself on top of him, trailing kisses that lingered down his neck. Peter groaned low in the back of his throat, his body responding to mine. The pulse of his arousal stirred against me as he let out a shaky breath and then gripped my hips, gently rolling me off him.

"Peter?" Confusion swam around in murky puddles as I lay there, feeling his rebuff like the sharp sting of a slap.

He leaned over me and ran his fingers through my hair, cupping my cheek in his hand. "I just want to hold you, okay?"

"Of course." My voice shook as he pulled me into his arms. The warmth of his breath was a whisper on my neck as I nestled my back against his chest, allowing the soft silence of words unspoken to percolate around us.

The moon trailed across the sky as I lay enfolded in Peter's embrace. The slow, rhythmic breathing as he slept rose and fell in my ear. I delicately curled my fingers around his and placed them over my heart, pressing myself tighter against him.

How I longed to merge into his skin, to slip into his mind and cradle the depths of his thoughts. He could hold me forever like this. But it wasn't enough. I wanted all of him. I wanted his pain, and the dark places that lay in the shadows. I wanted the complexity of his emotions, the vibrant fire that smoldered behind the veil of his eyes.

Tears bloomed, traveling a silent trail down my cheeks. Awash in his sorrow that lay beside us, I allowed this aching vulnerability to spill out, and the tears I shed did not feel like my own.

Late morning sun streamed into the room, the light blinding me as I opened my eyes and found the space next to me empty. I got out of bed and bent down to retrieve my clothes, pulling them on as I wandered into the kitchen. Dusty stood waiting by the door to be let out, and a cold plate of half-eaten eggs sat on the counter.

Throwing on my boots and coat, I opened the back door and headed over to the barn, with Dusty following behind. A light wind blew against me, deceivingly warm as I made my way across the pasture. Shattered sunlight pierced through the rafters of the barn as I stepped inside, calling out Peter's name. Only silence answered back as I glanced around, finding Penny's stall empty, and Ginger pawing impatiently within hers.

I unlatched the door to her stall, stepping back to give her space as she tentatively crept past me and then bolted out of the barn, her tail flicking. I stood in the open doorway, scanning the pasture for any sign of Peter. *Where was he?* It was so unusual of him to take Penny beyond the field, and I tried to push away the growing sense of unease that settled and took root within my gut.

The moan of an engine in the distance grew closer, startling the quiet, and I walked out of the barn to see a man on a backhoe driving through the pasture from the direction of the aspen grove. He slowed down when he saw me, tipping his hat in my direction. The engine shuttered and fell silent.

"Morning, miss."

I looked up at the man, his weathered face cast in the shadow of his wide-brimmed hat.

"Hey there." I tried to stifle the concern in my voice with a small smile.

He leaned across the steering wheel and extended his hand; it was surprisingly warm against the chill of the morning. "My name's Rick. And you must be?"

"Lara."

He nodded with a small smile. "Nice to meet ya."

I gestured across the pasture. "Have you seen Peter?"

"Not since early this morning when he took off on Penny." He glanced toward the mountains with a puzzled look on his face. "Figured he'd be back by now."

I wrapped my arms around myself, feeling the cold pressing against my bones.

"Well, I'm all finished up over there." Rick cocked his thumb in the direction of where I knew Spirit now lay buried deep within the earth. "Will ya let Peter know when you see him?"

"I will." I glanced over at the fence line. "Let me get the gate for you." Heading over to the fence, I unlatched the rusty iron lock and swung open the large entryway for him to drive through.

Rick started up the engine once more, and with a wave made his way through the field and across the driveway. I watched him until he faded into a wavering blur down the dirt road.

I spent the rest of the morning in the barn, laying out fresh hay and feed for the horses, and refilling the water troughs. The day slowly went by in a state of restless worry as I retreated to the house, puttering around with Dusty at my heels. Every so often I would glance out the window, my eyes scanning the pasture, hoping to see the outline of Peter and Penny in the distance.

The shadows grew long, stretching across the field as the last of the sun's rays dwindled over the snowy peaks of the mountains. Dark, ominous clouds gathered over the horizon as I stood beside Ginger with a piece of apple held out in my hand, attempting to coax her back into the barn with slow steps and gentle clicks of my tongue.

"It's okay, girl," I softly cooed. "Let's get you inside." She cautiously trailed behind me, her hesitant gaze bouncing from me to the apple as I managed to lead her back into her stall.

Closing the door behind me, I leaned against the gate and held my hand out to her, feeling the soft velvet of her nose brush against my fingers. "I know, you're wondering where your mom is." I sighed and looked out at the darkening sky from beyond the door of the barn. "I am, too." The unease that had followed me around all day had shifted to a persistent, gnawing worry as the hours had crawled by and Peter still had not returned.

It started to rain as I headed back to the house with Dusty. Stepping inside, the loud, incessant thrum on the roof surrounded me as I paced the length of Peter's living room. *What if something happened to him?* I grabbed my phone from off the coffee table, clutching it nervously in my hand as I debated whether I should call Miriam. I didn't know what else to do as the nauseating grip of anxiety curled around me like a vise.

The sudden sound of Dusty scratching and whining at the back door drew my attention toward the kitchen as the door burst open and Peter walked in.

My heart leapt, and relief flooded me as I rushed over to him and wrapped my arms around him. His coat was soaking wet, and rivulets of water ran off the brim of his cowboy hat and onto the back of my neck.

"Where have you been?"

"I was just out riding." Peter's tone was tense and clipped.

"I was really worried."

He reached out and slid his hand down my arm, giving it a light squeeze. "I'm sorry. I didn't mean to worry you."

"Are you okay?"

"I'm fine."

Peter slipped past me and walked down the hall. Following him into the bedroom, I leaned against the door frame with my arms crossed, watching as he removed his wet shirt and sifted through the closet. "No, you're not fine Peter. Talk to me. What's going on?"

Peter sighed and sat down on the bed, his eyes distant, and a feeling of apprehension coursed through me.

"I think we need to put the brakes on all this."

Chapter Twenty-Six

My breath stilled.

I walked over to where Peter sat on the bed, wringing his shirt tightly in his hands. "What are you talking about? Where's this coming from?" My mouth was dry as I tried to swallow the growing lump in my throat. Why did it feel like he was about to rip my heart out of my chest?

Peter stood and moved away from me, pain slicing across his face as he vigorously ran his hand through his wet hair. I watched as droplets of water slid down his bare chest.

"I think you should go. I'm sorry. I just need to be alone right now."

"Please tell me what's going on?" The words felt like paper in my mouth as my heart began to beat erratically in my chest. "I know you're upset about Spirit, but don't push me away like this."

He stood there and shook his head blankly. "This isn't just about Spirit."

"What is this about, then?"

His words came out cold. "I'm no good for you, Lara."

A well of tears formed in my eyes, clouding my vision. "What do you mean?"

Peter's face contorted into an emotion I could not read, his words coming out harsh and cracked. "I mean, *I'm fucking broken!*"

I stared at him as a sudden anger rose up. "Oh, *you're* broken. Really? Is that what this is all about?" I stood and grabbed his shoulders, pulling my face close to his, wishing he could look me in the eyes, wishing that his blindness wasn't a barrier between us.

"I lost the best thing that has ever happened to me. I would gladly give up my sight, just for one minute. *One more minute* with my son again!" My voice came out strangled as tears slid down my cheeks. "Do you think this has been easy for me, letting you in like this? Being this vulnerable? Don't be such a *coward*."

Peter squeezed his eyes shut as he pulled away from me, his voice a broken whisper. "Lara, please."

"Please what? What the hell has all this been to you, then? Tell me!" I searched his face, looking for some sign of the Peter I knew, but all I could see was the impenetrable wall he had erected around himself. "Was I just someone to help pass the time? Someone to keep your bed warm?"

Peter flinched as if I had punched him in the gut. "No, Lara." He clenched his jaw as he spoke. "I care about you. I just never thought things would go this far. I got so swept away..." Peter trailed off; his voice choked as he sat back on the bed and leaned forward, placing his elbows against his knees, his bandaged hands grasping at his hair. "But you don't need someone like me weighing you down. I don't think I can give you what you want, and you deserve more than that."

I stood there, shaky and blindsided. "How do you know what I want?"

Peter didn't answer. He just sat there, clenching his hair tightly in his fists, while the things I longed to say to him were lodged in my chest. All I had was a red-hot anger that guarded me, and like a shield I wielded it.

"Fuck you, Peter." I spat out at him, spinning around, and leaving the room.

He called out my name like a defeated plea as I stormed into the kitchen. Grabbing my phone, I scrambled into my boots and coat before yanking the back door open and slamming it behind me.

I made my way down the steps, rain pummeling me as a loud crash rang out from inside the house, the furious sound of shattering glass piercing through the night air. My boots sunk into the thick mud as I ran down the pathway, away from Peter, away from all the emotions that rushed at me; loud, encompassing, and too heavy to hold.

Tears blinded me as I reached the cottage. I tore through the closet and drawers, throwing everything I owned into my suitcase. *I couldn't stay here.* Beneath all the anger was a deep pain that threatened to rip me open, leaving me exposed, and I had to get away. I couldn't sit with these feelings, so afraid that if I did, they would break me apart. And I was so tired of being fractured.

A dense curtain of rain poured down as I backed my car out of the driveway, the tires spinning frantically in the mud. I sat there for a moment with the engine idling, foot hovering over the gas pedal as I stared at Peter's house, willing him to come to me. But his door remained closed. Whatever kept him locked inside was stronger than the force of my own longing.

My headlights sliced through the watery darkness that bent and shimmered against the windshield as I drove away. My heart pulsed like a wounded bird, smashing itself against the bars of its cage while the sky wept above; the long trail of the highway once again stretching out before me, endless and indifferent.

The hours rushed by, and the familiar hum of the freeway pulled me forward as I passed mile markers and towns, driving further east into Montana toward Bozeman. My thoughts stretched out unhinged upon the asphalt, rushing by with a velocity I could not control.

Here I was once again, driving with no direction. Running from a man, from emotions that left me terrified, and I wondered, had I been running my whole life? Had I always chosen the path that was easiest? Had I only married John because he was safe? Because I knew he wouldn't challenge me? That he couldn't reach deep enough inside to break open the bare elements of who I really was?

Had it been myself I had been running from this entire time?

These thoughts consumed me as I drove, spinning in a perpetual loop I could not dispel as the car devoured mile after mile. And all the while I ached for Peter with an intensity that burned so hot and deep it physically hurt. These feelings were familiar, yet at the same time, so foreign and vast. I had no compartment to put them in. My mind compelled me to keep driving, while my heart screamed for me to turn back.

Something had broken open inside, and what spilled out was a grief that enveloped every part of me. Forced to sit beside the loss of my son, my mother, the parts of myself I had neglected for so long, and all the wasted years I lived trapped in a dying marriage. There was nothing left but my own visceral anguish purging me as I drove further and further away from the one thing that had made me feel whole again.

Somewhere outside of Laurel, my foot released its grip on the gas pedal. I took the exit toward Billings, passing through dark quiet streets swathed in puddled reflections of orange light. Guided by the soft glow of a motel up ahead, I pulled into the half empty parking lot and stared up at the vacancy light above me, hoping that a room filled with silence would wash out the pain.

The older man at the front desk eyed me with concern as I

stood before him, my eyes puffy and red, face streaked with tears.

"Just one night, Miss?"

I nodded as I silently slid my card across the counter and grabbed the key from his hand. "Just let me know if you want your check-out time extended," I heard him say as I quickly retreated out the door.

I walked down the outside corridor of the motel, following the buzz of the flickering lights above me, until I found my room number and pushed open the door. Stale air with a hint of mildew hit me as I took in the stark silence, punctuated only by the occasional drone of cars in the distance. It was cold, and that familiar smell of emptiness permeated the room as I clicked the heater on and burrowed beneath the blankets. Clinging to the thin life raft of the sheets, I waited for the relief of sleep to carry me away.

A sharp knock at the door jarred me from the depths of a fragmented sleep.

"Housekeeping."

I dragged myself from the bed, bleary-eyed and momentarily confused as to where I was. As I fumbled with the lock, the night before hit me with a sudden wave, and nausea gripped my gut. Whatever moorings I had managed to anchor my life to were suddenly gone. I was once again untethered and adrift.

I opened the door and squinted up at a chipper looking older woman with the name of the motel embroidered across her crisp white uniform shirt.

"Oh, I'm sorry. I thought this room was a check-out." She glanced down at her clipboard with furrowed brows.

"It was. Can you let the front desk know I would like a later check-out, please?"

"Why certainly. You take your time, love." She beamed at me, her voice light and cheerful, the blue of her eyes full of a happiness that crackled around the edges. She reminded me of the type who would have her kitchen full of sunlight and cookies baking in the oven.

The door closed, its hinges sighing in protest. Retreating into the bathroom, I shed my clothes onto the floor and stepped into the shower. My sleep had been restless and void of dreams, only hazy images which replayed themselves like feverish whisperings, and I allowed the forgiving warmth of the water to cascade over me, washing away the night's residue.

Wrapped in a towel with my hair still wet, I lay on the bed, savoring the momentary quiet in my mind. I knew I needed to get up, to arrange myself once more and retrieve the growth inside of me that had taken root. But for now, I floated in between it all, listening to the sound of my breath rise and fall like the tide, hoping the answers would wash upon the shore.

The sudden ring of my phone from my purse startled me, and I sat up to answer it. Miriam's name flashed across the screen and my heart lurched in my chest.

"Lara. Are you okay? I just got a call from Peter; he sounded pretty upset, but he wouldn't give me any details. He just said you left last night."

I inwardly flinched, my fingers picking away at my nails. "I'm sorry. I was going to call you."

"It's okay." Miriam's voice was low and full of concern. "Do you mind me asking what happened between you two?"

Hot tears brimmed to the surface. "I really don't know." My words came out choked as I struggled to articulate to Miriam what Peter and I had become. "Lately, we have been getting… close."

"Uh huh…" From the tone of Miriam's reply, she appeared to understand what I was implying.

I took a shaky breath. "And then last night, he just flipped a complete one-eighty on me."

There was a long pause on the other end before Miriam spoke.

"I'm so sorry, Lara." Her words were heavy with empathy. "You know, his ex-wife really did a number on him."

"His ex-wife?" My mind scrambled to process this new information. "He never told me he was married."

"Oh, yeah. He was married." Miriam's voice came out tense. "She started messing around on him right after his accident, and then left about a year later."

"*Jesus.*" I began to pull at the loose threads of the thin towel wrapped around me as Miriam spoke, the complexities of Peter beginning to connect themselves into a pattern of tightly woven strands.

"Yep, a real piece of work that one was, and it screwed him up pretty bad. As far as I know, he hasn't had any sort of relationship with a woman since then. I mean, there were women that would come over from time to time throughout the years. But they never even stayed the night."

Miriam paused as if waiting for me to say something, but all my words were locked up tight within my throat. Perhaps Peter and I were both too broken to find happiness with each other? Like two lost souls being thrashed around in a current that took us in opposite directions.

Miriam sighed. "Lara, I don't know exactly what Peter is battling with right now. But he has *always* felt things very intensely, ever since he was a kid. And when he lost his ability to paint, he also lost one of the things that kept him grounded… I'm *so* sorry he pushed you away like that."

Tears, which had begun to feel as natural to me as my heartbeat, slipped down my cheeks, the gentle outbreath of my sorrow.

"I understand you needed to leave. You know, Peter can be such a stubborn ass fool sometimes, and communication has never been his strong point. Losing Spirit like that may have just pushed him over the edge. I just wish there was something I could do."

"It's okay." My words tumbled out against the unsettled rush of my exhale. "I have a friend out in New York that I've been meaning to visit for a while now. I think this is a good time for me to take a trip out there."

"New York, *really?* Well, you do know that's my neck of the woods these days." Miriam's voice grew light, as if trying to dispel the note of gravity that clung to the line. "You definitely should give me a call when you get out here. I would love to see you. We could have a girl's night out... go cause some trouble?" I could picture Miriam winking as she said that, in the same fluid way that Peter would wink when he was being playful, and my heart collided with itself all over again.

"That sounds good. I'd like that." I tried to hide the tremble in my voice.

"Okay then, it's settled, and promise me you'll be safe out there, okay?"

"I will."

"And Lara..." Miriam's voice grew serious. "I'm really sorry this happened between you and Peter. This whole thing just breaks my heart."

Images flashed through my mind like a movie reel. The way the sunlight would hit the peaks of the mountains in the evenings, the whispering grass of the pasture. The stillness that enfolded me like a blanket, and the warmth of Peter's touch as he drew out all my yearning and gave it a name. *Love.* I had stumbled into love; beautiful, fleeting, and gone before it even had a chance to begin.

Hushed words fell from my mouth as I choked on my tears. "Me too."

I threw my bag onto the back seat of the car and pulled out of the motel parking lot. Judging by the map on my phone, I could make it to Belfield, North Dakota before nightfall. A part of me looked forward to the long hours ahead, with nothing but the continuous stretch of road between me and my tangled thoughts. Driving had become therapeutic, and I welcomed the emptiness it brought, stripping me of all the weight and leaving me bare.

Somewhere outside of Miles City, my phone rang, and my heart accelerated, clutching the hopeful possibility that it was Peter calling. I glanced down to see Sasha's name lighting up the screen.

I had a tentative plan to surprise her. To show up at her tiny, one-room apartment in Manhattan and fall into her sturdy arms, which had never failed to catch me. To lose myself in her witty banter and infectious laughter. She had always been like sunshine to me, peeking through the clouds of my rainiest day. But when I answered the phone, the whole story spilled out of me like a raging flood.

"Lara, are you driving?"

"Yes."

"Pull over, right now."

"I'm on the freeway."

"Just find a place to pull over."

I spotted a sign for a rest area half a mile up ahead and flicked my blinker on. "Okay, I'm pulling over."

My car rolled to a stop beneath an old oak tree, the steady

swoosh of the freeway engulfing me with its soothing murmur. Through my windshield, I watched the wind as it picked up and brushed over the tall grass like a gentle wave that stretched out and buffered itself against the highway.

"Okay, sweetie. So, here's the deal… as much as I would absolutely love for you to show up in New York and stay with me right now, you need to turn the car around and go back."

"Sasha, what are you talking about? I have nowhere to go back to."

"You need to go back to Peter."

"I'm not going back there. He made it *very clear* that he can't do this with me."

"Lara. Did you fight for him?"

"What do you mean, did I fight for him?"

"Did you tell him how you feel?"

A long pause swept over me as I leaned back in the seat; the silence heavy with the realization that I hadn't. I had been too angry, and too stunned to speak, to lay my feelings down at his feet like some fragile offering.

"You need to go back and tell him how you feel."

"Sasha, I'm not driving eight hours just to tell Peter how I feel, that's ridiculous. If he wanted to talk to me, he would have called by now."

"What is eight hours to you, Lara?"

"What do you mean?"

"Eight hours is nothing compared to *years* of wishing you had done things differently." Sasha's voice had grown grave, a quality I was generally unaccustomed to hearing in her. "You remember why I left California, right?"

"Of course."

"I loved the crap out of Phillip. You know that. But I was too proud and too scared to tell him. And now he's married with kids, and I'll never know what could have happened if I'd just stayed and fought for us. It's been six years, and no man has *ever* come close to making me feel the way he did. I regret leaving. *Every day.*" Sasha's voice cracked on the other end. "Don't you dare make the same mistake I did."

I sat in my car long after my conversation with Sasha had ended, staring out into the blankness of the overcast sky, trapped between the cracks of indecision. Should I risk going back and potentially plunging the knife in deeper? Could I afford to unravel the delicate filaments of healing I had so painstakingly sewn together? And if I didn't turn around, if I kept driving east, and traded in my trembling vulnerability for the blank slate of safety, could I live with that decision? Could I cast aside all the possibilities of a life with a man who made me feel things I never thought possible?

My mind stared at these choices like deeply carved inscriptions I could not erase, weighing these options between uncertain fingers. What was more important in the end. The exposure of love? Or the shelter of healing? And could one really exist without the other?

Taking a deep breath, I started up my car and pulled out of the rest stop.

Chapter Twenty-Seven

The hours flew by as the deep greens and russet browns of the landscape rushed past me. I drove with my pulse thrumming wildly as each mile brought me closer to Peter.

Night had descended across the sky, staining it a pale pink as the familiar range of the Bitter Root mountains loomed above, stark and embracing. I passed the sign for Missoula and took the long, winding road off the freeway.

I drove down the rutted dirt road in the dark, my hands shaking as the shadowy outline of Peter's house came into view. Shutting off the engine in the driveway, I sat there for a moment with nothing but my breath filling the space. So much hope trembled inside my chest as I stared at his house. Somewhere within those walls was a man enclosed in the kind of darkness I knew I could never share, but one I wanted so desperately to understand.

I had so many words carefully rehearsed as I walked up the steps and knocked on the chipped white paint of his screen door; but as it opened and Peter stood there, his face tense and awash in the glow of the porch light, they all disappeared from my mind and disintegrated into fragments of silence.

"Who's there?" His voice was gruff and he looked tired, his eyes rimmed with red as he stepped closer to me.

My heart jackknifed in my throat at the sight of him, my voice coming out in a whisper. "It's me."

"Lara?" The look on his face was a mixture of relief and a sadness that swept across his eyes as he tightly gripped the doorframe. "What are you doing here?"

Dusty scrambled past Peter, almost knocking me over with his enthusiasm, his cold wet nose frantically nudging my cheek as I bent down and wrapped my arms around him for a moment, seeking comfort in his wiggling, joyful body. I took this moment to gather my thoughts, wishing I had the ability to be so effortlessly transparent with my own emotions.

"I came back to talk."

Peter nodded solemnly, raking his fingers through his hair as he held the door open. I cautiously stepped into the darkness of the living room, watching as Peter moved to turn on a lamp for me, casting the room in yellow light.

"I wasn't expecting you to come back." Peter stood beside the couch; his hands hung awkwardly at his sides.

"I wasn't either. I was really angry at first. But now I'm just hurt."

His eyes flashed with sorrow as he tentatively took a step in my direction. "I never wanted to hurt you, Lara."

"Well, you *did*." The bitter bite of emotion stung my eyes as he moved closer, his hand reaching for me, fingers grazing against mine; eliciting a sharp wave of longing that ripped me open inside. I yanked my hand away from his. "And *please* don't give me that bullshit line."

"What do you want me to say then?" Peter held his palms up in defeat.

"I want you to tell me why you pushed me away."

What filled the room was a crushing silence that made me want to scream, and all the anger I thought I had put away came rushing back to the surface.

"God *damn* you, Peter. You owe me at least that!"

He just stood there, his hands tightly clenched, trapped

within his own self-imposed prison; and I was only banging at the bars in a futile attempt to reach him. All my hopes crumpled, and an anguished disappointment flooded in as I realized I had been a fool to come back.

"You're breaking my *fucking* heart, you know that?" My vision wavered with the threat of tears as I wheeled around for the door and swung it open.

"Lara. Wait!" Peter jerked toward me suddenly, his voice frantic as he made contact with the door and slammed it shut. He gripped me by my shoulders, and I turned to face him, his eyes wide and pleading. "You want me to tell you why I pushed you away? You said it yourself, I'm a coward. I'm a *goddamn* coward, Lara."

I grabbed his arms, feeling something about to break within him. His wall was fragile, and I could see the cracks around the edges. "Why?... why are you so afraid?"

Peter's face flashed with intensity, his eyes dancing with tears. "Because I need you, dammit! And I *can't* need you like this." He pulled away from me, stumbling against the couch as he did, his hand gripping the back of it. "I feel like I can't breathe without you, Lara. And that terrifies me."

His words plunged in, deep and sharp, his confession like an offering, laying himself bare before me.

I crossed the room and drew him close, sliding my hands up his back and feeling the heat from his body against mine; the beating of his heart like a frantic metronome as he tensed for a moment and then relaxed, wrapping his arms tightly around me.

My fingers traced along his jaw, touching the wiry softness of his beard, and brushing away a tear which had slipped down his cheek. "Why didn't you call me? Why didn't you reach out to me?"

"Because I was scared." Peter ran his hand up my shoulder, his fingers brushing across my neck and hovering against my cheek. He slowly shook his head as his thumb caressed me and gently cupped my face. "I have spent the last five years not needing anyone. I have grown very comfortable with my solitude." He leaned in closer, his voice a coarse whisper against my ear. "And then you rushed in, and I can't seem to find that place anymore."

Peter's lips rested against my ear, his breath warm and enticing against my skin, and everything within me cried out for him. "I don't want you in that place, Peter." My fingers tangled themselves into his hair as I pressed his forehead against mine, my voice shaking. "I want you here with me. Do you understand that? I *need* you, too."

"Lara." The way he said my name was like a gentle breeze that wrapped around my heart, filling it up with a renewed hope as we stood there clinging to each other. His breath hitched as his fingers traced along my cheekbones and rested softly against my lips. "I'm so sorry. I've been such a fucking fool."

His mouth found mine, gentle and hesitant at first, like an apology delicately traced along my skin, drawing out a tenderness I thought had been lost. Then his kiss became fervent and consuming, and my entire body ignited with a frantic, clawing hunger as Peter sunk to his knees, taking me with him.

We collided against each other, grappling upon the floor in a reckless, frenzied blur of lips, skin and eager hands tearing at our clothes. Whatever words were still in us, had been replaced by a primal need to find each other again, our bodies seeking solace through the unspoken language we articulated so well.

Peter held me close against him, crying out as he buried himself in me. Deep, urgent thrusts that completely devoured my senses. An intensity burned between us that had not been there before. It was as if we were ripping away at the thorns and uncovering the places inside that we had both been hiding.

"I need you, Lara." He slowed his pace, matching the rhythm of my heart as his breathless words entangled in my hair. "God, how I *need* you."

Bliss ignited within me, and his name spilled out like an impassioned chant as my desire reached its peak and I exploded beneath him. I took Peter with me as I felt him shudder and release himself deep inside, tasting the salt of his tears on my lips as they merged with my own.

We lay undone together on the floor, coiled in the aftermath of our fire. Rolling onto his side, Peter drew me up against his chest. "You're trembling," he said as he ran his hand slowly along my back.

"You do that to me."

Peter stood and took my hand. Leading me into the bedroom, he wrapped us up in warm covers and enfolded me in his arms. My head nestled against his chest as we lay together on the bed, my fingers running lightly over the bandages on his hand. "How do your hands feel?"

"Better." Peter dipped his head down close to my ear. "I can't believe you're here." His voice was a whisper as he placed a lingering kiss on my brow, his breath trailing through my hair. "When you left last night, it felt like something died in me."

I slid on top of him, my lips teasing the lobe of his ear. "You *are* a fool, you know that? You never should have let me leave in the first place."

Peter ran his hand down the length of my back. "I never wanted to push you away like that... I just panicked." He paused, letting out a long sigh. "That day when I had to put Spirit down, there was so much pain, and all I wanted was to be with you. The need for you was like this ache in my gut that consumed me."

His confession made my breath hitch, and I reached up to run my finger across his lips, tracing the soft fullness of his skin. "Then why didn't you come to me? I *wanted* to be there for you so badly."

"Because I was afraid. I was afraid of all these feelings you woke up inside me. And then when you came to me that night and wanted to make love... I knew that if I did, I would completely lose myself. I was so terrified that if I let you all the way in, you would see the broken mess I really am." Peter shifted himself beneath me, rolling onto his side. "I don't want you picking up my pieces, Lara. You need a man who is strong and whole inside."

"But you *are* strong. And nobody has ever made me feel this way before. I don't need someone who is whole. I need *you*." My lips fell to his shoulder, brushing against his skin. "I'm broken inside too, but when I'm with you, I don't feel so... lost anymore."

Peter ran his hand down my chest, trailing past my stomach and across my thighs. "The blind leading the blind," he said with a faint chuckle.

"I'm serious." Sitting up, I took his hand, intertwining it with mine. "I know I didn't handle myself very well either. I had some realizations last night. I realized that running has always been my way of avoiding the hard moments in my life. But I can't do it anymore. I'm done running."

He squeezed my hand, his eyes full of warmth. "I've been a runner too, Lara. I think that's part of the reason why I felt such a connection with you when we first met. We both share the same affliction." A smile played on the corners of his lips. "Why do you think I like riding horses so much?" He pulled me back down onto the bed and clasped his arms around my waist. "I'm just glad you came back."

"Me too." I nestled against him as the words tumbled from my mouth. "Peter."

"Yeah."

"Why didn't you ever tell me about your wife?"

I felt him tense at the sudden reference. "How do you know about her?"

"Your sister called me this morning."

He released me and sat up, running his fingers through his hair as agitation flashed across his face.

"Hey." I reached for him and wrapped my arms around the sturdiness of his chest, resting my head against his back. "I'm divorced too, remember? I know how ugly these things can be sometimes." Peter relaxed against me as my hands trailed down his torso, feeling his muscles contract and release.

"What do you want to know?"

"Whatever you want to tell me."

A wary sigh escaped him. "Me and Cherise, we had been married for about eight years. Right after my accident is when she started cheating on me." Peter sounded distant and strained as he spoke, and I wondered how much of that pain still sat beside him like a flightless bird.

"She would go out to bars and come home late at night, but I didn't know at the time that she was seeing other men. It wasn't until she left me about a year later, for someone who worked in her office, that she told me everything. A part of me didn't blame her. I was pretty miserable to be around at the time. She told me that she couldn't be married to someone who was so damaged inside. That it was my fault she cheated. The truth is, I don't think she ever really knew me. She just knew the parts of me that she wanted to see, and when those parts were gone, she left."

"Did you love her?"

Peter turned in my direction, his hair falling into his eyes, catching the bits of moonlight that played across the room. "Honestly, I think I loved the idea of her. She was spirited and wild, and she made me feel alive. But she lived on the surface of herself, and I never really got to see inside. You can live with someone for years, and then wake up one day and find out that you never really knew them at all."

His words burrowed into the memories of me and John, and I realized how true that was. Our marriage had been built on the foundation of an idea, both of us seeing only what we wanted in the other.

Peter's hand searched for me, sweeping his fingers across my brow. "What I find so endlessly mesmerizing about *you*, Lara, is not just who you are on the surface, it's what's hidden beneath that. You have shown me the deeper parts of yourself... and those parts are *so* beautiful."

I rested my head on his chest. "You make me feel beautiful," I whispered against his skin as he pulled me close, the comforting rhythm of his heartbeat merging with my own.

The hours passed as we lay in bed talking, our words spilling out and mingling together upon the sheets. It was as if I had come back from a long battle with myself, and the tight knot I had been carrying within eased its pulsing ache as I rested within the safety of Peter's embrace.

"The sun is rising." Harbored in a room bathed in dawn, I lay curled up with my back against him while his hand traced lazy circles across my thigh.

"Tell me what it looks like."

I sighed wistfully. "It's *so* beautiful. It looks like the peaks of the mountains are painted in gold."

"What else?" His voice was a soft caress in my ear, sending goosebumps up my arms.

"The clouds are a wispy pink against the dark blue and purple of the sky."

"Sounds beautiful," Peter murmured, "in my mind I can see the way the light is hitting you right now." His fingers hovered against my cheek as if capturing the image through touch. "It's breathtaking."

I turned to face him as he drew me in for a long kiss, caught in the delicate moment between the edge of night and the promise of a new day; his hands paying homage to every part of me like a reverent dance, while the sun shifted its blanket of colors across the awakening sky.

Chapter Twenty-Eight

I awoke to a gentle kiss on my forehead. My eyes fluttered open to see Peter sitting on the edge of the bed with a coffee in his hand.

"This is for you." He held the cup out to me as I sat up and stretched, my body drowsy and relaxed.

"Thanks." I took the coffee between my hands, breathing in the rich nutty aroma. "What time is it?"

Peter slipped his hand underneath the blankets, trailing it up the length of my calf. "It's about mid-afternoon." He threw me a smile as his fingers continued their slow journey up my leg. "I'm sorry I kept you up so late."

I set the cup on the nightstand and leaned in close to him, my voice a teasing whisper in his ear. "Oh, I don't think you're sorry at all."

With a groan, he bent down and ran his lips along my shoulder, his hands slowly traveling up the curve of my hips. "You're right. I'm not."

I grinned and managed to extract myself from Peter's intoxicating caress, moving to the edge of the bed. "I really need to go take a shower right now, I stink."

"I think you smell absolutely amazing."

I snorted as Peter grabbed me, nuzzling his face against my neck. He let out a low growl as he breathed me in and gently nipped at my skin. "I love the way you smell, Lara."

"That's because you're an animal." I laughed, and playfully poked at his stomach as I stood up, enjoying this lightness between us, as if the night before had purged all the weight away.

"Well... you bring it out in me." Peter replied, reclining against the bed with a wink as I made my way into the bathroom.

Closing my eyes, I let the hot spray of water cascade down my back. Thick steam curled through the air as images from last night washed over me like a delicious dream. There was no denying the overwhelming connection we had, but I wondered, would it be enough? Was it strong enough to reach past all the pain? Would he pull away from me again? Would I *want* to run? All these questions left me with a feeling of being stranded on an island of unstable ground.

Toweling off, I stepped out of the bathroom and padded down the hall to where I found Peter standing in the middle of the bedroom with all my luggage on the floor beside him.

"Oh, thanks for bringing that in for me," I said, bending down to unzip my suitcase and grab out some clean clothes. "You didn't have to do that, you know." Peter rested his hand on my back as I stood.

"Lara." His face grew serious. "I want you to unpack your clothes." He nodded his head in the direction of his dresser, where half of his drawers lay open and empty.

My mind stumbled around, trying to grasp the sudden, heavy implications of this while my eyes darted to the bags at his feet. Bags that I had been carrying around for months like a safety line, anchoring me within the turbulent waters of my life.

"What are you saying, Peter?"

"I'm saying, I don't want suitcases and bags between us anymore." He ran his hands up my arms, grasping my shoulders. "I thought I lost you, and by some miracle, you came back to me. And I'll be damned if I screw this up again." Reaching up to cup my face, he ran his thumb along my cheek in that delicately tender way of his that never failed to make me ache inside. "Maybe we'll both make a mess of things, but I want the mess. I want every part of you, every day."

Something cracked within me, allowing the rush of relief and joy to filter through as the anxious clawing of my heart let go of its hold. I wrapped my arms around him, all my fears suddenly longing for release. I couldn't hold them in any longer. I didn't want to. I was so tired of running from them. I wanted to live again.

"I would love nothing more than to unpack my bags."

I gazed up into the wildness of Peter's eyes. Like a mirage, they were glimmering and beautiful, but at the same time, untouchable. How I wished he could look back at me. All the unspoken things I longed to communicate were lost within those walls of darkness I could not reach. So I drew him against me, allowing my body to speak in the language I knew he could understand.

A light shimmered inside me, and within its center lay the bright spark of happiness as Peter's lips fell on mine with an intensity that stilled my breath. He picked me up and placed me onto the bed, his kisses tender and full of devotion, leaving trails of honey and silk across my skin.

The last of the day's light traveled across the room, throwing shadows against the walls. I lay wrapped around Peter, drawing silent words with my fingers across his bare skin. He was good at this game and turned to me with a teasing smile. "Oh, you're hungry, huh?"

I traced the word YES across his chest in big, bold strokes. "I'm always hungry around you."

He chuckled, rolling me onto my back, his voice a deep

rumble against my neck. "Well, I guess I need to find a way to satisfy this hunger of yours."

"No, I'm serious, I'm starving, Peter!" Laughter trickled from me as he ran his lips down my chest, his beard tickling the flush of my skin.

We managed to untangle ourselves from each other and throw some clothes on, his hand cradling mine as we made our way into the kitchen. Shards of glass pushed to the corners of the kitchen floor reflected the light of the late afternoon sun, and the night I left came flooding back to me; the sounds of crashing as I ran blindly toward the cottage.

"Do you know that you still have glass all over your floor?"

He grimaced, his face pulling into a frown as he moved toward the refrigerator, his arm slipping into the narrow space alongside the wall in search of the broom. "That night was not my finest hour, Lara."

"It's okay, I got this." I took the broom from him and began to sweep up the remaining pieces he had missed. "So, you like to break things, huh?" I asked him in a teasing lilt, trying to soften the tension on his face as I dumped the glass into the garbage bin.

Peter found me, wrapping his arms around my waist, and burying his face into my hair. "Only when I'm acting like a stupid fool."

"We're both stupid fools," I said as I turned around and kissed him until he relaxed against me.

We stood in the kitchen holding each other as the last tentative beams of sunlight spilled across the sky, piercing through the windows, and dancing across our skin like whispers of renewal. Blood, tears, and words had been shed, and like hesitant dancers taking our first steps, we were learning this rhythm between us. I knew my heart still trembled with uncertainty, and much of Peter's walls were still there; I could see them in his eyes, layers of pain like hardened stone. But he had opened up a door for me, and I had walked through, allowing the delicate filament of potential to come creeping in. And it was enough for now.

Early afternoon sunlight flirted with the clouds, teasing me with flickers of warmth that pierced through the chill of the winter sky. Peter dictated vague directions to me as we walked through downtown.

"So, where are we going?"

"You should see a blue door coming up real soon."

I stopped us in front of a cheerful-looking shop. "Ice cream? This is what you've been craving? Isn't it a little cold for ice cream?"

Peter grinned. "It's never too cold for ice cream. Besides, this happens to be the best ice cream shop this side of Montana."

"You sure do talk this town up, don't you?" I said, giving him a playful nudge.

"It's all about perspective, Lara."

"I'm rolling my eyes at you right now."

"Thanks for letting me know," he chuckled as I led us into the store.

Only a few people stood waiting in line at the counter as we entered. The air was sweet with the scent of sugar that brought memories of my childhood rushing back to me.

"What's your favorite flavor?" Peter spoke close to my ear as his lips swept against my hair, making such a simple question feel so sensual and intimate.

"Coffee."

"Really?" he said with a small smile. "I would have pegged you for more of a strawberry kind of gal."

"Well, I'm full of surprises."

Peter pulled me against his chest as we got in line. "Yes, you are," he said, nuzzling into my hair. "You are definitely full of surprises, Lara."

I sank into his arms, realizing that the feeling of discomfort that always used to accompany any public display of affection with a man was nowhere to be found. Being with him like this felt as natural as breathing.

"What can I get you two?" A young woman's voice jolted me from our little moment, and I extracted myself from Peter's arms, stepping up to the counter.

Retrieving our order, I weaved us around the rows of tables and headed for a booth in the far back beside the window. Nestled close to Peter, I watched as he enthusiastically dug into his ice cream combination.

"Chocolate, pistachio and peach, huh?"

"It's good."

I crinkled up my nose. "It sounds a little gross, honestly."

"Oh, no, Lara. It's *good*." A wide grin spread across his face as he waved a big spoonful in my direction.

"No thanks."

"Come on, I know you want to try it."

"I actually don't." Laughter tumbled from me as Peter leaned in closer, managing to smear his ice cream across my cheek.

"Oh, I'm sorry. Did I get some on you? Let me help you with that."

He puckered his lips, and I pushed him away playfully, grabbing a handful of napkins next to me as the front door jangled open and a rush of cool air trickled through. Wiping ice cream off my face, my heart lurched for a moment as I turned toward the window and saw a yellow school bus parked out front and a long line of children filing into the store.

The room filled with the cacophony of jubilant chatter as

the teacher, an older rosy cheeked woman, was wrangling her class into two lines. She must have recognized Peter, because she suddenly beelined straight for us.

"Why if it isn't, Peter!" she sang out as she approached our table.

Peter cocked his head in her direction, his face lighting up. "Mrs. Denshire."

She grasped his hands in hers, squeezing tight before she whipped around and clapped loudly. "All right, kids. You remember the rules we talked about. Only one scoop each, ya hear?"

A chorus of mumbles filtered through the room as she turned back to us with a wide smile. "It's so good to see you, Peter." Her eyes bounced over to me. "And who is this lovely lady?"

Peter placed his hand over mine, his voice growing soft. "Someone very special to me."

I found myself blushing as I extended my hand out to her. "I'm Lara."

"Well, it's a pleasure, Lara. You know I used to teach Peter way back when he was a boy."

"Oh, really?" A smile stretched across my face as my gaze slid over to him. "I'm sure you have all kinds of stories."

"Oh, yes, I do. He was quite a handful back then," she said with a chuckle. "He was always getting into some kind of trouble." She reached over and patted Peter's arm affectionately. "Never a dull moment with this one, I tell ya."

Peter laughed and slipped his arm around my waist. "Still doing the annual ice cream outing, huh?"

"Yep. Every year on schedule. Speaking of which, I should probably get back before they plan a mutiny." She cocked her thumb out to the line of kids beginning to break away and wander around the room. "But it was so nice running into you. And wonderful meeting you as well, Lara."

"You, too." I nodded to her with a smile before she glided off to rejoin her class.

A tender longing stirred inside as I watched her with the children. That part of my life which I thought I had buried so many years ago, dislodged itself and hovered delicately against my chest.

As if reading my thoughts, Peter folded his hand over mine. "Do you ever think about teaching again?"

I took a deep breath and threw a wavering smile at a little boy who ran by the table with his face covered in sticky chocolate, his hair the color of Caleb's. "I don't know."

I looked down at my ice cream, realizing it was beginning to melt, and took a bite, feeling the cool sweetness slide down my throat. "I thought that part of my life was over." I turned to Peter, feeling an unexpected rush of possibility gather within. "But maybe it's not."

He squeezed my hand. "It doesn't have to be, if you don't want it to be, Lara."

The days passed like a languid dream as the holidays approached. The frigid hold of winter brought frost that clung to the windows, encasing us in a hushed world of silver and grey.

We were out working in the barn together, refilling the horses' water trough, and placing fresh hay into the net which hung against the wall, when Peter abruptly stopped and grew quiet. He stood beside Spirit's empty stall, his hands trailing slowly across the wooden fence as his eyes flashed with sorrow.

Coming up to him, I wrapped my arms around his waist, resting my head against his back. "I miss him, too," I whispered.

He turned to me, threading his fingers through my hair. "You know, he was a catalyst."

"What do you mean?"

Peter sighed, his eyes shifting through the dark spaces only he could see. "His death made me face parts of myself I had been pushing down for so long." He brushed his hand across my cheek, his fingers lingering against my skin. "My anger with the past. My fear of being vulnerable." He drew me against him, burying his face in my neck. "The way you make me feel."

The heat of his mouth on my skin caused a rush of arousal, and I arched my head back, wanting more as his lips trailed down my neck.

"And how do I make you feel?" My words came out breathless as he gently walked me backward until I was up against the barn door.

"You've opened me up in ways I never thought possible. You make me feel whole again. His voice was a soft caress as he trailed his hands up my shirt, his touch teasing my nipples through the fabric. "I think this is it for me, Lara. *You're* it."

My heart stretched with a joy that longed to release itself, and I slid my fingers through his hair, allowing the potency of my feelings to spill out, unguarded and resolute. "I love you, Peter."

"Oh, Lara." The deep green within his eyes seemed to flicker with a buoyant light. "I love *you*. So much."

A sigh spilled out as he pressed me against him, his lips on my skin like gentle confessions. I grappled with the enclosure of his pants, needing to feel him inside me with a desire that grew reverent, aching to solidify what had just been claimed between us.

The sting of the cold air was a sharp contrast to the warmth of his body as he slipped my pants down and lifted me up into his arms, holding me tightly as he pressed my back against the barn door.

"*God,* you are heaven," he groaned against my neck as he found his way into me. With each thrust, Peter took me deeper into that wild, beautiful place that shattered all my walls. My cries pierced through the air, and the sound of Penny and Ginger neighing and pawing at their stalls echoed through the barn.

"Shhhhh." He breathed seductively in my ear, nipping it lightly. "You're going to spook the horses." His mouth found mine, stifling my moans as I succumbed to an orgasm so intense, it felt as if my entire body was dissolving, leaving only the exposure of my heart behind.

We tumbled into the house together, flushed from the heat of our lovemaking in the barn. I glanced down at my phone which lay on the kitchen table, ringing loudly.

"Hey, Sasha," I answered, an elated smile resting on my lips.

"Hey, girl... What are you doing in a few hours?"

I looked over at Peter who had retreated down the hall, shedding his shirt as he walked into the bathroom.

"Um, I don't know. Why?"

"Because, I have a surprise for you."

Chapter Twenty-Nine

I stood by the window of the airport, the warmth inside the waiting room fogging up the glass as I watched the small plane touch down upon the tarmac. The late November sky slanted dark and ominous above me as an angry gust of wind tugged at the trees. Sasha's vibrant red hair peeked out from the depths of her hood as she descended from the plane, her stride long and brisk as she made her way into the airport terminal.

Suddenly, Sasha's arms were lifting me up and spinning me around in a flurry of laughter and rose perfume. "Girl! Am I so glad to see you!" Sasha's deep brown eyes sparkled as she smiled down at me, placing her hands on my shoulders. "You look different. You look really *happy*, Lara."

"That's cause you're here, silly," I said, giving her arm a squeeze.

"You know what I mean." Sasha picked up her bag and slung it over her shoulder. "I can't remember the last time I've seen you like this." She waved her arms dramatically around me, flashing a wide smile. "It's like you're glowing."

A flush rose to my cheeks as I recalled my moment with Peter in the barn earlier that afternoon.

"Well, I can't wait to meet the guy who makes you look like *this*." Sasha threw me a playful wink as we weaved our way through the terminal and out into the blustery chill of winter's pallid grip.

"I'm so excited you were able to surprise me like this for Thanksgiving," I said with a wide smile as I unlocked the car.

Sasha threw her bag into the back seat and slid into the front with me. "Me too. I was able to shift the family obligations to Christmas this year, so you get me all to yourself."

Sasha chattered enthusiastically the whole drive back to the house. She entertained me with tales of her manic Manhattan taxi driver, and the slow talking cowboy who had asked her out on a date during her flight.

"He gave me his number," she said, fishing out an airplane napkin from within her purse. "Apparently, he lives just outside of Stevensville."

I glanced over at Sasha with a raised eyebrow. "Are you going to call him?"

She grinned at me. "Maybe. He *was* pretty cute."

Sleet had begun to hit the windshield as we pulled into the driveway. Cutting the engine, I pointed to the cottage nestled beyond the farmhouse. "You get to stay out there, it's really cozy. You'll like it."

Sasha peered through the window. "This place is straight out of some home and garden magazine, Lara. It's so beautiful."

The sky had opened up, and thick slush pummeled us as we ran across the driveway and up the steps of the farmhouse. The door opened and Peter walked out onto the porch with Dusty beside him.

"So, you must be the infamous Peter?" Sasha broke into a wide grin and extended out her hand for him to take. It hovered in the air awkwardly before she dropped it, her eyes skirting over to me as a gentle blush rose to her cheeks.

"It's so nice to finally meet you, Sasha," Peter said as he stepped forward and held out his hand.

Sasha took it with a sheepish smile. "Thanks for letting me come and stay here for a bit. This place of yours is really nice."

Peter nodded as he held the door open for us. The living room was filled with the crackle and hiss of the fire that burned steadily within the hearth. Sasha crouched by the fire, spreading her hands out over the flames. "Gosh, how I miss real fires." She sighed wistfully as Dusty nudged his way underneath her arm, his tail wagging in excitement.

I sat down beside her as Peter headed into the kitchen. "You ladies want some wine?" he called over his shoulder.

"Oh, yes please," Sasha replied as she turned to me with a slow, mischievous smile, the fire illuminating her face. She dropped her voice down to a whisper and nudged my arm. "Jesus, Lara. You never told me he was so *gorgeous*. That's one tall drink of water you got yourself there. Does he have a brother?"

I raised an eyebrow up at her as recollection flashed across her face. "Oh, right... I don't want that."

"No," I said, shaking my head. "You definitely don't want that."

We sat together in the living room, wine glasses resting in our hands as we talked. Peter was beside me on the couch, his fingers lazily trailing across my thigh. As our intimacy had blossomed and stretched into something ripe and nourishing, I realized that his hands were his way of looking at me. Instead of a loving glance, his fingers would stroke my skin; an understanding look became a gentle squeeze. His touch was the thread that connected us, and I never grew tired of him watching me.

"So, Sasha... Lara mentioned that you're a dancer."

She took a large swig of wine and nodded. "Yes. I do mostly modern and jazz, with a little bit of hip hop thrown in. I'm teaching classes for kids right now." Sasha's gaze flickered over to the wall, motioning toward Peter's paintings. "Did you paint all these?"

There was a beat of silence from Peter, and I noticed Sasha grow uncomfortable for a moment. Sensing her unease, a warmth played across his features.

"If you're referring to the paintings on the wall? Then, yes, I painted those."

Sasha twirled the stem of her wineglass in between her fingers. "Well, they're really nice. Have you ever sold any of them?"

Peter nodded. "Yes, quite a few, actually. When I was actively painting, I used to display my work in a few art galleries in Missoula. I also taught an art class at the community college."

I turned toward Peter. "I didn't know you used to teach?" I found myself surprised by his disclosure. His art had always felt like such a sensitive topic that I never brought it up with him.

"Yep. Painting has always been a big part of my life ever since I was a kid." He shifted himself on the couch, drawing me closer against him. "I remember my sixth-grade art teacher once asked the class to paint *what your mind would look like if it was a landscape*. It gave me something to focus on, and I was unable to stop after that." A reflective smile crept through. "I think art saved me in a lot of ways."

"Exactly!" Sasha leaned forward in enthusiasm. "My childhood was pretty messed up, and I think dance was the only thing that kept me grounded." Her gaze flickered over to me, the tangled history of her past hidden in the depths of her eyes.

I sat back and listened as the two of them exchanged stories. Animated and hearty, they dove into the intricacies of self-expression and all the ways it had saved them.

My mind drifted back to my childhood; when I was ten and wanted to be a circus performer. I had set up a trapeze act in the backyard, with a jump rope and a swing; my mother's makeup splashed across my face as I envisioned myself soaring through the air like a beautiful bird, all the joy and possibility of life coursing through me. What happened to that little girl who was not yet afraid of heights and believed she could fly? Was she gone? Or had she always been there, just patiently waiting for me to remember her again?

Sasha and I walked down the pathway toward the cottage. Snow lightly fell around us as we treaded across the frozen ground, following the thin beam of light that shone from the porch.

"I really like Peter," she said to me, her breath billowing out in white clouds. "He's definitely a keeper, Lara."

"He is, isn't he?" I opened the door and turned on the light. "Being with him, it really feels like a dream to me sometimes. One that I'm scared I'm going to wake up from."

Sasha took my hands in hers, her eyes growing serious. "But it's not, Lara. This is life, giving you back some joy. *Take it,* run with it. It may not always be easy." A softness spread across her face. "But you know that the best things in life aren't. It's the things that challenge us which become the most important. It's what allows healing to take root."

I squeezed her hands, emotion welling up inside me. "Since when did you get so philosophical?" I asked with a teasing smile.

She shrugged, her eyes bright and beaming, cheeks rosy from the wine. "Let's just say I've been trying my hand at a little meditation these days. It's really amazing how much perspective you can get when you learn to let go of all the chatter in your mind."

I nodded and sank down onto the couch. "I don't know why

I never tried that." I leaned my head back against the cushions. "All those years I spent, just... *lost*."

Sasha sat down next to me, folding her hand over mine and giving it a light squeeze. "You were grieving, Lara. Grief takes up *all* the space inside you."

"It does, doesn't it?"

With a sigh, Sasha curled up her knees and laid down, resting her head in my lap. I smiled and ran my hand through her hair, twirling my fingers through her thick auburn curls. "Do you remember when we were kids, and I used to make you sit for hours while I played with your hair?"

Sasha let out a snort. "Yeah, I remember. I hated people messing with my hair back then, but I let you because I knew how much you loved it."

I laughed. "Oh, the compromises of childhood friendship."

"Worth *every* French braid," Sasha murmured with a chuckle.

A tenderness washed over me, grateful for the kind of love we had always shared, effortless and unwavering. So much of myself was entwined with her, and I wondered who I would have been if I never had her in my life. In the end, she was the one who had kept me alive through all the darkness.

"I love you, Sash."

The gentle cadence of her breath was the only reply, filling the space beside me as I sat there, smoothing back her hair, and watching the delicate flakes of snow fall out the window.

I didn't want to wake her just yet.

The smell of onions cooking and the delicious aroma of spices wafting through the air stirred me from sleep. Rolling over in bed, I glanced out the window to a world covered in white. Delicate sunlight sparkled like glitter on the new snow.

Quickly pulling on some clothes, I walked into the kitchen where I found Peter at the stove making stuffing for the turkey.

"Good morning, handsome." I leaned against him, resting my head on his back.

Peter turned to me, his hair rumpled and smelling like sage and thyme, as he tucked me under his arm and placed a kiss on my forehead. "I'm glad you got some good sleep last night. You conked out on me pretty early."

"I did, didn't I? I've been so tired lately." I reached up to run my fingers through his hair. "I guess I just can't keep up with you."

A mischievous smile slipped across his face. "Is that so?" He ran his hands down my back and cupped my bottom firmly, his lips teasing my neck. "Should I start taking it down a notch then?"

"Oh, god no. *Please* don't," I whispered as I pressed myself against him, feeling a sharp wave of desire surge within.

"When does your friend usually get up?" Peter growled low into my ear as he fumbled with the knob on the stove, turning it off.

"She usually sleeps late," I breathed as he slowly slid his hands down my breasts and across my belly, his fingers inching up the fabric of my shirt.

The back door burst open, startling us as Sasha walked through, trailing a gust of cold wind behind her. "Damn! It's freaking cold out there!"

I reluctantly released myself from Peter as Sasha's vibrant energy filled the kitchen.

"Oh my god, did I sleep well last night though, and thanks for helping me into bed after I passed out in your lap like a drunkard." Sasha said to me with a laugh as she walked over to the pot of coffee percolating on the counter. "It's *so* quiet out here. And that little cottage is adorable."

I smiled at her as I reached up to grab a mug from the cupboard. "Peter built that himself, you know."

"He did?" Sasha glanced at Peter, who had turned the stove back on with a click. "Well, aren't you multifaceted?" She poured coffee into her cup, throwing me a wink. "Gotta love a man who is good with his hands."

Peter chuckled as I threw Sasha a look. "What?" She asked in mock surprise. "Did I say something?"

"Oh, I think Lara appreciates what I can do with my hands," Peter retorted with a sly grin.

Rolling my eyes, I backed out of the kitchen. "That's enough out of you two. I'm going to take a shower now."

I retreated into the bathroom with a smile, the light banter between Sasha and Peter trailing down the hall behind me.

The house was rich with the inviting fragrance of turkey roasting in the oven. Through the fogged-up windows I could see snow beginning to fall once more. Sasha and I bundled ourselves up and stepped outside into the wintry landscape, opening the gate to the pasture and watching Dusty as he ran around in loops, his tracks crisscrossing against the fresh snow.

"I can see how this place works for you, Lara," Sasha said, wrapping her arm around my waist. "It's beautiful and peaceful. A lot like you," her eyes flashed with emotion, "I've been thinking about what Peter said last night, about finding the landscape of your soul. I really think you've found yours." She glanced off into the distance. "I hope I can find mine one day."

I rested my head against her shoulder. "You will."

"I hope so." She sighed and went to brush a loose strand of

hair away from her face. "But you know me, it's so hard to stay in one place for too long."

"You know I've always admired your ability to reinvent yourself."

Sasha turned to me with a faint smile. "It's only because I have to. I have no other choice. Life forces you one way or another."

"I guess it does." I looked up into the grey of the sky. "I've actually been thinking about teaching again."

Her face lit up. "Do you know how happy that makes me to hear that? I know how much you loved teaching, and you were always so good with the kids." She squeezed my hand. "I remember being really sad when you decided to stop. I mean, I understood that it was just too hard for you after Caleb died, but I know how much joy and purpose it gave you."

I nodded. "Yeah, it did. And I think I might finally be ready to find that joy again."

She linked her arm in mine. "Searching for joy despite what life throws at us... *that's* what gives us strength. That's what makes life worth living."

I leaned against her with a smile, a peaceful silence settling over us as we made our way toward the aspen grove with our arms entwined. The trees stood like silent, unclothed figures, the dark etchings on their bark like gentle eyes observing us as our boots crunched in the fresh snow, leaving tracks like shadowed brushstrokes upon a canvas of white.

That evening, we sat around the table together, full of food and easy laughter. It had been so long since I had enjoyed myself like this, and a rush of warmth enfolded me. The last three years of holidays had been saturated in so much misery. John's parents, a rigid and aloof couple, would make the obligatory drive across town to join us for a dinner filled with silence and tension. A dinner at which I would drink way too much wine and stumble into bed afterward, wrapped up in a hazy, painful fog of emptiness.

Peter rested his hand on my knee, giving it a light squeeze before he reached up and ran his fingers through my hair. His thumb brushed over my cheek and found a tear that had snuck down. "Are you okay?" he whispered into my ear.

"Yes," I said, wiping away the tear. "I'm just really happy right now."

Peter brushed his lips against my temple. "So am I."

"Oh, well aren't you two cute," Sasha cooed, startling me from our moment.

"You know..." She leaned across the table with a playful grin, gesturing toward us with her wineglass. "I think I should get a little credit for all this."

Peter turned in her direction with a quizzical look on his face as she continued. "I mean, I *was* the one who convinced Lara to turn around and drive back to you."

"Is that so?" Peter slid his arm around my waist. "Well, I guess I owe you one then, Sasha. Though I do like to think that at some point I'd have pulled my head out of my own ass."

Sasha raised her glass in the air. "Well, I certainly hope so. Shall we drink to that?"

"What exactly are we drinking to?" I asked with a chuckle as our glasses clinked softly against each other.

Sasha looked at me with a small smile. "To facing life head on."

I awoke to moonlight streaming in through the darkness of the bedroom and falling on my skin in fragmented patterns. I rolled over, taking in the soft outline of Peter asleep next to me, his arm draped across my waist.

My hand ran down to my stomach, feeling around for the source of discomfort which had stirred me from my sleep.

Careful not to wake him, I quietly slipped out of bed and crept into the bathroom. My eyes squinted as I adjusted to the glare of the overhead light and searched for a source of blood that was not there. Confusion washed over me once more as I took in a deep breath and clutched my abdomen, grimacing as another dull grip of unfamiliar cramping pain lanced through me.

Chapter Thirty

"Sounds like a UTI to me, hun," Sasha said as she reached across the seat and gave my leg a squeeze. "Otherwise known as honeymoon cystitis."

I glanced at her with a confused look, causing Sasha to chuckle. "It actually can be pretty common when one is engaging in... shall we say, *a lot* of sex." She playfully raised her eyebrow at me. "I can't believe you've never had one before."

Gripping the steering wheel, I tried to distract myself from the pain in my bladder. "I guess I wasn't having enough sex until now."

She let out a little laugh and then stopped herself. "I'm sorry. I know it's not funny, and I'm only teasing you about the sex part. Don't worry, you just have a little imbalance going on. You'll be fine, just go into one of those walk-in clinics and get some antibiotics. It'll clear itself up in a few days."

I pulled the car into the departure terminal, cutting the engine while Sasha grabbed her bag from the back seat. "Well, I guess this is it?" I shot her an exaggerated pouty face as I stepped out of the car.

With a smile, she drew me into a long embrace, the sweet smell of her perfume drifting around me. "It was *so* good to see you." She placed her hands on my shoulders, clasping them tightly. "You got a really good thing here, Lara. Peter is amazing, and the energy between you two... well, it's *intense*." She shook her head, a lightness playing in her eyes. "And honestly, it's been a little hard to watch sometimes. But you deserve happiness more than anyone I know. Don't you *ever* forget that, okay?"

I nodded and squeezed her hand in mine, stifling the tears that rushed to the surface. "I wish you could stay longer."

"Me too." She gazed longingly out across the expanse of prairie in the distance before lifting her bag over her shoulder and turning to me. "But I have a feeling I'm going to see you again soon." She rested her hand on my shoulder. "You're my favorite."

I smiled at the phrase she always used in moments like these. A tender reminder of the bond between us, larger than any goodbye. "And you're mine."

"Sasha," I called after her as she turned to leave. "You'll find your happiness too."

She looked back, throwing me with a wide smile. "You know, I think I have found my happiness, Lara. I just wish I had someone to share it with."

"Well, you got me," I said with a grin.

She chuckled. "That's true. Maybe you're all I really need."

I watched her as she strutted into the airport, blowing me a kiss before she disappeared behind the sliding glass doors.

I sat in the harshly lit exam room of the walk-in clinic, nervously twining my fingers as I waited for the doctor to come back with my test results. The door swung open and in walked a woman, her dark hair neatly pressed back into a tight bun.

"Lara Peterson? I'm Dr. Fadden." She quickly glanced down at her clipboard before settling herself in a chair next to me. "Well, you were correct. You do have a urinary tract infection." She paused for a moment, pressing her glasses against the bridge of her nose. "And were you also aware that you are pregnant?"

My whole world came crashing to a standstill. *Pregnant.* That word was like a knife in my gut. I shook my head at her in disbelief. "No, that's not possible, I have an IUD."

"Well, though uncommon with IUDs, things have been known to happen on occasion," she said, rolling her chair over to an instrument cart and pulling out a gown. "I know you're not feeling very comfortable right now, but I need to take a look at what is going on." Her warm gaze rested on mine, and she gave me a reassuring smile. "Regardless of what you decide to do, we are going to have to remove the device."

The doctor left the room, closing the door softly behind her as I undressed in a state of shock. My hands shook as I lifted myself onto the exam table to wait for her to return, rearranging the flimsy gown across my legs. My mind flashed back to three years ago, right after Caleb had died. I had been sitting in a room much like this one, waiting for a doctor to insert a device that would guarantee I would not have another child. The very thought of being pregnant again had filled me with such crushing pain and anxiety. I knew I could never do it again. I had my chance at being a mother, and it was ripped away from me. I could never replace Caleb, and I didn't want to.

The door opened, jerking me back to reality. One I did not want to confront. The doctor must have seen the look on my face, and she placed a warm hand on my knee in an attempt to soothe me. "I know this is a lot to take in right now, and we can go over all your options after the exam, okay?"

I nodded blankly and laid back on the table; the paper crinkling loudly underneath me. I tried to think of anything other than what was happening right now as I felt the cold metal of the speculum slide up inside me.

"Do you know who inserted your device?" the doctor asked in a gentle tone.

"I don't remember." My voice came out strangled. "It was some clinic out in California."

She looked up at me with concern in her eyes. "How long have you had this in for?"

"A little over three years."

She frowned. "And you have been sexually active this entire time?"

I shook my head. "No, not until recently."

"Well, that explains things, then. It looks like what has occurred is something called a partial expulsion. The IUD has moved away from its position at the top of the uterus. This is one of the most common complications that can occur with this device. This is why it is important to check the strings on a routine basis."

"The strings?"

"Yes, the doctor who inserted this device should have gone over this with you."

I looked over at her from my awkward position on the table, vaguely remembering a pamphlet the doctor had given me that in my veil of fresh grief I had never read. "Yes, of course." I squeezed my eyes closed, feeling like an idiot.

"And just so we can get a better idea of how far along you are. When was your last period?"

I shook my head. "I don't really know. The past three years, my periods have been really irregular. I think I had some light spotting a few months ago."

"Okay." The doctor paused for a moment and then grabbed something from the tray beside her. "I'm going to be removing the IUD now. You will feel a little pressure," she said as I felt a sudden sharp pull within my uterus.

The rest of the appointment went by in a blur of information that I struggled to process. I dressed hastily and grabbed the pamphlets and the antibiotic prescription the doctor had given me. My mind a sea of raging emotions I attempted to choke down like bile in my throat.

The doctor stood beside me, her hand resting briefly on my

shoulder. "We have a very safe and discreet service available to you if you need it; all you have to do is call, okay?" With a gentle nod, she opened the door and strolled down the long, empty hallway.

The hours passed by in a haze. I vaguely recall standing in line at a pharmacy and then driving down the freeway back toward Stevensville. My heart was a throbbing mess of panic and grief that felt as fresh to me as the day Caleb died.

I swerved to the side of the road and shut off the car, allowing splintered sobs of their own volition to spill out of me.

Night crept across the sky as I relinquished myself to the unavoidable. My phone had not stopped ringing, and I knew it was Peter wondering where I was. I needed him, but at the same time, I didn't know if I could face him. The heaviness inside was too much to bear. How could I explain this? How could I drag him down to the depths of my complicated pain and ask him to stay there with me?

Pulling my car back onto the road, I drove recklessly toward the house, my foot pressed hard against the gas pedal as if the violent velocity of speed could extract all the thoughts from my mind.

Peter was sitting on the couch when I walked in. "Lara, where have you been? I've been calling all day." Peter's face was pinched with worry as he stood and strode across the living room, his hands seeking me out and grasping my shoulders tightly. "Are you okay? What happened at the clinic?"

The words lodged themselves in my mouth, brittle and dry. I didn't have the strength to tell him. So, I settled for the half-truth. "I apparently have a bladder infection. So, I was prescribed some antibiotics."

Peter tilted his head, looking confused. "What took so long?"

"Oh, you know how walk-in clinics are," I said, pulling myself away from him, my words coming out flippant as I attempted to hide the shakiness in my voice. "Spent an hour in the waiting room, then I had to go to the pharmacy."

Peter followed me into the kitchen as I poured myself a glass of water, taking out the container from the pharmacy bag and dispensing a pill into my open palm.

"Lara, what's wrong?"

I flinched. "Nothing. I just don't feel good right now." I placed a quick kiss on his cheek. "I'm going to lay down for a bit."

I slid beneath the cool sheets and buried my head into the pillow, hoping to muffle the chaos in my mind. I could hear Peter pacing in the living room, and I felt terrible for shutting him out.

Eventually, Peter came into the room, the mattress shifting slightly as he sat down next to me and slid the covers back. "Lara. Don't think that just because I can't see you, I don't feel you. I know you're upset about something." He reached his hand out, his fingers brushing against my forehead. *Talk to me.*

I lay there, curled up in the fetal position, his touch dragging me back to myself as tears slipped down my cheeks. I knew I couldn't hide this from him.

"I'm pregnant."

The look that flashed across his face was one of surprise, and then a fleeting glimmer of elation, and my heart broke all over again, a loud sob escaping me. "But I *can't*, Peter. I can't do this." I choked out, watching as flecks of sorrow swam in his eyes. "I can't be a mom again. It's just *too* painful."

Peter lay down on the bed beside me, taking me into his

arms. "Okay," he whispered into my hair. "It's okay. We'll do whatever you need to do."

The next few days were a blur. I couldn't think straight. It was as if my mind had been ripped from me and all that remained was the animal inside, telling me to run. There was no room for logic. I knew that not having this child would be a loss of its own, but when I thought of going through with it, the claws of fear rushed in, and my heart broke in a language I could not decipher.

Peter tended to me gently, holding space for the tumbling inside me. But his face was etched in a mask of sorrow, his eyes full of emotions he wouldn't speak out loud, and questions I didn't have the strength to ask. The silence that encompassed us was heavy, and we orbited around it without a compass, lost to the gravity of our own uncertainty.

I burrowed into my coat as I walked through the pasture; the snow crunching loudly beneath my boots. The icy grip of winter pierced through me, the wind biting at my skin, incessant and bitter. I found Peter out in the barn, brushing down the horses, his face tense. He looked startled when he heard me approach.

I placed my hand on his arm. "Do you need any help in here?"

"Nope, I'm all finished." He set the brush down on the shelf by the door. "But I'm going for a ride." He leaned into me, placing a brief kiss on my forehead. "I'll be back in a few hours."

Peter lifted himself up onto Penny, taking the reins in his hands and slowly trotting her out of the barn before digging his heels in and racing off through the field. Snow flew up like bursts of clouds as he disappeared from my line of sight.

We had both been tiptoeing around each other the past few days, and I could feel the space that was growing between us. It was an ache that tore into me, and I wondered if we would be able to get past this.

I made my way back into the house and wandered into the bedroom. My phone sat untouched on the nightstand, full of missed calls from Sasha. It was one more thing I was not confronting, but I knew I had to call her; she was a lifeline I desperately needed right now.

"Sasha." My voice cracked as I opened my mouth and let the last few days spill out in a frantic rush. She remained silent while I purged all the guilt and fear from my gut until I was empty and still.

"And how is Peter doing with all this? What does he want?"

I began to pick at my nails, which had started to grow out for the first time in years, tearing away at the tips and exposing the sensitive skin underneath. "I don't know. He's been really quiet. And when I ask him, he just says that he's here for me and will stand by whatever decision I make."

"Lara." Her voice was cautious. "Have you considered the possibility of having this child?"

I closed my eyes for a moment, trying to shut out the question that had been following me for days now. "I don't think I can do this again. How can I have another child, knowing that at any moment I could lose them?"

"You know that's just your fear talking." Her words came out measured. "Listen, I love you, and I'll support you no matter what you choose to do here. But I really think this could be a way for you to fully heal and move on."

"I can't just *replace* Caleb, Sasha."

"Of course not, and that's not what I'm saying. I'm talking

about moving on from the pain. You can't keep carrying it around with you forever. It's eating you up inside."

I gazed out the window, watching the faint silhouette of Peter and Penny appear, bending, and dipping as they ran against the backdrop of the hills. *Why was the trajectory of healing so unsteady? Would I ever find a place inside me I could rest against?*

"I know it is. But I don't know where to put it."

Sasha's voice grew soft. "You don't put it anywhere, Lara. You just... let it go."

The racing of my heart woke me from my restless sleep. The gentle press of Peter's body against mine was like a beacon within the darkness, and as much as I wanted to seek refuge there, I couldn't. The isolating prison of my turbulent thoughts swept over me, carrying me farther away from him.

I stumbled from the bedroom to the bathroom as the crippling weight of panic consumed me. Turning on the shower, I shed my clothes and stepped into the spray, hoping the warmth would wash away the anxiety clawing around inside.

Leaning my head against the tiles, I attempted to breathe from deep within my abdomen, summoning up all the years of therapeutic tools I had paid for. But my anxiety was a relentless villain, and its sword was always much stronger than my shield.

My limbs trembled as the insistent flood of adrenaline crawled through my skin. *What was wrong with me?* My mind rushed back to Sasha's words on the phone, and I knew she was right, but I didn't think I had the strength to do this again. What kind of mother would I be? Broken, bruised and terrified all the time. Afraid of every scrape, fall and fever. Every fear a brutal reminder of what I lost. All these thoughts swirled inside like a hurricane, smashing against the walls of my mind.

The sound of the shower curtain opening startled me, and I turned to see Peter standing there, steam curling around him. I reached my arms out and instinctively pressed my body into his comforting solidity.

"You're shaking, Lara."

I buried my face into his neck. "I'm scared... *why am I so scared?*"

Peter stepped into the shower with me, the water soaking his clothes. "I'm here." He drew me tightly to him. "I'm not going anywhere. I'm here."

As he stood in the shower holding me, a stillness gathered around the tight spaces inside. My heart slowed its frantic pace and fell in time with his, like the rhythm of a drum calling me back home. His arms cradled me while he kept whispering the same words. *I'm here,* until I finally realized what he was trying to say. I didn't have to do this alone anymore.

We sat together in the hushed and chilly waiting room of the abortion clinic. My hands were clammy as my fingers clenched tightly around Peter's, his body tense beside me while he tapped his foot upon the tiled floor. My eyes flickered to a stack of magazines on a table, where the smiling faces of women stared back at me with their vapid, airbrushed happiness.

The room was empty, except for another woman who sat across from us, staring into the glow of her phone, her face awash in a look I knew all too well. I wondered what her story was, and I suddenly wanted to reach out to her in solidarity, to tell her that she wasn't alone. How much of the choices in our lives are governed by fear, like a monster lurking within the darkened places of our mind? And what kind of bold life could we live if we did not succumb to it?

The sound of a door opening caused both of us to look up as a nurse walked into the room with a clipboard in her hand.

"Lara Peterson?"

Chapter Thirty-One

I shoved open the exit doors of the clinic, my heart hammering as I beelined toward the car. Glancing up, I saw Peter making his way out of the building with a look of confusion on his face. "Lara, where are you?"

"I'm over here," I called out, leaning against the car, trying to calm my breathing. "I just want to go home, okay?" I held my arms tightly around myself, trying to block out the chill of the wind and all the quarreling emotions lurching around inside.

Peter stood there looking slightly agitated, until I walked over to him and placed my hand on his arm. "I'm right here. Sorry about running off like that."

He furrowed his brow, concern flashing in his eyes as he took my hand. "What happened in there?"

"I don't know," I drew in a shaky breath, "when the nurse called my name… I just froze."

Peter pulled me close, and I sunk into the refuge of his arms. "We can reschedule if you want."

I looked up at him as the words fell unrestrained from my mouth. "I don't think I want to."

He moved to cup my face lightly, his thumb grazing my cheek. "What are you saying?"

Swimming in a sea of inner conflict, my heart scrambled around in avid desperation, trying to battle against the powerful narrative of my mind. "I have no idea. I'm so confused right now."

"Lara." Peter's face grew earnest. "Do you know what my first thought was when you told me you were pregnant?"

I took a deep breath, ready to finally hear all the words he had kept at arm's length. "What was it?"

"I felt this rush of hope, like my whole life had been leading up to this moment." As he spoke, his eyes began to dance with tears. "Truth is, I never thought of having kids, until you came into my life."

Pierced by the realization of this, my heart trembled with a resolution that suddenly felt much larger than myself. "Why didn't you tell me this before?"

He sighed. "How could I? The last thing I wanted to do was add to the burden of your decision."

My hands shook as I trailed them down Peter's chest. I realized I had been so selfishly lost within my own trauma that I had shut him out of his emotions.

The tears I been holding back finally released. "I'm *so* sorry."

"It's okay." Peter tenderly stroked my cheek. "I know all of this has been really hard for you. And this decision needs to be something that *you* want."

I looked into his eyes, and what flowed from them came from something much deeper than sight. He saw possibility.

"Do you really think we can do this? I mean, how are we supposed to raise a child when we are both so broken inside?"

Peter clasped my hands tightly in his. "You know, Leonard Cohen once said it perfectly… *there is a crack in everything, that's how the light gets in.* I'm beginning to believe that. I think it's the broken pieces inside of us that make us stronger in the end."

Peter rested his lips on my forehead, running his hands through my hair. "All I know is that I love you. And I honestly never thought I could feel this deeply for someone, but I do. You've opened up something in me." His voice trembled. "You've given me the ability to see in ways I never thought I could. I've been scared of *a lot* of things in my life. But I'm not scared of this... this feels right. There's nothing I want more than to go on this journey with you. I want to meet this child we've created together."

A lightness rose within, like a heavy fog lifting to reveal a clarity undefined until now. "I want to meet this child, too," I whispered as the strong grip of fear eased itself, slowly unraveling around me and allowing the idea of a new beginning to boldly rush in. Life was offering me a gift, something precious and profound, and I could feel myself reaching for it.

"Are we gonna do this, then?" Peter asked, a tentative smile creeping across his face.

"*Yes*... I think so."

My heart soared with joy as Peter lifted me up into his arms, spinning us in a circle. "We're going to have a baby!" His voice was ardent, exhilaration burning within his eyes as he lowered me to my feet, his lips falling on mine and drawing me into a kiss that made the whole world fall away; solidifying this decision we had just made together, standing in an empty parking lot under a cold, grey winter sky.

The sound of someone walking past startled us from our fevered embrace, and Peter leaned down, speaking into my ear. "Let's get out of here."

I walked us to the car, my limbs weak as I fumbled with the keys and pulled out of the parking lot. As I drove, my thoughts hesitantly circled around this new reality between us, causing a concentrated silence to fill the car.

Peter turned in my direction and placed his hand on my knee. "Lara, will you pull over for a minute?"

I slowed the car to a stop by the side of a field. Clouds hung thick and low over the horizon, obscuring the view of the mountains. Peter slid the keys out of the ignition, his face full of tenderness. "I want you to know that no matter what, I'm always going to be here. For you, and for this child."

I unclipped my seatbelt and climbed across the console, settling onto his lap. "You promise?"

He wrapped his arms around me. "I promise."

I buried my face into his jacket, breathing in the earthy, grounding scent of him. "I'm still scared, you know."

"I know. It's okay to be scared. But you don't have to carry that fear alone anymore."

I sat up and traced my fingers down his cheek, my eyes swelling with gratitude. All my roads had led me here, to a love that brought me back to myself. "God, I love you."

A smile washed over Peter. "I love you more."

The windows lost their clarity as the warmth of our breath surrounded us. A misty rain began to fall, tapping lightly against the car roof in a rhythmic pattern as we held each other. This new life together stretched out before us, unknown but filled with possibilities.

Standing in the bathroom, my hands ran over the subtle rise of my belly. My body was already shifting, adjusting to this child within me, my breasts tender and full. Stretch marks from Caleb threaded across my skin like thin, silver strands of memory, and my heart stirred as I recalled his first, faint movements, like the gentle wings of butterflies dancing inside. The feeling of holding him in my arms. The beauty of his eyes meeting mine for the first time. Gratitude bloomed within me as I sat with all the ache and joy this new life had awakened.

Wrapping a robe around myself, I stepped into the hallway, where I found the door to Peter's art room ajar. Afternoon snow fell outside the window, filling the space with a soft white light as I watched him place his paints and brushes into a box.

"What are you doing?"

He turned in my direction, running his fingers through his hair. "I'm clearing out the space."

"And what are you going to do with all your supplies?"

"I'm thinking of donating them to the local high school art department."

I leaned against the doorframe, wondering where this was suddenly coming from. "Are you sure you want to do that? I mean, I know how important painting was to you."

"It was. But art has endless opportunities for self-expression. I'll find a new way to create." Peter walked over to where I stood and ran his hands along my arms. "It's time to let go of this part of my past and make room for something even more beautiful to take its place." A smile crept across his face as he moved down to stroke my belly. "I'm thinking this would make a nice room for our child."

A flush of elation rushed through me. *Our child.* There was something so deeply sacred in those words. We had created life out of our own visceral longing to strip away at the rubble and reveal the tender shoot of renewal, magnificent in all its imperfections. I placed my hand on his chest, and glanced around the space, envisioning a crib, and rocking chair by the window; songs I had once sung to Caleb filling the walls of the room. "I think so too."

I could never replace Caleb. He would always be the loss I reverently carried with me. But I could honor him by giving this child all the love which had been trapped inside for so long, patiently waiting for wings to give it flight again.

Chapter Thirty-Two

The living room was ablaze with colored lights, strung from the evergreen Peter and I had brought into the house that morning. I stood beside the fireplace, reaching into an old dusty box full of Christmas decorations I had found out in the barn. I hung the ornaments on the branches of the tree, while the gentle notes of Miles Davis played in the background. The cozy ambiance and the crackle of the fire filled me with nostalgia and a sense of contentment that was punctuated by a bittersweet sorrow.

Peter walked in through the back door, bringing with him the chill of outside. "You in here, Lara?"

"Yeah, I'm over here just finishing up the tree."

He came up from behind, smelling of fresh hay from the barn as he wrapped his arms around me, his hands cradling my belly. "How does it look?"

"Really nice." I sighed and reached out to finger an ornament of a tiny angel wrapped in silken thread hanging from a branch. "You know, this will be my first Christmas without Caleb." I turned around to face him. "John and I, we stopped celebrating after he died."

Peter's hand traveled up my neck, brushing his fingers along my cheek. "You know, I haven't found much to celebrate either, these past few years..." his thumb traced along my temple, "until you came along." Peter broke out into a soft smile.

I tangled my fingers in his hair, still wet from the snow

falling outside. "You're going to be an amazing father, you know that?"

Peter's eyes lit with emotion as he ran his hands down the curve of my belly. "All I know is that I'm going to love this kid with everything I've got in me."

"God, you make me so happy," I whispered against his lips as he drew me into one of his deep, slow kisses that never failed to make me dizzy.

The door suddenly opened to a flurry of Miriam and Clive, bringing a burst of cold air rushing into the room with them. "Oh, I saw that, you two lovebirds!" she called out in her joyfully infectious lilt. "Making out by the Christmas tree... so quaint." Miriam knocked the snow off her boots before stepping inside with Clive, leaving their bags on the front porch.

"You're early," Peter grumbled with a playful smirk.

"Well, I'm sorry to break up the party. Our plane came in ahead of schedule." Miriam threw me a wink as she spread her arms out wide. "Get on over here, Mamma," she said with a large smile. "It's so good to see you."

The house came alive with the bustle of activity as Dusty ran in looping circles around our legs. Making my way into the kitchen to check on dinner, I overheard the hushed tones of Miriam speaking with Peter over the sizzle of food cooking on the stove.

"I've been meaning to thank you for doing that, Peter. I know it wasn't easy for you."

Miriam shot me a knowing look as I walked in. "Something tells me that Lara here, may have had a small part to play in all this."

"In what?" I asked.

Miriam leaned against the counter. "In our brother's early release. He's in a really great rehab facility up in Missoula now."

Peter shook his head as he extended his hand out to me. "She did, but not in the way you think. I've realized that a lot of my resentment with Greg had more to do with my own issues." Peter ran his hand down my back. "And I'm not angry with him anymore."

"Is this the healing power of love talking, Peter?" Miriam asked with a warm smile.

He chuckled as his lips swept over the top of my head. "Something like that."

That evening, after an animated dinner around the table, I found Miriam staring into the open doorway of Peter's art room. The previous week we had finished clearing out the space and painted the walls the bright color of sunshine.

"Looks a lot different now, doesn't it?" I said, standing beside her.

Miriam turned to me with a look of elation. "Oh, Lara." She took my hands in hers, giving them a squeeze. "I remember having this really intense feeling I could not shake the day I met you at the diner. It was like I *knew* you were going to have some profound effect on our lives." Miriam's eyes wavered with tears. "And I was right. Not only did you change Peter's life, but you changed mine as well." She brushed away a tear that snuck out. "I've always wanted children, but I've never been able to conceive. But now..." She glanced down at my stomach with a tender smile. "Now I'm going to be an auntie."

I pulled Miriam into a tight hug, feeling the delicate strands of her loss. So different in color than mine, but the language remained the same.

Miriam released me with a soft laugh as she wiped away her tears. "You know, I've never seen my little brother so happy, Lara. He's just head over heels about you."

I smiled as that rush of joy I was beginning to get used to collided with my heart. "I'm pretty crazy about him, too. I think in some ways he saved me."

She nodded, her eyes twinkling. "I think you saved each other."

Clive appeared next to us, placing his hand on Miriam's back. "What are you two girls chatting about over here?"

I watched as Miriam looked up at him with a lighthearted grin. "Oh, we're just talking about love."

"Love, huh?" Clive said as he stifled a yawn.

Miriam smirked and leaned in close to me, placing an affectionate kiss on my cheek. "I'm going to get this old man over here into bed. We'll see you in the morning."

Clive chuckled and playfully ruffled Miriam's hair as they walked down the hall together.

I awoke to Peter trailing light kisses down my back. Out the window, the early morning sunlight bloomed over the thick expanse of snow. I rolled over in bed, snuggling into the warmth of his arms.

"Morning, beautiful." Peter's mouth found mine as his hand moved down to the gentle swell of my belly, tracing lazy circles against my skin. "I'm really loving this, you know."

I looked at him from across the pillow. "Loving what?"

With a grin, he bent down and traced his lips over the rise of my stomach. "I'm loving how voluptuous you are."

I laughed. "Well, lucky me then, because I'm only going to get more voluptuous."

"I know." His voice was a low growl as he ran kisses up my breasts. "What I would give to be able to paint you right now."

"Really?" I threaded my fingers through his hair. "Did you paint any nude women back in your day?"

Peter rose above me, his dark hair sweeping across his brow and falling into his eyes. "No, I never painted a woman before. You would be my first and *only*." He leaned closer, his lips against my ear. "I think I would start here. Right where the curve of your neck meets the lobe of your ear."

His whispered words caused the tiny hairs on my arm to raise. "And then what would you paint next?"

"Your lips, and then the adorably perfect arch of your nose."

"You like my nose?"

"I love your nose. I love every single part of you."

I nestled against him and drew the covers up around us, resting my head against his chest. "I never thought I would find this, you know?"

"Find what?"

My fingers traced spirals down his arm. "The kind of love I saw in my parents. The kind I stopped looking for long before I even met John."

He slowly ran his hand up my back. "And what would you call this kind of love?"

I rose onto my elbow, taking in the depths of his eyes, which stared up at the ceiling and brushed my fingers across his cheek, causing him to turn in my direction. "The kind that feels like home."

Peter's face lit up in a wide smile as he enfolded me in his arms. "I'm honored to be your home."

A peaceful silence fell over us as we lay entwined, the rise and fall of our breath syncing together like the waves of the ocean while the light of the morning danced across our skin.

The sound of Miriam and Clive moving around in the house stirred us from our private world, and Peter spoke softly in my ear. "You think it's time we go join the living?"

I sighed and reluctantly rolled out of bed, padding over to

the closet. I glanced back at Peter who still lay there, sprawled among the sheets, beautiful and enticing. I smiled and tossed some clothes beside him. "Well, you better get dressed then, before I get any ideas."

He growled and slid off the bed, his hands seeking me out. Grabbing me by the waist from behind, he buried his mouth against my neck. "Oh, but what if I have some ideas of my own?"

Peter trailed his hand down to my sex, and I gripped the frame of the closet as he slipped his fingers inside, causing my legs to buckle.

"What are you doing?" I gasped as a hot flush of arousal cascaded over me.

"Would you like me to stop?" he whispered seductively in my ear.

I closed my eyes and lost myself to his touch, so achingly perfect in its execution. "No, please don't."

Turning around, I cupped the length of him, which stood erect before me, but Peter shook his head, pressing my back gently against the wall.

"No, I want to feel *you* let go."

So, I did. The voices of Miriam and Clive in the other room drifted underneath the door as Peter touched all the tender, aching places inside, molding my desire into something that was sanctified, and for him alone.

"Yes." He groaned against my lips. "Let go for me, Lara."

His words were a tantalizing push that sent me over the edge, and I dropped my head against his chest, stifling my moans as I succumbed to the sweetness of momentary oblivion before the waves of pleasure washed me back to shore.

"God, I love listening to you," Peter murmured, running his hand through my hair.

I smiled languidly, my legs trembling and weak, my body

humming; awash in the intimacy between us. I rested my forehead against his. "You do, huh?"

"Yes. It's intoxicating." Peter ran his mouth down my neck. "It's not my pleasure that I desire. It's *yours*."

Longing rushed through me all over again as his words teased my skin. "You need to stop." I whispered, gripping his hair in between my fingers. "Or we'll never get out of this bedroom."

"Okay, okay." With a chuckle, Peter released me and walked over to the bed to retrieve his clothes. "Apologies for the detour."

Slipping on my pants and a sweater from the closet, I leaned against the wall and watched him dress. "You're the first person who has ever made me feel that."

"Feel what?"

"Feel like my pleasure was important."

He came up to me, his eyes soft as his fingers ran across my cheek. "*Everything* about you is important to me. The happiness, the pleasure, the anger, and the sorrow. I want it all, Lara."

"Careful what you wish for," I said with a laugh.

"Oh, I am *very* aware of what I am getting myself into." Peter cracked a playful smile as he entwined his fingers through mine and led me out of the bedroom.

We found Miriam and Clive in the kitchen, the room rich with the aroma of coffee and eggs.

"Merry Christmas!" Miriam called out to us as we entered. She stood beside the stove with a big grin on her face, waving a spatula in the air. "I figured you two lovebirds would be taking your sweet time, so I made breakfast."

"Thanks, Sis," Peter said, bending down to place a quick kiss on top of her head.

I settled into the chair by the table as Peter handed me some tea. The steam from the cup rose into the air as I let my gaze drift out the window. The gentle sounds of Peter and Miriam talking together floated around me as I sunk into the cozy warmth of this life I had stumbled upon, like a rare gift delicately unfolding.

That evening, we sat beside the fire exchanging gifts. Peter, with an enthusiastic smile, traced over the braille lettering of the three vintage Led Zeppelin albums I had painstakingly scoured the web for.

"Where did you find these?" he asked, pulling me into his lap and playfully showering my face with kisses. "My life is now complete."

"Well, I'm glad to know that's all you were missing this whole time," I laughed as Peter felt around under the tree for a small box, placing it in my lap.

I unlaced the bow around the box. Inside, nestled among some tissue paper, lay a carved wooden bird with intricate designs etched into the wood. All along the plumage swirled flowers and creeping vines. The detail was breathtaking, and in the center of its chest lay an exposed heart.

"This is *so* beautiful, Peter. Where did you get this?"

"I made it." A sneaky smile flashed within his eyes. "I've been working on this one for a while now. All those times you thought I was out with the horses; I was actually making this for you."

Tears sprang to my eyes, and a wave of emotion washed over me as I envisioned him carving this out in secret, hunched over his creation in the chill of the barn. "I *love* it."

Miriam leaned in close to get a better look. "Wow, this is really incredible work. How did you manage to do this?"

Peter shrugged. "Turns out carving is a lot like reading in braille for me."

Miriam traced her fingers along the engravings in the wood. "And what made you decide to do a bird? Is there some sort of symbolism there?"

Peter ran his hand up my back, his fingers slipping through the strands of my hair. "Well, Lara reminds me of a bird. A rare, beautiful bird that flew into my life, stole my heart, and decided to stay."

Miriam looked over at me with a smile, swiping at a tear that had materialized on her cheek. "Well, Jesus, Peter. You just got me all misty-eyed here." She stood up from the floor, grabbing the empty glasses in front of us. "When did my little brother become such a sappy romantic?" She chuckled to Clive as she disappeared into the kitchen.

"You stole my heart too," I whispered as I wove my fingers through his and leaned against him, resting my head on his shoulder. Firelight played upon our skin as I watched the life of the flames leap and collide with one another, seeming to disappear among the embers and then reemerge once more, in an endless dance of rebirth.

The car sped along the open stretch of highway. Against the backdrop of spring's optimistic blue sky, mountains gave way to towering evergreens that enclosed us in a palette of emerald and jade. Peter rested his hand against my leg as I drove, his thumb every so often stroking me in soft circles.

I shifted in the seat, trying to find a position that would more comfortably accommodate my growing belly. At five months, I was much bigger than I had ever been with Caleb. Peter, noticing my discomfort, placed his hand on my lower back, gently kneading the tender muscles. "Why don't you pull over for a bit? You've been driving for a while, and I would like to give you a proper massage."

I groaned, my eyes rolling back as he hit all the right places. Peter's intuitive ability to locate my tension and draw it out never failed to amaze me, and I had been joking with him lately that he should look into massage therapy as a new career path.

"It's okay," I said. "We're almost there."

"You're still not going to give me even a *hint* as to where we're going, are you?" Peter asked with a smile.

"Nope, it's a surprise. All you need to know is that you're going to meet my brother and his family."

Peter sighed. "You're a stubborn one, you know that?" His hand swooped across the taut rise of my belly, his eyes suddenly lighting up as they always did when he felt the quiet stir of our child inside. "She's kicking, Lara."

I let out a laugh. "Yes. I am *well aware* of that. She loves to kick me when I'm trying to drive."

I spotted the exit for Westport, Washington, and flipped on my blinker. We drove through the quaint seaside town, past the tourist shops, with their paint faded from the relentless sea spray. A thin film of fog snaked its way along the coastline, shrouding the view in a hazy mist as I drove toward the ocean. Pulling into a parking lot that hugged the shoreline, I spotted Mitch's Subaru and the faint outline of them down by the water, four bodies weaving in and out of the surf.

"We're here." I opened the door and came around to his side as he stepped out.

Peter tilted his head back, taking in a deep breath as the wind whipped his hair wildly around his face. A wide smile broke out as he turned to me.

"You drove me all the way to the ocean."

"I did," I said, wrapping my arm around his waist and taking in the view of the crashing waves from the parking lot.

Peter turned to cup my face in his hands, his eyes swimming with happiness. "God, I love you."

"I love you more."

Peter shook his head, his finger playfully tapping my nose. "I don't think that's possible. I got the market cornered on this one, Lara." He closed his eyes in silence for a moment, as if he were drinking up all the sensations around him.

I took his hand in mine. "Are you ready to meet my family?"

Peter opened his eyes and smiled. "Of course."

I led him down a set of stairs and onto the soft sand below, watching the outline of Mitch appear through the fog as he jogged toward us. He attempted to draw me into an embrace, deep laughter spilling from him as my belly jutted between us, making it an awkward endeavor.

Mitch held me at arm's length, his eyes sparkling with joy. "You look absolutely radiant, Lara."

I placed my hand on Peter's arm. "Peter, this is my brother, Mitch."

Mitch reached out and clasped Peter's hand. "It's so good to finally meet you. Welcome to the family."

Peter smiled and allowed Mitch to lead him down the beach, where Steven and the girls stood along the water.

Evie and Josie ran to me, their tiny arms grasping for a hug, their faces flushed with effervescent glee. "Auntie Lara! Your belly is *sooo* big!" Evie giggled with wide eyes as she ran her hands in little circles down the rise of my stomach.

"Yes, the baby in there is growing really fast, and very soon you'll get to meet her."

Josie tugged on my arm. "Does the baby have a name?"

I glanced out to the water, where Peter, Mitch and Steven stood together talking, the spray of the water swirling around them. I looked down at Josie with a smile. "Hope. The baby's name is Hope."

"Ooooh, that's a pretty name," Eva cooed as she skipped

around me. "We're hunting for buried treasure, Auntie Lara. Come hunt with us!"

I chuckled with a nod. "That sounds like a lot of fun, girls. I'll join you in a bit, okay?"

"Okay!" Evie sang out as she grabbed Josie's hand and raced down the beach with her.

Steven turned to me, holding his arms out with a big smile as I walked up to him. "Thank you, guys, so much for meeting us out here," I said into the stiff fabric of Steven's windbreaker as he held me against him.

"We'd meet you anywhere, Lara. I'm just so happy we get to see you in this beautiful state. You look like an absolute goddess," Steven said with a twinkle in his eye as he released me.

With a warm smile, Peter slipped his arm around my waist. "That's because she *is* a goddess."

Mitch mouthed the words *this guy* to me while fanning his face in a mock swoon. Steven playfully hip checked him and turned to Peter with a grin. "It appears my husband may be a bit smitten with you already."

Their laughter rang out and collided with the rush of the waves that lapped upon the shore, teasing our feet. A joy pulsed within me as I looked out into the boundless, churning life of the sea. Our family was tenderly growing once more, and while there were pieces missing, memories that would always ache, there was a tremendous beauty in it all. For I was beginning to understand that you cannot truly appreciate the moments of light until you have sat in the darkness.

Watching the waves crest with turbulent grandeur, I felt Caleb and my mother beside me, like two bright, burning sparks of love encompassing my entire being. And I knew they would always be there, quietly guiding my heart.

The girls ran up to Peter, tugging on his arms. "Peter, Peter!" they chanted in unison, "come play hide and seek with us."

A wide grin stretched across his face as his hands fell to the top of their heads, sparkling with drops of water from the ocean. "And where did these two sea creatures come from?"

With a chuckle, Mitch shoved his hands into his pockets. "I think you girls may have a bit of an unfair advantage, here."

They giggled and broke away from Peter, only to weave back around. "Try and find us, Peter, we're over here!" Evie called out, laughing as she and Josie circled him.

I stood there, watching Peter as he played beside the water with the girls. My hands curled around my belly, feeling the gentle kick of our child as she stretched and bloomed inside me.

I knew there were no happy endings. Only new beginnings. We were imperfect creatures, learning how to walk again, learning how to let in more light among the shadows. I knew there would be days when I would lose Peter momentarily to his darkness, as there would be moments when I would fall into mine, but we would always find a way back to each other. Life was too delicately beautiful not to make room for love.

Epilogue

The blush of spring flirted with the richness of summer, followed by another vibrant canvas of color unfurling; giving way to a winter steeped in the hush of white, while springs growth waited patiently beneath the snow. Time had swept me away in her arms as the seasons spun by, and life had become so full.

Hope banged her spoon against the highchair, babbling gleefully as food splattered onto the floor and all over Dusty, who stood beneath her, eager to assist in the cleanup. The back door to the kitchen was propped open, allowing the cool early morning air to filter into the house, a temporary respite from the sweltering heat of August.

The day Hope was born had been a summer morning much like this one. Despite my initial fears of something going wrong, I didn't want bright lights and sterile walls to welcome her; I wanted the soft sanctuary of home, just as I had given Caleb. After a long night of labor, darkness had released itself into the open arms of sunrise, flooding our bedroom in shades of gold and pink as the midwife slowly guided Hope out into the world. Her cries were like the flight of birds as I held her in my arms. The memory of Peter's face as his hands met her skin for the first time was something I would never forget. Tears had spilled from his eyes as he gently trailed his fingers across her cheeks, entwining his hand around hers, reveling in the tiny, miraculous perfection of her.

Drawing myself from my thoughts, I turned to the window

to see Peter strolling in from the barn, his cheerful whistled notes carrying across the pasture. Hope's wide blue eyes swiveled in the direction of the door. "Dada!"

I smiled. "Yes, sweetpea. Daddy's coming."

"Where's my girl?" Peter called out as he entered the kitchen.

Hope giggled and kicked her chubby legs against the chair as Peter drew close to the sound of her laughter, showering her mess of tangled, dark hair with kisses before bending down and lifting her out of her highchair.

"Hold on," I said, coming over with a towel. "She's covered in food."

I wiped her face and unclasped her bib as she wiggled in Peter's arms, grabbing handfuls of his hair in her elfin fists. The light in his eyes danced with an earnest tenderness as I watched the two of them together.

"Where's Sasha?"

I glanced out the window toward the cottage. "Still sleeping, I suppose. She got in pretty late last night."

"And when will Mitch and the gang be showing up?" he asked, bouncing Hope around the kitchen.

I threw the towel onto the counter and leaned against it. "He texted me early this morning and said they should be arriving sometime before noon."

"Great." Peter placed a big, loud kiss on Hope's forehead, causing her to squeal. "Miriam and Clive will be here by eleven, I think."

"And your brother?"

Greg had been sober and out of rehab for almost a year now. I had witnessed the delicate repair between them through long, late-night phone conversations, but this was the first time Peter had invited him back to the house.

Though a whisper of reserve twisted around me, I knew this

was the next step in healing the fractures of their past, and I was prepared to welcome him with open arms.

"He should be here a little after twelve." Peter lowered Hope to the ground, where she tottered off into the living room in search of Dusty. Moving to where I stood against the counter, Peter ran his hands down my arms. "Are you absolutely sure you're okay with him coming today?"

I brushed a strand of hair out of his eyes. "Of course. I know you two need to work things out."

Peter nodded and placed a kiss against my forehead. He smelled of hay and pine as I slipped my arms around him, breathing in his scent and all the steady assurance his love encompassed. I lifted myself onto my toes, and found his lips, momentarily falling into a soft, drawn-out dance, speaking in that silent language we navigated so well.

"Is there anything you two do together besides make out?" Sasha's exuberant voice broke our embrace as she stepped through the back door.

With a playful grin, I pulled away from Peter. "Yes, we can also make really cute babies."

Sasha glanced around the kitchen with a laugh. "That is *very* true, and where is my adorable little monkey, anyway?"

I tipped my head toward the living room. "Most likely lying on the dog."

She breezed by us and peeked through the doorway. "Yep. You're right."

I smiled as the gentle lilt of Sasha's voice addressing Hope filtered into the kitchen, surrounding me with the sound of laughter that played in between the early morning light.

Standing precariously on the ladder, I threaded streamers through the branches of the large oak tree outside. Balloons tied with string swayed optimistically in the breeze, pink and yellow against the bright blue of the sky.

"Oh, will you get off that damn thing, Lara, and let me help you with that?"

Miriam's voice startled me from below, and I looked down at her from my perch. "It's okay, I'm almost done."

"No, you're not." Miriam chuckled. "And Peter told me you're afraid of heights, so get your little booty down right now."

With a sigh, I guided my wobbly legs down the ladder rungs. "I'm trying to get over it, you know."

Miriam patted me on the shoulder playfully. "I know, but I think Mitch and the gang are here, so why don't you go greet them while your nerves are still intact."

The sound of car doors slamming, and the gleeful chatter of the girls rang out across the driveway as I came around to the front of the house. Evie and Josie crashed into me in an enthusiastic tangle of limbs and dark curls that smelled of sunshine. I breathed them in, crouching down to shower their faces with kisses as Mitch and Steven stood above me with warm smiles against the towering backdrop of mountains and sky.

"I'm so glad you guys were able to make it," I said, pulling Mitch and Steven into a tight hug.

Evie tugged at my shirt, her big brown eyes full of excitement. "Auntie Lara, where's Hope?"

"The birthday girl is inside, making a cake with her daddy, but I think they might need some help," I said with a wink.

Steven ushered the girls inside as Mitch slid his arm around my waist. "So, how's motherhood treating you these days?"

I turned to him with a soft smile. "It's been easy on me so far."

Mitch nodded. "Well, you look really happy, Lara." His

expression grew thoughtful as his eyes flickered over to his car. "I actually have a little something for Hope. It's from John."

Mitch walked over to the car and retrieved a gift wrapped in bright silver paper. "He stopped by for a visit with us a few weeks ago while he was attending a trial in town, and he wanted me to give you this."

My heart froze as my hands wrapped around the lightweight package.

"I figured you might want to open it in private."

I stared at Mitch, my mouth growing dry. "What is it?"

He shook his head slowly and shrugged. "I don't know."

I stared down at the gift, my fingers cautiously hovering over the paper as if its contents held the possibilities of explosives. I was not yet ready to see what was inside.

Sasha and I stood together beneath the oak tree, enjoying the cool caress of a momentary breeze against our skin.

"How's teaching been going?" Sasha asked, cradling a glass of beer in her hand.

I watched Hope tumble through the pasture with Josie and Evie beside her, their laughter ringing out through the field. "It's been really great. I love my class. We were able to find this amazing woman who comes and helps with Hope while I'm gone, and once a week, Peter comes in and does finger painting with the kids."

"Oh, that sounds like so much fun," she said with a wide smile.

"It is, and the kids love him."

Sasha glanced past me at the sound of footsteps coming up the driveway. "Who's that guy?"

I turned around to see Greg approaching.

"Wait, that's Peter's brother, isn't it?" Sasha whispered, leaning in close to my ear. "My god, he looks so much like him."

I nodded, my eyes falling to Peter, watching as he tentatively greeted his brother, followed by Miriam, who enfolded him in a long, crushing hug. "He does, doesn't he?" No longer gaunt and washed out looking, Greg had put on weight and looked healthy; a startling contrast to the man I remembered stumbling into the cottage, his eyes glazed over with drink.

I threw Sasha a look, and she raised her hands up in mock defense. "I didn't say anything."

"You don't need to," I said, giving her a playful smirk. "I know what you're thinking."

Sasha set her beer down on the table and ran her hands through her unruly curls. "I'm just going to introduce myself, that's all."

I rolled my eyes as Sasha sauntered over to Greg and Peter with a cheerful lilt in her voice, sunlight dancing off her hair.

Turning around, I went to grab the stack of plates and napkins by the back door and began to place them on the picnic table when Greg came up beside me. "Can I help you with that?"

He looked slightly sheepish as he glanced down at me with the same sharp hazel eyes as Peter, and I found the resemblance startling. Handing him some cups, I motioned toward the table. "Sure, thanks."

"No, thank *you*." His tone was somber as he stood there, regarding me with a look that seemed sincere. "You saved my brother, you know."

I attempted a playful smile, brushing a strand of hair out of my face. "I don't know if he was the one who needed saving, Greg."

He tilted his head at me, his face earnest. "We all need saving once in a while." He glanced up into the tree above us, watching the wind as it played with the leaves. "You helped open up his heart again, and he's now willing to repair things between us." Emotion pooled in his eyes as he began to place the cups along the table. "And because of that, I have my brother back, and that means the world to me."

Placing my hand on his arm, I gave it a gentle squeeze. "I'm really glad you came."

A warm smile lit up his face, softening the edges of the remorse which hovered in the depths of his eyes. "Me, too."

The sun sank behind the mountains; the day shifting its colors and washing the sky in a dusky golden glow as the sounds of laughter and conversation trickled in from outside.

I stood in the bedroom beside the open window, watching Sasha in the pasture as she walked through the grass with Hope in her arms, swaying to a silent song. Evie and Josie stood beside Penny, delicately threading their fingers through her mane as she gently bumped her nose against Josie's chest, sending her tumbling to the ground in a fit of giggles.

Closing the bedroom door behind me, I sat down on the bed and took a deep breath as I hesitantly reached for the package from John that I had placed on the nightstand. I could not still the frantic beating of my heart as I began to carefully remove the paper. The night we had torn open the scars of our marriage and watched them bleed out onto the ground had never stopped haunting me, all the bitterness and pain we had thrown at each other, leaving nothing behind but the silence of regret.

My fingers felt something soft, a familiar cloth of faded dusty blue. My breath caught in my throat, and tears gathered in my eyes as I pulled out Caleb's baby blanket.

A note fluttered to the floor beside my feet. Picking it up, I unfolded the letter and began to read John's tight, blocky script.

Lara,
As I was cleaning the house the other day, I found Caleb's blanket. Can you believe that? It was lodged behind that old bookshelf in the hallway. Remember how we spent days turning the house upside down, frantically looking for it? How upset Caleb was? We could never figure out what happened to it. And then you came up with that beautiful story about the fairies, and how they needed his blanket to keep their babies warm. You always had such magic with him.

Tears stained the paper, bleeding the ink of the words John had so carefully written me. I held Caleb's blanket to my chest, curling my fingers around the fabric. Memories of him as a baby washed over me, caressing the delicate place inside that I had finally found the courage to open up once more. Taking a shaky breath, I continued reading.

So, I thought your little girl might like to have this, so she can keep a piece of her brother beside her always.
I am so glad to hear that you are a mother again.
I am doing well these days. I have been going to therapy, and trying to piece myself back together. And I want you to know that I never stopped loving you, even though I had a hard time showing it.
I wish you nothing but the best in your life. You deserve all the happiness in the world. I'm just sorry I couldn't have given you more when we were together.
John.

The door opened, and Peter's gentle voice called me back to myself. "Lara, are you in here?"//
Wiping the tears from my cheeks, I stood up from the bed and walked across the room to where he was, slipping my arms around him. "Yes, I'm here."

His hands ran up my arms and into my hair, his thumb brushing against a stray tear. "Are you okay?"

"Yes. I was just reading a note from John."

A look of concern flashed across Peter's face as he furrowed his brow. Moving to grab the blanket from the bed, I placed it in his hands. "John wanted Hope to have this. It was Caleb's."

He fingered the cloth, and then drew me close to him, pressing his forehead against mine. "Do you need a moment?"

I shook my head. "No. The only moment I need is right here."

Peter's lips rested on mine, tender and lingering as the sound of tiny toddling feet came into the room.

"Mama... Dada."

I looked down at Hope holding a balloon in her tiny hand. Bending down, I scooped her up into my arms and wrapped Caleb's blanket around her shoulders, enfolding her in the fabric of a past she had yet to understand.

"You have a new blankie from your brother, Caleb."

She stared up at me, grasping at the cloth with her chubby fists before resting her head on my chest, the feel of her against me like the beautiful promise of renewal. A promise born of life's fervent potential.

Delicate, wild, and endless.

www.ingramcontent.com/pod-product-compliance
Lightning Source LLC
LaVergne TN
LVHW041624060526
838200LV00040B/1431